THE LAST BASTION

Peter C. Wensberg

THE PERMANENT PRESS
Sag Harbor, New York 11963

Library of Congress Cataloging-in-Publication Data

Wensberg, Peter C.
    The last bastion / by Peter C. Wensberg.
        p.   cm.
    ISBN 1-877946-58-3 : $22.00
    1. Men—Massachusetts—Boston—Societies and clubs—Fiction.
2. Sex discrimination against women—Fiction. 3. Boston (Mass.)—
Fiction. I. Title.
PS3573.E56L37 1995
813'54—dc20   94-11243
                                                                    CIP

Manufactured in the United States of America

First Edition, March 1995 – 1,200 copies

THE PERMANENT PRESS
Noyac Road
Sag Harbor, NY 11963

*To Craig, Erik, Ander, and Peter J.,
members of an exclusive club.*

The author's thanks to Andrea, Patrick, Esther, Lorraine, Donna, and most particularly to my brother, Erik.

The verses to Mademoiselle Yvonne were written by Lawrence Dame. I have not been able to track down the author of the lines beginning, "They talk about a woman's sphere as though it had a limit." My thanks to Jack Thomas for his researches into Boston tours as reported in his column in the *Boston Globe*. Homage to Alexander Williams and his charming and invaluable *A Social History of the Greater Boston Clubs* (Barre Publishers, 1970), which has provided inspiration. (When Alex and I were working together at a Beacon Hill publishing house, he a senior editor, I the most junior promotional assistant, we had an exchange which has since passed into legend. In the old mansion which served as our offices I asked, "Mr. Williams, could you tell me where the Men's Room is?"

"Actually, I'm not sure. I always go down the street to the Somerset.")

Several real clubs in Boston and other cities are mentioned in this tale. The Charles Club, the Pilgrim Club, and the Elks Lodge in Somerville, however, are entirely fictional, as are all the events and characters recounted here.

I don't think women are clubbable.

Member of the Garrick Club of London quoted in the *New York Times* after an overwhelming vote against admitting women as members.

It's not that we discriminate against any body or group, but we are very partial to our own.

Member of the Boston Club of New Orleans explaining in a deposition why the club has admitted neither women nor blacks, as quoted in the *Wall Street Journal*.

Because it smells like my father.

Former woman member of the Tavern Club of Boston when asked why she resigned, as quoted in the *Boston Globe*.

Chapter 1

Leslie Sample drained the coffee from her mug and hit a key on her speed dialer. The mug was decorated with a large capital L garlanded with lilac blossoms. The dialer stored thirty numbers in memory. Once a month without fail she re-programmed it with the names and telephone numbers of her current A list. There were five things she did once a month without fail. She did most of them on the first Saturday of the month no matter how busy she was. Saturday could be very busy. Most of her clients worked during the week and wanted to look at property on the weekend. But somehow Leslie found the time without fail. Then, when she was done paying bills, sorting her lingerie drawer, cleaning the refrigerator, re-programming her speed dialer and giving up coffee, she could look at her month and her life with some small satisfaction. *I may have screwed everything up, but at least I'm well-organized,* she told herself. No love life, no non-business socializing, no plan, no fun, no spare time, no excitement. The list of nos usually occurred with her head in the refrigerator finishing the least pleasant of the five tasks. But she didn't slam the door until it was spotless.

The telephone murmured in her ear, and her large eyes lit with interest as the top of her A list answered. "Jerry? Leslie Sample. Are you wide awake? I know it's early morning but I have something special for you . . . yes, very special . . . No, pour some coffee, I want your juices flowing when I tell you about this one." Her voice was husky, surprisingly deep, emanating as it did from a diminutive frame. She was the most strikingly attractive woman in the John Coster and Co. office, a position she worked conscientiously to maintain. Heavy dark brown hair hung smoothly in sculpted planes around her slender neck. Her skin was pale against the dark scenery of hair, eyes and brows. All her life people had told her she sounded like Tallulah Bankhead, like Bette Davis, like

Tammy Grimes. She had a vague idea who Tallulah Bankhead was and had seen Tammy Grimes once and Bette Davis several times on television. It was not really important, however, since Leslie did not much care who she sounded like. What she cared about was what she was good at, which was closing.

"Yes, Jerry, now picture this, a floor-through in a 1920s building on a good corner, not the sunny side, but great light because it has windows on three sides, the back, the street side, and the front which is Commonwealth. Of course deeded parking, two spaces. Good ceilings, about ten feet, nothing ridiculous and hard to heat, good dentil work in all the rooms, three, count them, three fireplaces, marble, working, Eurotrash kitchen with all the bells and whistles . . . " A sound like a knock on the earpiece she cradled between her ear and shoulder intervened. "Jerry? Could you hold for a sec, please just let me clear this?" She hit FLASH. "Hello? yes it is, can I call you *right* back I'm just finishing a call . . . Yes, give it to me . . . Got it, back in a click." She stabbed FLASH again. "Sorry Jerry. Look, it is a must see, just and I mean really *just* now on the market and mine alone . . . Of course, who do you think you are talking to, only the best that's who . . . No, I won't tell you anything more except that the elevator opens right into the apartment. Think about it, your dream come true and if you will buy me lunch at the Copley I will show it to you today at two . . . Of *course* cancel, because if you miss this you will never forgive yourself, let alone me, and we don't have a lot of time because the word somehow got out and the wolves are circling . . . Yes a couple from Hingham, they're desperate to buy, but if we *move* . . . Right, see you at one at the Copley. 'Bye."
Leslie extracted the phone from beneath hair the color of old mahogany. "Coffee," she said as she stood and stretched her back. Looking for her note with the other number, she jumped as the phone rang beneath her hand. She snatched it up. It was going to be a money day, she could feel it.

Seymour Gland pulled his dark blue Mercedes-Benz convertible out of the Brimmer Street Garage and immediately parked it in a space beside a fire hydrant, the engine running, the seat heater keeping the leather beneath him snug. He consulted an address book, clumsily turning the pages with his driving gloves on. When he found his number he peeled off the right glove and began to dial. He urgently wanted to talk to a man named Lester who owned several adult book shops and a special-audience movie theater.

After one broken headlight and a second close call Seymour had given up trying to operate the phone and the car simultaneously. He had been appalled to discover that a single "headlight set," as it was called, for his 560SL cost four hundred and eighty-five dollars before it was installed. Now he initiated his morning calls from just outside the garage before starting the eight-block drive to his office. The phone worked well from this spot and no one he spoke to was aware he was not driving. Occasionally a passing car honked, adding verisimilitude to the conversation of a busy venture capitalist touching bases on his way to work.

His friends and clubmates complained ceaselessly about the expense and difficulty of keeping a car in Boston. They, of course, in the best Brahmin tradition tried to do it on the cheap. They parked their pathetic ten-year-old Volvos in alley spots inherited from dead aunts, or worse yet on the street where roving bands of radio collectors broke the windows, heedless of NO RADIO signs posted on every side. "Of course, they can't read," muttered Seymour as he re-dialed the number. Increasingly of late he had experienced difficulty distinguishing the numbers and letters on his carphone keypad. Often he had to dial several times to get his number. He was painfully aware that each attempt cost one dollar and seventy-five cents. He had gone so far as to have Ms. James, his secretary, inquire at several electronic stores if a rotary car phone was available. "There's one the Japs haven't thought of," he told her when she reported back empty-handed. In Seymour's mind all key-operated devices were associated with Japan. He had five vintage black Western Electric instruments in his West Cedar Street house and could dial them without squinting. Lester was not in.

His broker's number was busy, so Gland called Ms. James to get his day's schedule. He glanced back at the sedate entrance to the Brimmer Street Garage which returned, as it always did, a glow of satisfaction. In the early seventies this unprepossessing building had been acquired by an enterprising developer who had turned its six floors of parking spaces into automobile condominiums. When a friend told Seymour that he had paid six thousand, five hundred American dollars for an oblong of concrete outlined in yellow paint with his name stenciled in it Seymour was aghast. Once again he glimpsed cracks in the foundation of Western civilization. In 1982, however, when his friend moved to Florida and sold his space for twenty-two thousand, Seymour reconsidered. He had, after all, built his career on a clear understanding of the Greater Fool Theory. The car thing, as it had been formulating for some time in his mind, was going to be expensive. Why not make it self-liquidating to use one of his favorite phrases? He had checked the market. There was almost no other indoor parking available on the Hill. Shopping carefully he bought a Brimmer Street Garage space for nineteen-five; then the Mercedes, a slightly used repossession, for forty-two thousand; then the carphone, installed, for one-sixty-nine, ninety-five plus tax. Since he owned the building on Milk Street where he worked he requisitioned the best of the twelve parking spots in its basement. Now, five years later, he still had less than ten thousand miles on the car whose top had never been lowered. The carphone was, of course, an expense charged to his business. The value of his one hundred and twenty square feet of oil-stained cement had increased to ninety-eight thousand dollars in the most recent transaction. That was over eight hundred dollars a square foot, much, much more even than his historic eighteenth century Colonial house was worth, the best investment, by God, he had ever made. The car was worth twenty-five to be conservative, and the phone well, throw that in with all the excise tax and the confiscatory insurance charged by the state-supported gougers and he was still ahead almost one hundred thousand dollars. Who said a car in Boston was expensive? Just those poor saps at the Charles Club where he was to lunch at one o'clock, that's who. He wondered how he could bring the subject up at the Long Table. He didn't want to sound superior to the pitiful nincompoops, even though everything in life told him he was. Seymour Gland flicked the accelerator with his handsomely shod toe. The Hun machinery within responded instantly. He jerked the selector into drive and the car shot ahead alarmingly, narrowly missing the fire hydrant. Gland gripped the steering wheel with driver's gloves of iron, tamed the beast, and by fits and starts made his way over Beacon Hill toward Milk Street.

Chapter 2

Owen Lawrence and Tasha walked briskly toward John Glover, heading for Alexander Hamilton and George Washington, dimly to be seen in the November dusk a block ahead. Owen, as was often the case, was not setting the pace. A leisurely amble would have better suited his mood, compounded as it was of fatigue, disappointment that he would not be dining at the Charles Club that evening, the desire for a drink, and a nagging concern not only about his ability to pay his life insurance premium but whom he should designate as his beneficiary. Tasha, a white dog with the conformation and curly tail of a husky, had her shoulders into the work and her head down. She was pulling with a determination and an enthusiasm that would have pleased her Siberian ancestors, the *Bjelkier*, which in the language of the Samoyed tribe means the white dog which breeds white. Owen's left hand gripped the nylon leash above the choke chain. His right hand held the loop at the other end of the lead. He felt his briefcase slipping from under his elbow. "For Christ's sake, Tasha," he grunted as she lunged sharply off the sidewalk that stretched down the center of the broad Commonwealth Mall and, nose to the tired grass, began to search for the perfect spot

Grateful for the respite, Owen adjusted the briefcase. It contained the thin intellectual fare that would sustain his evening, a business plan for a young company which argued, not entirely unpersuasively, that gold and glory were to be found in the freight forwarding business. He was tall and lanky, his shoulders broad enough to carry his tan raincoat like an oversized coathanger. Most of his clothes seemed to flap below his shoulders. His frame, a little over six feet, appeared taller because it was so slender. All his life people had told him to stand up straight. Hatless, his sandy hair ruffled a bit by the restless night air, Owen peered at his dog with a trace of impatience. Tasha examined the earth with her nose, moving forward with powerful little crowhops until she found what she sought. Owen relaxed the tension on the leash, flexed his left hand and stared thoughtfully at the statue looming above them.

JOHN GLOVER
OF MARBLEHEAD
A SOLDIER OF THE REVOLUTION

announced the tablet on the granite pediment. The further details of Glover's service were obscured by a device overlaid in a kind of Mongoloid handwriting exercise in white spray paint across the plaque. BORGO it proclaimed, as best Owen could decipher. The officer himself stood at ease, surveying the urban battlefield from his vantage, one foot resting on a cannon barrel, his sword drawn but invisible since it had been snapped off at the hilt by a vandal who apparently accomplished what the Hessians could not. Owen was reminded that most male statues within reach of the public lost sword, nose, penis, or all three. Why do we emasculate our heroes, he wondered. Despite his loss, Glover looked cheerful in the uncertain light of the street lamp. A chill breeze rattled the last leaves in the oaks above them. On the side of Glover's pedestal just beneath his boot another message was inscribed in small black capitals: CHEVROLET GIRLS WERE HERE. SUICIDAL SINCE DAWN. FEEL THE CHAIN. Owen sighed. "Come on, Tasha." He looked down at the pile of turds steaming on the ground as at last his dog moved forward. He knew he should pick it up and deposit it in a trash can. Most of the residents of Commonwealth Avenue and the cross streets named alphabetically for English earls from Arlington to Hereford did pick up. Across Massachusetts Avenue, Owen knew, no one picked up. It was, he realized, a significant class distinction. No blue-collar Bostonian would touch dog shit. Only the young aspiring-to-be Brahmins of the Back Bay and Beacon Hill would stoop, literally, to the task. Well, he thought, where did that leave him? Although he had lived around Boston for most of his thirty-eight years, he knew his roots were still in the clay soil of his father's ranch in New Mexico, where fertilizer stayed on the ground.

When his mother had died, Owen had been sent to a boy's school in New Hampshire. That abrupt uprooting, his unarticulated grief for his mother, and the fear that his father wanted him off his hands had left Owen vulnerable to whatever mercies his new environment might or might not offer. Holderness School had in fact proved a refuge for the next four years. The masters were young, many with wives, some with small children. The little campus was overrun with boisterous boys, dogs, and babies. The boys skied during the long winter, played hockey in the arctic outdoor rink, ran the trails when the snow melted, climbed the little mountains in the exuberant spring. Most of Owen's schoolmates who had not been born in nearby New Hampshire towns had been sent up from Boston. Owen was mildly surprised to discover that he was viewed as the local representative of a friendly foreign power. It was widely believed that he needed a passport to return home to Santa Fe. He knew, however, he had been accepted more readily by the school, coming as he did from an exotic land, than the few who had journeyed to Holderness from Cleveland or Chicago. Early in their acquaintance his roommate had asked Owen if he knew any Indians. Since he did, the legend was confirmed and grew.

He returned to Santa Fe only twice during his four years at Holderness. Each time his father greeted him warmly, formally, and then seemed quietly to disappear. Owen sought out a few of the friends with whom he had spent his years at the ancient San Ysidro Grade School on Cerro Gordo Road. To them he looked and sounded Eastern. He spent most of those two summers working with the two Spanish-American hands who ran the little ranch outside the town. They laughed at him until he lost the inflections of his Spanish teacher and regained the easy New Mexican patois of his childhood.

It required an effort of imagination to continue to call the Lawrence place a ranch. It had been in the family for three generations before Owen's father, but it had withered and shrunk during his lifetime as a few acres were sold every year or so to developers or abutters to pay the taxes or, one year, to rebuild the barn. The two old vaqueros looked after a dozen horses, some beef cattle, a dairy cow and her yearly calf, a flock of migrant chickens, and many generations of dogs. Set on a pretty stretch of the Rio Grande that meandered between stands of aspen and cottonwood, the land itself changed little: alternately green and sere, occasionally dusted with snow.

Owen's father worked intermittently as a civil engineer, usually as a consultant to other engineering companies. His career had never been as active as in the period during the second World War, when he was intensely involved in the construction of the laboratory buildings and the attendant town of Los Alamos. He had never spoken to Owen of that experience except to say that he could not talk about it. Since 1945 he had practiced engineering about half of each year, fished the Pecos River, and read long hours in his study. He found little time for people, preferring horses, dogs, and books. His wife and only child saw him from a distance, or so it now seemed to Owen. His strongest memories of his father were associated with arrivals and departures. His mother, however, was as vivid to him as if she were still alive.

[13

She had died when he was fourteen, in the river near their house, drowned in a pool shallow enough to wade across. Her death was called an accident; no autopsy was held. One morning she was alive, fixing breakfast, toasting homemade bread, hurrying Owen to school with scoldings, kisses, cuffs, and caresses. That afternoon he came home to disaster, confusion, emptiness, and despair. His father was in Albuquerque. He didn't return for forty-eight hours. Owen wondered as he waited for him if he had ever loved his father. He wondered now. How long since I have seen him, he asked himself. Two years at least came the answer.

Tasha trotted along now, her head held to one side savoring the night smells, tracking the passage of an occasional jogger, questioning with her black nose a man sleeping on a bench. They approached Alexander Hamilton standing alone in the gloom, a toga draped over his officer's coat, staring sourly across Arlington Street at the magnificent equestrian statue of George Washington which dominates the entrance to the Public Garden. To Owen, Hamilton's visage and bearing suggested displeasure that he was afoot while his commander was so handsomely mounted. Owen rounded Hamilton, the usual limit of the evening walk, yearning for a stiff Jack Daniel's with a few cubes of ice to soften it. Tasha stopped to squat and christen the ground yet again. Owen studied Washington, softly illuminated from beneath, sitting lightly on his glorious bronze stallion, unbroken sword in his right hand resting across his left wrist, his gaze directed not at Alexander Hamilton, Owen, Tasha, or the expanse of the Commonwealth Mall that unrolled grandly from his charger's feet but at the front entrance of the Ritz-Carlton across the street. A bird sat on the brim of Washington's hat. Tasha and Owen started home. It was almost black now, the city's traffic subsiding, a siren echoing faintly in the distance. What killed her? Owen wondered. I wanted so much more of her, he thought. What would my father and I talk about if we saw each other again? What have we ever talked about?

They walked at an easier gait on the return leg past the dark statues that inhabit each block of the Mall: Hamilton, then Glover, then Patrick Michael Collins, an early Irish mayor whose bust glowered from between two goddesses, then William Lloyd Garrison sitting in a huge bronze chair, then Samuel Eliot Morison sitting on a rock. Just before the Hereford Street crossing they walked carefully across the grass avoiding mementoes of other walks, cut across the eastbound lane of Commonwealth, and descended the steps to the door of their basement apartment. As he dug for the key in his trouser pocket, Owen glanced in surprise at the mailbox by his front door. BORGO it said in paint still moist enough to reflect the light from his front window. "Bastards," said Owen.

Chapter 3

The skinny old man trotted along, through the cellar of the Charles Club, muttering to himself. This dark, damp, cavernous maze extended well beyond the walls of the clubhouse. Rooms had been excavated from the mud which originally filled Back Bay beneath the Ladies' Entrance on Hereford and under the broad sidewalk on Commonwealth. With hasty, scuffling tread Nilson headed for his workbench behind the oil furnace. This monument to the engineering which made America a world leader in the nineteenth century had been converted in the golden year of 1925 from hot air to steam. Beside the fire chamber with its tangle of internal pipes extended a massive iron boiler. Nilson paused to tap the pressure gauge. The needle bounced and returned to sixty pounds. Although it was early November, the furnace ran more or less continuously, providing scalding tap water and copious amounts of steam which ascended the iron capillaries of the Charles Club to the slate roof, five stories above. The club was in fact overwarm in most seasons. A member unlucky enough to be forced to spend a night in one of the guest rooms on the fourth floor invariably began the evening by flinging open the window. Nilson ignited the furnace in October and shut it down in May. During this period an oil truck arrived once a week to replenish the massive tank. Only Miss Ontos, who operated the computer, ever spoke to Nilson about oil. He stared back impassively when she remarked in the pantry one day how little sense it made to her that as much money was spent on oil as food or drink in a club the size of the Charles. Cost weighed lightly among Nilson's responsibilities. His life at the Charles Club was a series of skirmishes. Like an elderly but still agile jungle fighter, he darted from tree to tree. Furnace firing, pressure up, no problem here. He jerked a string above the cluttered bench and light flooded down on his narrow head, heavily but irregularly thatched with iron-colored hair. Quickly he grabbed a crescent wrench, a short prybar, a ballpeen hammer, a huge screwdriver, and an electric drill, throwing them into his wooden tool carrier. As an afterthought he added a coil of heavy wire, a disk of electrician's tape, and a toothbrush. He pulled the light cord and plunged the cellar again into semi-darkness. As he scuttled past the oil burner it faltered for an instant. He kicked it hard with a mailed boot, grunted as it picked up the cadence again, then ran for the stairs up to the back hall.

His urgency was prompted as much by fear as by the debacle which had again befallen the elevator. He stopped short of the wooden steps as a gray torpedo shot past his foot. With a cry he dropped his tool container and, snatching the ballpeen, hurled it like Wotan's hammer at the departing shape. It struck with a gratifying clatter. Hearing nothing but his own harsh respiration and the echoing roar of the furnace, Nilson approached with silent steps. There, in the angle of the cement floor and the granite foundation, lay his victim. Skulled but not squashed, observed Nilson with satisfaction. He picked it up by the tail and deposited it with the tools. A good foot and a half from tip to tip. Now, they'll listen, he exulted as he pounded up the stairs. His passage through the pantry was punctuated by a shriek of outrage from Old Jane. "Serves you right for sticking your nose in," panted Nilson as he entered the front hall, dodged his way through a gaggle of concerned members and headed up the front stairs to the disaster on the second floor.

One of the amenities added by the club in 1925 to the already handsomely equipped townhouse was a diminutive elevator which travelled in a shaft circumscribed by the main staircase. The most decorative small model in the Otis line, the elevator moved in a channel of brass filigree, its cage a bower of rods, leaves and branches interwoven to afford the occupant glimpses of his ascent. Only the floor of the car was solid. From within and without the elevator in use suggested nothing so much as a bird being lifted in its cage to be hung on a hook somewhere at the top of the house.

The elevator alone had not been converted to alternating current, which now animated the rest of the building. A Westinghouse motor in the attic had functioned without failure since its installation. Years of use, however, had worn the brass hardware and the copper contacts of the controls and switches in the cage itself. The floor-selection buttons in the ornamental panel had acquired a comfortable concavity from millions of jabs by thousands of impatient Yankee digits. Least trustworthy were the switches and latches on the doors. A sad story had repeated itself.

Well launched on the cocktail hour with several friends in the Library, Roger Dormant was possessed with an important desire to visit the lavatory. His most obvious choice lay just off the entrance hall. Spacious, comfortable, warm, this chamber was a Back Bay landmark. The plumbing fixtures, unequalled for their originality in Boston, included a fine set of oak water boxes activated by brass chains with porcelain pendants. A commodious shower bath with a bench, loffas, and an English back brush beckoned. The line of sinks, a full half dozen, boasted German silver water spouts, massive valves, various levers and plungers, suggestive of the control bridge of a zeppelin. Reflected in the mirrored wall was a matchless array of aids to masculine beauty, including hair oil, talcum, combs soaking in a glass of mild antiseptic, cologne from Cologne, glycerine soap from London, jojoba oil soap from Paris, and stacks of large soft towels. The massive urinals stood like porcelain buttresses, proudly stamped "American Standard," glacial, spotless, a sanctuary of rest and relief to kidneys whose production sometimes demanded haste, sometimes patience. Finished in white hexagonal tile, its wooden stalls many times painted, the great room offered every comfort except privacy. Men often walked blocks out of their way to enjoy the elegance of the Charles Club's *grande salle de bain*.

Other than the Ladies' Room, inaccessible of course to Dormant, the ground floor offered one alternative. This small chamber adjacent to the front door resembled a coat closet, which in fact it had once been. Refitted in the early years of the club, it contained a marble seat with one hole shaped in the country fashion, a chamber pot beneath. A discreet card bore the legend, "For emergency use only."

Dormant, however, sought neither the camaraderie of the large bathroom nor the Spartan convenience of the closet in the foyer. He felt a little rocky and decided to use the toilet on the second floor, a facility with no particular distinction except a lockable door. Unsure of his balance, he elected to take the elevator rather than risk the stairs that curved up from the marble lobby. As he boarded his eye passed unseeing over the card affixed by Nilson to the inside of the door:

IMPORTANT!
CLOSE DOOR TIGHT.
DONT PRESS BUTTON
UNTIL DOOR IS LATCHED.
ALL THE WAY. REALLY SHUT.

The outer door banged. The pantographic door shot home with the authority of a guillotine blade. The huge rocker switch above the door crashed down, sending a surge of direct current into the magnets of the motor high above. The old cables stretched a bit then jerked mightily. The birdcage rose, momentarily staggering its occupant. Dormant was a small, unprepossessing man who nevertheless often reminded people of someone else. On numerous occasions friends and acquaintances, of whom he had many, asked him if he had recently shaved off his moustache. This puzzled him since he had never worn a moustache, but he had come to accept it as one of the vagaries of the restless, contentious, uncertain time in which he lived. Dormant watched the cornice and the graceful ornament of the ceiling approach, then passed into the opening confident that he would arrive with time to spare. At that moment the front elevator door, not latched, popped open. The circuit broken, the rocker switch sprang up. The motor, drained of life, slowed and stopped. The birdcage bounced. Dormant, his legs and feet visible in the ceiling—attributed by some to a pupil of Bulfinch—let out a wail. Nilson, sitting in the pantry, dropped his copy of the Boston *Sphere* and headed for the cellar.

By the time he had the man's head in sight Dormant's cries had subsided. Not unfamiliar with this problem, Nilson called down to him, "What do you need?"

"My topcoat. And a stiff bourbon and soda."

Nilson turned to Old Jane, who had followed him, avid to add another to the lexicon of Charles Club stories with which she entertained the inner circle of her favorite bar in Allston. "Get his coat. Abel knows which it is. And bring the booze."

"Should I bring up some hors d'oeuvres?"

"God damn right. Bring the menu too. This is going to take a while." He reached for the prybar and the bloody hammer. "Maybe you'll walk up next time," muttered the jungle fighter.

Chapter 4

In a sense, Owen reminded himself as he scraped the chin of his reflected image, Seymour saved my life. The thought of being beholden to Gland was repugnant enough, but the realization that he had fallen so far so fast after the divorce made him wince. He lifted his razor and stared curiously at the face whose grimace confronted him. The tiny bathroom enfolded his lean frame in a grasp of pink plastic tile. He was clad in pyjama bottoms, leaning over the little sink which as usual had produced water which was hot, but not very hot. Was I so dependent on her, he wondered.

Ten years of marriage had fractured in ten weeks. Try as he might, he could not remember specifically what had caused the first crack. Perhaps it had been the dog. She had never liked the dog, never had a dog, even when she was a child. A dog had always been an essential element of his own life. He remembered events in association with the dog which was present at the moment; the brown bitch named Emma, for instance, who waited with him for his father to return. He saw himself and the dog sitting together on the worn wooden step in the shadows of the *portal* watching the road. He didn't have a strong sense of how the boy looked, but Emma was a clear, complete image: narrow muzzle, yellow eyes, lop ear, feathered tail. The two of them had studied the empty dirt road for two days until his father had returned. Em's single sharp bark preceded the sight of the old Chrysler by three minutes.

Another dog watched him from the open bathroom door, her black eyes regarding him from behind a white mask. Tasha rarely barked, but whenever she did in the five years since Owen had brought her home from the Animal Rescue League his wife covered her ears. "Why is the dog barking?" she asked. No answer seemed to suffice. Each bark took her by surprise. So did white fur on the carpets of their house in Weston, the need for a kennel whenever they travelled, the dog walk that always ended Owen's day. Maybe she was keeping score, he thought.

His lawyer was a classmate who warned Owen that he never took divorce cases unless his friends insisted. When he learned that the case would be heard by a certain judge in the Norfolk County Court Owen's counsel sighed. "It's all over, Champ. I know this one. She's got an agenda." His prognosis was correct. By the time Owen had begun to school himself in phrases like ex-wife and former residence, the house, the furniture, the Volvo, the summer cottage in Mattapoisett, his modest portfolio, and the fourteen-foot catboat had sailed out of his life. The boat was sold as a package with the beach house which was put under a sales agreement a month after the decree became final. Owen had been able to claim a few furnishings out of the cottage. Now he felt like a badger holed up under the tree roots in a tiny basement apartment which had been described in the listing as a studio. Studio sounded right for a place in which he would begin to learn about his new life, but it lacked the north light he might have hoped for. In fact, its front windows opened on the street six inches above grade with a view of the blue mailbox, the green pedestal which supported the traffic light on the corner, a prickly bush, and the feet and legs of passersby. The apartment's other pair of windows stared at the furnace room. If he parted the lank curtains above his kitchen sink, Owen was confronted with a naked bulb burning beside the fuse box flanking the furnace. The rumble of the furnace and the clank of steam in the pipes were not uncomforting, however, and masked the sounds of the street as he slept.

The Mattapoisett cottage had yielded several birch log chairs and a matching table. An old Navajo blanket covered his bed. Books overflowed shelves arranged from boards and bricks. A wrought-iron floor lamp peered over the largest of the log chairs. On a wicker table a black-and-white television set, near the end of a long career, rested quietly. The table, which had existed on the front porch of the cottage, smelled of the sea. A shallow fireplace framed in iron with a narrow marble mantel proved, after careful investigation with spills of burning newspaper, to be unencumbered. If he was careful Owen could burn the sticks Tasha brought back from their walks and Presto Logs from the market at four ninety-nine each.

If the living space of his studio had become, through a process of random acquisition, comfortable and welcoming, the kitchen remained a grisly chamber. Sink and drainboard seemed designed for sinister medical purposes. The small gas stove and half a refrigerator crouched under open shelves. The room was decorated with cans of dog food, ketchup, a box of cereal. Glassware and crockery had been collected in a cardboard carton before bidding good-bye to Mattapoisett. The mushroom anchor from the catboat propped the kitchen door so Tasha had access to her bowl and water dish under the sink. Owen felt the open door added dimension to the living room. He could see the electric clock above the stove without difficulty from his birch chair in front of the fire. The clock told him when it was time to eat, a signal no longer issued by his stomach. Not a bad badger hole, Owen thought as he towelled his face, but it's unfortunate that I owe it all to Seymour.

When they met in a hardware store on Charles Street five months ago Owen was, in fact, wondering how he was going to pay his rent. As he waited for the clerk to finish a telephone call, Owen twisted his MIT ring, which seemed to have become larger, on his left ring finger. The second thing he had accomplished after his divorce decree, on the day he returned from Mattapoisett, was to quit his job with Portman and Sells, Consulting Engineers. An undemanding position, it paid $78,000 a year and offered the prospect of steady employment with regular small salary increases. Working with an assortment of clients in research and manufacturing companies around New England provided enough variety to help Owen postpone his ambitions of creating a company someday. Certainly the problems and disasters of his clients offered him a continuing seminar on the mismanagement of American industry. His last act on the day he quit was to explain again to the owner of a laser printer patent that his principal competitor, by negotiating a manufacturing agreement with a Korean conglomerate, had achieved a potential price advantage that might be difficult to overcome. Owen left the client hoping that the Olympics might be a disaster, went into his father-in-law's office, and resigned.

"What do you need?" asked the hardware clerk, downing the telephone with a sigh. The answer momentarily overwhelmed

Owen. As he struggled to find his list, which he remembered included bathtub caulking and D-Con, a familiar voice intruded.
"I am looking for an elegant mailslot. Heavy brass. The sort that is affixed in the panel of one's door. A pivoting flap. Wide enough for large envelopes and periodicals. One that speaks of . . . " the voice paused in full flow, then erupted in a giggle. "Owen? Owen Lawrence?"
Owen had not seen Seymour Gland since a party after their graduation from Harvard. That evening had begun badly and ended in the middle of Garden Street at three in the morning. Gland could not find his car. Owen walked many blocks with him searching fruitlessly for it. When he remembered that a girl had driven him to the party, Gland sank to the curbing in front of the Widener Library crying softly.
"Don't be sick on my shoes, Seymour."
"Of course not," said Gland between sobs and promptly ruined his own. They wandered into the Square together, had eggs, and persuaded a reluctant cabbie to take them to Gland's house on Beacon Hill.
"It's been sixteen years," said Owen.
"I hope you've spent them productively."
Owen grimaced. "So do I. Two years for an engineering degree at MIT. Ten years of marriage. A job with Portman and Sells here in town."
"Well why haven't you called me? Children? No? Well, I'm sure that dog intimidating the people outside is yours. You've always had some hound trailing you. Whom did you, ah, choose?"
"It hardly matters. We were divorced two months ago. Quit my job as well. Only a step ahead of a pink slip. I was working for her father."
"Portman?"
"No, Sells."
"Oh, Abbie Sells; then you're well out of it. An engineer? What sort of engineer?"
"The electrical sort."
"Beaver signet and all. Why don't you come work for me?"
"What do you do?"
"Venture capital. I need a smart engineer. We're constantly evaluating new technology." As he uttered several of his favorite words, Gland's voice rose a notch, causing a couple in the paint department to look up from the color chips. "There is an ocean of

money to be invested in technology, you know, several oceans, in fact, since we manage three distinct funds. We can't find enough good ideas to pour them into.'' Then, turning to the clerk, "Yes, yes, the perfect receptacle,'' Gland cried, bouncing several times on his small feet shod in gleaming penny loafers, "a wide opening, the pivoting flap.'' He snatched the proffered mailslot and tucked it under his arm like a relay runner receiving the baton. "Put this on my bill. You *are* a smart engineer, aren't you?'' This to Owen. "If I were to guess, you graduated third or fourth in your class, only because you were always pig lazy.''

"Fourth, as a matter of fact. I just might want to come in and talk to you, Seymour. I could use a job. Things have rather,'' he searched for the word, "surprised me lately.''

"Well, don't come in to talk. Be ready to start. There is a new desktop publishing something or other I want you to look at. Come by on Monday. We are at 95 Milk Street. I own the building myself. I do a little real estate on the side.'' He beamed with simple joy at the notion of real estate on the side and bounced out the door.

The couple returned to their choice of enamel. Owen watched as Seymour squeezed gingerly past Tasha and trotted up Mt. Vernon Street, brass in hand, remarkably agile as always despite his bulk. Paying for the rat poison, the thumbtacks and the tube of sealant, Owen untied his dog and headed home through the Saturday crowd of tourists, sleepy students, and ancient Boston dames. He felt a little lightheaded. He wasn't sure what venture capital was all about. He should have asked.

As he tied his necktie in the medicine cabinet mirror Owen frowned. He didn't exactly save my life, he thought, but he changed it. He made it workable again. "Workable is not quite the same as tolerable,'' said Owen aloud. Tasha nudged his knee with her nose, reminding him that she was due six blocks on the Mall before he left for Gland, Hollings Ventures, Incorporated. Owen sighed, remembering he was out of coffee. "Can I make a cup of hot water?'' he asked the dog. The answer was clearly no. Owen snapped the leash on the ring of her choke chain and let her pull him through the front door, up the short flight of cement steps into the bright cacophony of the fall morning. It didn't occur to him to wonder if conversations with his dog were a symptom of something.

Chapter 5

Leslie lowered her husky voice so that, in the luncheon clamor of the Dartmouth Street Restaurant, Ann Dormant had to lean forward to hear. "So, he smiles this sort of nice-nasty smile and says, 'You are one bright little Back Bay bitch.' Can you *believe* it? I go, whuh-oa! I do not *need* this. No sale is this important. There are plenty more where this one came from. Who does he think he is? Or," she said louder, the rhetorical emphasis lifting her voice to its usual baritone, incongruous from the slender throat and diminutive frame, "more important, who does he think *I* am?"

"The Great American Questions," said Ann, sipping her second glass of house white.

"I'll accept the 'little' part. God knows I've worked hard enough on it."

"You look fantastic."

"Well, I got down from a ten to a six. It took almost a year of starving myself and drinking nothing but water. And there's this great class at the BCAE. It concentrates on your behind. That's the problem area for me. It didn't do anything for me for the longest time, then it just *peeled* the pounds off. I'm buying my good things from Albert Fiandaca now. I've decided if I work this hard I'm going to make at least one investment a year, maybe two if I hit a big one, and they're going to be sixes so I can't backslide."

"On your backside."

"Right. With that kind of money you take a serious view. I bought a little suit from him the other day. Just very classic tailoring with some nonsense," she waved her long red nails in the vicinity of her throat, "around the lapels. Beautiful wool and silk in a taupey, grayish, greenie sort of shade with gold buttons. Fifteen hundred. But it's worth it. I'll wear it forever."

"It sounds adorable." Ann buttered her second slice of French bread. The noise of the Dartmouth Street echoed around them as Boston's advertising community tore into the most *nouvelle* of menus. "Did he apologize?"

"I should say not. He told me he was giving me a special price because it looked so perfect on me. He said he had me in mind when he designed it. Now that's not true, because this was only the third or fourth time I had been in there, but I think he meant that my figure and my coloring . . . ''

''I mean the client. The one that called you a bimbo.''

''Not a bimbo. I wouldn't stand still for that either. I'm no bimbo. I'm a very serious person and I am *good* at what I do. I handled almost three million in residential, well mostly residential, product last year. I think I'd resent bimbo more than the other. Bimbo means dumb in my book.''

''What does bitch mean in your book?'' asked Ann with a smile. Their salads arrived and she dropped her half-gnawed crust of bread on the little plate.

''I'm not that sure.'' Leslie looked up with a question in her dark eyes at her friend, half a head taller and possessed of more than half a college education.

''A bitch is a female dog. It doesn't mean dumb, but it is quite demeaning when a man says it.''

''Does it mean sexy?''

''When a man says it to you, it probably does.''

''Fresh ground pepper?'' The waiter wrung a cylinder smaller than a baseball bat above their plates.

''When a woman says it, it means she hates you,'' said Leslie with conviction.

''Quite likely, but this wasn't a woman.''

''Damn straight. He's a hunk. An Italian hunk.''

''That's the hunkiest kind, I suppose.''

''I'm not talking North End here. I'm talking New York. And London. And, you know, Italy.''

''No guarantee of manners,'' said Ann, glancing at the man sitting on the banquette beside her attempting a very hot pizzetta with his fingers and making a poor job of it.

''Well, his manners were lovely. He just had a rotten mouth. Anyway, I froze him with a look.''

''Good thinking. Probably more effective than anything you could have said. Then what happened?''

''Well he was *so* pleased with the deal. He loves the space. It's more than two thousand square feet. A penthouse on the water side of Beacon. He said you couldn't duplicate it in Manhattan for a million. And he is getting it for six twenty, down from six forty-five. With a great river view and an assigned parking space. So he just tried to, like, gloss it over. He was super polite to me after that.''

"Are you going out with him?"

"Of course not. What makes you think he asked?"

"Just a wild guess."

"He did suggest dinner. At the Charles Club of all places."

"Is he a member?"

"No. He has guest privileges from some club in New York. A friend of his, Avery Coupon, just joined the Charles. They, the Coupons, moved here from New York about five months ago. I showed them some things around here, but they wound up going to Hamilton. It did start me thinking, though."

"About the Italian hunk with the mouth?"

"No, about the Charles Club. I think I should join."

Ann put down her fork and stared across the table, her eyebrows arched in unaccustomed interest. The advertising noise had risen beyond the threshold of communication to levels more suited to self-congratulation and recrimination. "Leslie Sample, what an original idea!"

"I thought so. It would be good for business."

"You know, of course, they do not admit women members."

"I suppose not. I really don't know much about it. I went once last spring for lunch. There were other women there. I went to the 'Ladies' Entrance on Hereford."

"How did you like the food?"

"All right. Sort of French, I guess."

"You know, of course, that they are being pressured by the MLB?"

"What's the MLB?"

"The Mass. Licensing Board. To admit women."

"No, I didn't. There, you see? I think I'll apply."

"No, my child. You have to get someone to put you up. You can't just apply. It's not like the Diner's Club. But let us consider this more carefully. You know that the Charles Club is populated by one of the prize collections of old farts on the eastern seaboard?"

"I don't know any of this, Ann, I told you. Are they all old?"

"Well, actually not. There are one or two rather choice specimens, now that I think about it. I know of one in particular who is just divorced. Then there is a singularly dashing trial lawyer, not young exactly, but not oldish or fartish."

"How young is not young?"

"Young enough to deserve consideration in my humble opinion. So, perhaps your interests are not entirely confined to business?"

"I don't know. Maybe not."

"You'd find a far better selection in any decent health club."

"I don't like to talk when I'm sweaty, do you? I don't even like sweaty men."

"I have not perspired since I left Northampton."

"Well, I was thinking basically of meeting people for business, not pleasure."

"But we must accept whatever pleasure is placed in our path."

"How you talk sometimes."

"Yes. Well, you are the one who came up with the idea. How many times have you been married, Leslie?"

"What has that got to do with anything? Once. Well, not counting the first time when I was still in school."

"Why don't you count that?"

"Because I don't. He was just a kid."

"What were you?"

"I don't want to talk about it. Pregnant, if you must know."

"Why was that a problem?"

"Because I was going to St. Michael's at the time. I really don't want to talk about it."

Ann Dormant applied herself once more to the remnants of her salad. There was a silence between them, if such a state could be said to exist at the Dartmouth Street. "You could be famous," she said thoughtfully.

"I am famous. My picture was on the second page of the *Boston Real Estate Journal* last week. The rest of the office was livid."

"I mean famous beyond your wildest dreams. Famous beyond real estate. Famous beyond Andy Warhol."

"He was very famous. The *Sphere* had his picture on the front page when he died."

"I don't mean *as* famous as Andy Warhol, I mean famous for more than fifteen minutes. Forget it. I mean famous enough to get your picture in the *Sphere* without dying."

"How?" asked Leslie checking her make-up in a small gold mirror.

"Fame will be thrust upon the first woman member of the Charles Club."

"Well, that's not why I thought of joining, to get my picture in the *Sphere*."

"Even if you're wearing the Fiandaca suit?"

"Well, it's not the basic reason. Do you want coffee? No? Then let's go." As they were retrieving their wraps, a pair of account executives squeezed by. One of them paused to help Leslie slide into her coat. "Love your perfume," he murmured. Leslie froze him with a look.

On the sunswept brick sidewalk, as she was about to say goodbye to Ann, Leslie paused and looked at her questioningly. "What are you thinking?"

"There's not a feminist bone in your body, is there?" said Ann, hands deep in pockets, staring at her friend.

"I stick up for my rights. I compete with men," said Leslie.

"I know you do. Very successfully, too. The Italian was right. You'd be perfect."

"Perfect for what?"

"Perfect to make history. Don't worry about it, leave everything to me. I'll find you a sponsor, an *agent provocateur* within their ranks. I'm sure I know one, perhaps more than one. Then, when the sands of time have run out for the Charles Club, you will be there to upend the hourglass."

"How you talk sometimes."

"Yes, don't I."

The two women leaned toward each other, almost touched cheeks and then parted; one bent on business, one pleasure.

Chapter 6

Tall, deep-chested, wearing a jacket with ridiculously wide shoulders that hung almost to the hem of her short skirt, blonde straight hair unashamed of dark roots. As he approached her Owen was conscious of ticking off the features of the woman who stood under the big chandelier in the lobby of the Parker House: cheekbones, beautiful legs, a nose. He could not seem to interrupt the inventory. "Excuse me, but are you Demetria Constantine?" She smiled. White teeth—more than the usual complement, Owen thought. He felt himself squinting as into a source of illumination. A wide jaw that makes you more conscious of those cheekbones. He studied the planes of her face, sanded by some master carver in a light smooth wood like birch. He was not sure of the color of her eyes. She looks less like my wife than almost any woman I've ever met, said Owen to himself, speaking as it were for the record. He had forgotten that he once thought of his wife—petite, dark, soft—as very beautiful. "I beg your pardon?" he said since he had not heard her reply.

"Yes," she repeated in the voice people use for the hearing impaired, "I. Am. She," her eyes darting a quick glance at the Tremont exit. The opulent lobby was not crowded. An Aer Lingus flight crew chatted quietly as they waited for transportation to Logan, otherwise escape from this cretin would be unimpeded.

"Have you got the plans?" Owen asked in a strangled voice.

"What is the password?" They looked at each other for a moment then burst into laughter

"Martini?"

"No."

"Scotch and soda?"

"No. If you do not have the password, I cannot give you the plans." She tightened her grip on a manila file folder tied at the mouth with string.

"White wine? Margarita? Some kind of stupid water with a stupid lime?"

"No, no, no." She started toward the revolving door.

"Manhattan? Sidecar? Screwdriver? Wine spritzer? Light beer? Dark beer?"

"None of the above. Only pregnant women drink dark beer."

"I'm glad you're not pregnant"

"So am I."

"Please, may I start over?" Before she could answer he rushed on. "I am Owen Lawrence. I know you were expecting to meet Seymour Gland and deliver some plans for an office building to him. I am an associate of Seymour's; we're old friends actually, and he couldn't get over here, so he asked me to pick them up for him. He said you would be the best-looking girl in the room."

"How nice of Seymour. And was he right?"

Owen glanced around the lobby; except for one of the Irish stewardesses the competition was minimal. "No."

"Oh."

"He should have told me you were the best-looking girl in Boston."

"Oh. Girl?"

"Could I buy you a drink?"

"Well, perhaps, since you're a friend of Seymour's. But just one. I have a date." She looked at him thoughtfully.

"What *do* you drink?" he asked, as they walked up the stairs to the little bar with the low soft chairs.

"Jack Daniel's on the rocks."

"What a coincidence," said Owen, taking her arm. Until now he had never believed much in coincidence.

The drink had become two drinks. "I've really got to be going." They listened for a moment to the good piano on the balcony overlooking the big dining room. "I told you I had a date." Waiters were dispensing Parker House rolls to the early diners.

"When I graduated from Harvard, I didn't really know what I wanted to do. My father was paying the bills, but he wasn't much help in pushing me to make up my mind. I suppose parents never are. Or, if they do try to get you to become a dentist, you decide to join the Peace Corps or start a band."

"It's actually not a date, it's a class."

"So, I entered MIT and decided to become an engineer. In a sense, that *was* my father pushing me. We never talked about it, but it suddenly seemed so obvious to me. He's an engineer, you see. Not an electrical engineer, but a civil engineer, the kind that builds buildings, bridges, structures like that. I had no interest in civil engineering, but EE at MIT is an exciting, *intriguing* field. They probably have the best people in the country. Cal Tech, of course, everyone says Cal Tech and Stanford, but my guess is that MIT is actually head . . . " She stood up.

"I really have to go. I'll be late for my class as it is."

"You know, I haven't even asked you what you do. That's very Western, you know. Where I come from, the first question people ask is what do you do."

"In Boston, the first thing they ask is where do you live."

Owen paid the check and picked up their coats. "Well, what do you do, and where do you live?"

"I'm a lawyer and I live in Brookline."

"You're a lawyer and you're still going to class?"

"Yes, at the Boston Center for Adult Education."

"I know where that is. On Commonwealth. It's just a couple of blocks from where I live. Can I drop you? We'll grab a cab." He knew he was babbling. She had hardly said a word, hardly been given the opportunity. He had a strong sense of playing the fool. In the cab heading up over the Hill Owen made a conscious effort to let this creature speak. "What class are you taking?"

"Great Buns."

"I'm sorry?"

"Great Buns. It's an exercise class."

"Should be teaching it," muttered the Irish cabbie who had watched her climb aboard.

"I thought you said Great Books."

"We all have our priorities. In fact, I took that at Boston University. Right here." The cab pulled up, double parked as she stepped out. Owen mentally agreed with the driver. "Thank you for the drink, Owen. Drinks. You've ruined me for aerobics tonight, I'm afraid, but I enjoyed it."

"I'm sorry I did all the talking. I really wanted to hear about you. I don't know what came over me."

"It was interesting. But you could use a workout yourself. You're very tense."

"What about my buns?"

"You don't have any, as far as I can see."

"That's because I grew up on a horse."

"I'm afraid of horses."

"I can fix that."

She looked down at him. "I doubt it."

"Can I call you?"

"Yes. Good-bye." She ran up the steps of the building, a townhouse whose ornate windows blazed with light. Owen knew the bliss of a patient who thinks he may have been cured of a terminal disease.

"Did you get her number?" asked the cabbie with interest.

"God *damn*," said Owen.

Chapter 7

"She's a stunner, isn't she, I told you, I know, I've had experience in these things, my lad, I recognize a real beauty when I spot one, not the face you'd find on the cover of a fashion magazine, mind you, but a great deal of power, sexual power, that's what that face radiates, sheer, raw, unadulterated, mind-warping, mouth-watering . . . "

"Be quiet, Seymour. Have a piece of cheese." Owen cut some pieces off the wedge and passed the platter to his friend. Gland sat in the largest chair in the library, a solid scotch clutched in one fist, leaning forward, spitting for emphasis, his soft, handsome face composed into a charming mask of boyish lust. Light from the windows behind him filled the room with the glow of dusty wood, reflections from the spines of books, the cheerful colors of the better of the Sargents.

"Well, wretch, don't say that I have never done you a favor. First, I rescue you from the gutter . . . "

"Thank you again for the job, Seymour. I know you are too smart to hire me unless you think I am going to make a lot of money for you."

" . . . then I install you in one of the better clubs in the city . . . "

"The Charles is not the best club?"

"Of course not. The Somerset is the best club. Everyone knows that. You have to be put up for the Somerset at birth. It sometimes takes twenty years for your name to come up. I'm sure, by the way, that no one belongs to the Somerset who was born wherever it was you were born. Most of the members I know are from the Hill or the North Shore."

"Are you a member?"

"No, actually not. I belong to the Club of Odd Volumes, the Charles, of course, the Harvard Club, and I'm a Proprietor of the Atheneum."

"Why aren't you a member of the Somerset? Did someone blackball you? Or were you never put up?"

"And then I introduce you to an authentic ethnic beauty, and what is the thanks I get? Carping, disparagement, complaints, ironic shafts hurled my way, barbed darts, cynicism, ugly irony, and that sort of Gary Cooper bullshit you always pull on me, looking sorrowful and talking with that dreadful Western twang.''

"Blackballed from the Somerset, who would have believed it of a Gland of the Pride's Crossing Glands?"

"Not blackballed, damn it. Never blackballed in my life, ever. Just never put up. I can't be a member of every club in Boston. I'm a member of the Lotos in New York too, by the way, did I mention that, and I was invited to join a London club as well, but it isn't as good as White's or one of those, so I put it on hold. I'll have to make a decision when I'm over there in April.''

"Where did you meet Demetria?"

"You know I don't have much time to spend outside the business sphere. And my social obligations are very demanding. It takes a man at some considerable leisure to do the right thing by one club, let alone, what is it—Charles, Odd Volumes, Harvard, Lotos, the Atheneum, which isn't a club, of course, but it might as well be. That's five clubs. Good God, man, what do you expect of me? I'm not made of iron, you know."

"I know, Seymour. You're made of several hundredweight of suet, encased in pink elastic. Where did you meet Demetria?"

"In court. Press the bell, will you, that's a good man."

"What court?" The Jamaican barman came into the library, a dignified presence, who despite his rather severe expression, suggested a wellspring of good humor somewhere within his comfortably padded, bottle-shaped exterior. At a signal from Gland, he returned to the bar without a word. "You know, I really don't need a second drink, Seymour. I've got a lot of work to do this afternoon. Let's go in to lunch.''

"Oh, for Christ's sake, one more drink won't hurt you, although you have never had much of a head for it, to be sure. Let that silly bunch finish first who are arguing about aid to education, or whatever it is. I could actually hear them as I walked in the front door. It's grotesque to have members shouting at each other in the clubhouse, over lunch, at that. There is a rule, you know, that requires decorum at meals, not that most of those relics know the meaning of the word."

"I think they're discussing AIDS. In what court did you find Miss Constantine?"

"The Federal District Court in Post Office Square. Ah, yes, there we are. Good boy. No, the scotch is mine. Right. I was

[33

appearing as a witness for the Iguana Computer people in a class action suit. You know, Owen," as he glanced at the bartender's departing back, "you've got to cultivate a warmer attitude toward the help. We have a devil of a time holding on to these people. A cheerful word now and again does much more than a raise in pay. You're in here a lot; you've got to do your part."

"I know Abel and he knows me. I'm sure a health insurance plan would do more to ensure his loyalty than cheerful words from the members."

"We're discussing that. Far more expensive than you imagine, and these people, many of them, couldn't pass a rudimentary physical examination. They live in terrible neighborhoods. Not brought up with vitamins, good diet, exercise. No real understanding of sanitation.

"Let's skip lunch."

"Well, of course, Anton keeps the kitchen spotless."

"What was that item in the current budget, the one headed 'pest control'?"

"Nilson, the custodian, has a morbid fear of rats. He's been after us to get an exterminator down in the cellar."

"And drive them upstairs? How did you meet Demetria?"

"No, no. They have this new little pellet that is irresistible, but causes pathological diarrhea. They die in their holes like, like . . . "

"Why doesn't the club just get another cat from the Animal Rescue League, instead of paying a crew to fill the cellar with rats expiring in their own excrement? I'm quite sure, as a matter of fact, I don't want lunch." Owen rang the bell. "It's your company, Seymour. If you find me asleep on my desk this afternoon, you have no one but yourself to blame. Abel, could we have another round?"

"Directly, Mr. Lawrence."

"As I said, it was one of those silly suits in which a crooked lawyer gets a couple of avaricious shareholders to sue about insider trading, or lack of proper disclosure, or some such garbage. I was appearing for the defendant, of course, since I'm on the Iguana board. I don't know what she was doing there. We both sat waiting all day long. It transpires that her brother and I went to Harvard Law together. She is a lawyer too, you know, but she wasn't altogether up front, although," Gland began to giggle, his large balding head wobbling on its invisible pivot in alarming fashion, "she is very up front, if you know what I mean. Oh, *very* up front." He lapsed into a fit of damply suppressed mirth.

"I'm surprised she would talk to such an obvious chauvinist."

"I am not, *not*, I repeat, in the least chauvinistic to women or other minorities."

"The last I heard, women constitute the majority. Even in Boston."

"Well, of course, if you are talking about sheer head-count or, if you prefer," he sputtered, "tailcount. But they are always representing themselves as being as downtrodden as the blacks, and, and, and . . . "

"Seymour, you have always trod with a heavy tread. You know it, I know it, the world knows it. It's one of your endearing traits, perhaps the only one: you are uncompromisingly, unashamedly rotten to anyone below what you consider to be your station."

"Well, thank you, Gary Cooper! Why don't you go to Washington and make speeches about democracy, like you did in that movie?"

"That was Jimmy Stewart."

"Well, you wouldn't be so holier-than-thou if you knew what I know is about to happen unless a few men of principle can find the courage to get up on their hind legs and fight for their rights."

"Rights to what, Seymour? What rights are we fighting for now?"

Gland smiled slyly and held up his glass. The tumbler caught the light and flooded the room with amber. "The right to this stuff, dear boy. The right to drink. Does that hit home?"

"To drink? You mean like Prohibition?"

"That's exactly what I mean. That and the right to privacy, the right to have a men's club, the right to limit the membership to those with whom we want to drink, or lose the right to drink at all. If the Charles Club does not vote to change its bylaws to admit women as members before the end of the winter, they're going to shut us down. Dry us up. It's the same thing, you know. Take away our liquor license. Oh, the bastards," he hissed, his lips fibrillating wetly. "It's the Massachusetts goddamned Licensing Board." Gland's suffused head seemed about to burst like a squeezed pustule. "Of course, it's the *women* who are behind it all."

Owen, who had been a member of the Charles Club for all of two months, listened to this outburst in some surprise. None of the members had mentioned it either during the period when Gland was introducing him as a candidate or since. Thomas Appleyard, a rather stiff corporation lawyer, had been Owen's other sponsor. Appleyard had said nothing about a threat to the Club. Seymour had a history of vivid paranoia. This was likely just the latest episode. "Calm down, Seymour. It'll never happen," Owen said. They did not go in to lunch after all.

Chapter 8

Along Commonwealth corner houses hold pride of place. Larger, more ornate, grander in concept and materials, like giant bookends they keep the discipline of the block. Because of their privileged position they enjoy light on three sides and, as is often the case, four sides in the upper stories. The lesser brownstones have sunlight only in the morning and the late afternoon from street and alley windows. Hallways and middle rooms are often dark in the daytime.

The Charles Club wore its privilege gracefully. A four-story Georgian house of brick and granite, its slate roof and virile chimneys crowned the corner of Hereford Street and Commonwealth Avenue. By no means the largest, it was often named among the handsomest houses on the Avenue. It was constructed in 1879 for a young man from Marshfield who had achieved his success building ships in the North River for others to risk at venture. By taking a small share of each of his vessels, in addition to enough cash to cover his costs and show a profit, he became a wealthy man at an early age. Realizing his talents lay in arranging for others to earn money for him, he commissioned a house in the new neighborhood of Back Bay, recently created by dumping trainloads of gravel from far-away Needham into a noxious tidal swamp. He chose an architect who had finished his studies only the year before and was eager to establish his name in the town. The shipwright struck a sharp bargain, then oversaw the construction with his eye for good workmanship. The result was a house with the uncommon virtues of taste and quality. The shipwright and the architect eventually built three more houses whose inhabitants had reason to bless them. The Charles Club, recently evicted from their rented quarters on Charles Street where the building had been pulled down around their ears, was the eager purchaser of the Commonwealth Avenue house when it came on the market again in 1881. It stood for forty-four more years with little or no change. Then in 1925 the mechanics of the building were brought into the modern age. Fortunately nothing of the exterior with its generous windows, simple ornament, and elegant proportions was touched. Once a day the door knocker, a huge hand whose extended forefinger touched a brass plate, was polished until it gleamed in the center of the front door like a beacon. Around the corner a small door gave access from the side street, a doorbell set like a dimple in the doorframe.

Celia and Ann Dormant, arms encumbered, stepped quickly out of the cab. Grimacing against the rain whipping along Hereford Street, they dashed under the little green awning into the Ladies' Entrance of the Charles Club. They were late, but not too late.

"Foul, foul, foul," laughed Celia in her smokey voice as she dumped parcels and shopping bags decorated with bunches of violets on the faded silk of the couch in the anteroom. Shedding her red Burberry, she glanced at her reflection in the oval mirror over the fireplace, blurted "Oh, God," and bolted for the Ladies' Room. Her daughter followed without comment. "How late are we?" asked Celia, as she jabbed at her dark blonde hair with discouragement.

"One drink," said Ann.

"Then hurry. One of the things that drives me crazy about this club is the service. It is *so* fast. Roger will be half in the bag by the time we sit down."

"Are you going to join?" asked Ann.

"Whatever do you mean?" Celia turned and looked at her twenty-three-year-old Smith College dropout leaning ungracefully against the doorway. As usual these days, the sight saddened her.

"When they have to admit women."

"Don't be silly, Ann. Roger has been a member for years. I have signing privileges as his wife. I can use the club whenever I want, which isn't, I'll admit, very often." She turned back to the mirror over the rickety vanity table to redefine her mouth. "Why would I want to be a member?"

"When Constantine makes them admit women, spouses may have to become members."

"Why would that be?"

"If they just continue the 'spouse tradition'—isn't that a choice phrase, I heard Daddy using it on the phone the other evening—it would mean that the husband of a woman member could automatically use the club. The men wouldn't like that."

"Well, I'm not sure I would, either."

"Or a significant other. They couldn't keep a boyfriend out. A marriage license doesn't mean anything now."

"Not to you, anyway."

"I suppose that's a crack about Ahmed," said Ann. "The fact that he's married is quite irrelevant."

"Perhaps not to his wife." Celia sighed. "You mean that if you became a member of the Charles Club, what's-his-name would be able to use the Club also, is that it? How about his wife? Could she use it too?"

"I would never join this stupid club. I can't imagine why any woman would want to."

"Frankly, I can't either. All of this controversy is really rather puzzling. If it wasn't so silly, it would be a little sad. I suppose the poor old Charles is just another trophy. One of the last white elephants. Someone is going to gun it down sooner or later. Do you really think I'd have to become a member to continue to use the Club? It *is* convenient to take one of those little rooms upstairs if you want a late evening in town."

"I just realized you can't become a member, Mother."

"Why not?"

"Seymour Gland would blackball you. I'm sure he hasn't forgotten what you said to him at the Monet opening."

Celia smiled at the memory. "Thank you, darling," she said, rising and walking past her lanky child into the hall to the lobby.

"For what?"

"You've just given me a reason to want to be a member of the Charles Club."

"Roger, is it true that wives will have to become members if this club admits women?" They were seated in the Other Dining

Room in a cozy alcove whose bay window looked out on a court-yard, barren and wet. An alley tree of the species that no city indignity can discourage lounged in the shadows. The alley beyond was empty except for a large trash truck, whose driver stared impassively at the Dormant family who looked as though they were eating lunch together. The usual clamor from the Long Table in the next room was unexpectedly muted.

"It's a very complex subject, dear. I'm not sure I can explain it to you. Would you like another drink?"

"No. Try."

"Well, as you know, wives and widows of members have the use of the club."

"Yes, I do know."

"They can sign for meals and drinks. They can stay in the guest rooms."

"Yes, yes, yes."

"They can do just about everything the men can, except vote."

"They can't come in the front door," said Ann, "or drink in the Library, or sit at the Long Table, or use the Baths of Caracalla off the lobby."

"What do you know about the Men's Lavatory?"

"I popped in there one afternoon when we were here for brunch. I've always wanted to have a peek, ever since you first brought me here when I was, what, nine, I think. It's positively decadent."

"I hope to God no one saw you."

"I was weighing myself on that old balance scale when someone came in. He ran away."

Dormant looked at his daughter and then his wife. Celia smiled at him. "Roger, please go on explaining. You're doing very well."

"Yes. Well, there has been a lot of debate, as you might guess. Of course, one element won't even consider the idea of women members. But some of us have been, well, exploring it a little."

"And?"

Dormant shifted in his chair. "There seem to be three alternatives, all of them a little sticky. If we were to admit women as voting members, we could continue to extend the current privileges to spouses, including the spouses of the women members."

"What is a spouse?" asked Ann.

"Why, a husband or wife, of course."

"How can you tell? If I brought Ahmed, for example, would he be my spouse?"

"Of course not. You're not married."

"He is," smiled Celia.

"You mean people will have to register the way they do at a hotel? You'll ask if they're married like they do in old movies? Even hotels have given that up, Daddy. That is pre*historic*. It's positively fifties. I can't believe what you're telling me."

"You seem to be telling me. I said it was sticky."

"Your daughter is pulling your chain, Roger. Please go on."

"Another alternative would be to rescind the spouse privilege."

"You mean," said Celia, returning a fork full of garden stuff to her plate, "you would have women members in a club wives can't use?"

"Well, yes. Actually, no one is advocating that tack." Dormant drained his drink and waved at the waitress.

"I'm very glad to hear it. Where are you going, Ann?"

"To Diego's. To have my hair cut. I'll meet you at the car at four-thirty. Thank you for lunch, Daddy," she said pushing it away untasted.

"Don't be late. The traffic will be wretched. And don't show up all spikey." Her daughter shot Celia an enigmatic look as she moved her angular frame among the tables toward the door. "Go on," said Celia to Dormant. "I can't wait to hear the next idea."

"Well, none of this is much joy for the members, I can assure you. It's an impossible situation. We really don't know what to do."

"Why don't you beg for mercy at the feet of the Greek goddess?"

"Do you think that would do any good?"

"No."

"Well, the Nominating Committee has discussed the idea of looking at both the prospective member *and* the spouse," said Dormant without much conviction. His corned beef hash had hardened as it cooled into the shape of a face. Two poached eggs stared coldly up at him.

"No one in Boston will ever be elected under those circumstances. Would the wives vote?"

"I don't know," he said. "If they were members, I suppose they would."

"In other words, make the spouses members."

"I imagine that is what it would mean."

"Just one big happy family."

"Yes."

"No more escaping to the Club."

"No."

"No escape at all."

"No."

"The last bastion falls."

"Yes."

"If it weren't so funny, Roger, I'd feel sorry for all you poor, old, harried, hapless men."

"We're not all old," said Roger.

Chapter 9

They sat across from each other, exhilarated by the white table-cloths, the silver, the two roses in the bud vase, the uncomfortable wooden chairs. Garlic and some less definable essence, perhaps almonds, perhaps basil, perhaps both, struggled unsuccessfully to overwhelm her fragrance. His senses reeled.

"What is your perfume?"

"Do you like it? It's Poison."

"I'll be damned."

"Well, do you like it?"

"I'm dying of Poison, even before dinner."

"I suppose that means you don't like it."

"No. It means I'm famished and a little drunk, and it has nothing to do with dinner."

"If that's a compliment, thank you."

Am I color-blind, he wondered. I can't discover what color her eyes are. She wore a large soft sweater with a gold chain and some sort of gold bar that hung between her breasts as she leaned a little toward him. He took a deep breath. "Why would they name a perfume Poison?"

"Why would they name a perfume Tabu, or Number Five, or anything? And who are 'they'?"

"The nameless, faceless They. Well, I'll never be able to buy you Poison." The proprietress smiled as she set two ponies of bourbon before them. "Cheers," said Owen.

Demetria sipped her drink and looked at him with her appraising gaze. "Don't buy me perfume, Owen," she said.

"Why not?"

"Because it is such a cliché. Perfume, flowers, a heart-shaped box of candy on Valentine's Day. Buy your mother perfume."

"My mother is dead."

"I'm sorry. I didn't mean to be flippant."

"That's all right. She died years ago, when I was a kid. I never gave her perfume. I wish I had. I gave her a pin-cushion once."

"That's sweet. What did your mother do?"

"I thought you were supposed to ask where she lived."

"Well, what did she do, and where did she live?" They laughed.

"We lived in Santa Fe. Well, in Tesuque, really. That's a little town just outside Santa Fe. We had, have, a place down by the river. She didn't do anything. I mean, she raised me, and looked after the house and the two hands who ran the place, and cooked for all of us."

"Who else was all of us?"

"My father."

"Was there a lot to do?"

"Well, not by current standards. She didn't have a career. She went to college, University of Colorado, but she didn't want a career."

"How do you know?"

"Well, I don't know. She never said anything about it. To me, that is. She baked bread."

"Was she a wonderful cook?"

"No. She baked bread, and she fed us well, but . . . " He stopped and took a drink.

"Was she a wonderful housekeeper?"

"No."

"I'm sorry. I'm asking all the wrong questions."

"She kept the place clean. But it was just a ranch house. There were always boots and pieces of tack and shotguns in the living room. It was, well, it was what it was. I haven't been back there in a while." They sat in silence for a moment, the noise of the room building slowly around them since they had arrived early, the late afternoon light on Tremont Street fading quickly into patterns formed of windows and headlights. "Tell me about your mother," he said finally.

"Well, she was a great cook," Demetria smiled wryly. "She was a serious cook. We came to meals prepared to *eat*. Moussaka, pastitsu, arni yemesto, amygdalopita—that's almond pie. She began cooking in the morning and only stopped to go shopping, or to clean the house. Once a week, she cleaned the whole house from top to bottom. It was a big old Victorian in Newton. The woodwork was worn from scrubbing. I mean, the paint was literally worn away in places."

"Are you a good cook?"

"I can cook. Every Greek girl can cook."

"You don't sound as though you enjoy it."

"I can do it. But I don't like to. I spent almost five years losing weight after I left home. And other things," she added.

"How many children in your family?"

"There are three of us; my brother, Stephan; my sister, Sophie; and me. Stephan is a lawyer. Sophie was married, but now she lives in Athens. I was supposed to get married, too. Raise children. My mother died brokenhearted because they brought up three healthy kids, stuffed them with food, bought them warm clothes, but no grandchildren happened."

"Why didn't you get married?"

"I wanted to be a lawyer. To go to law school like my brother. To do something."

"And you did."

"Yes. Let's order. You can't be interested in all this." She picked up the menu. "This is like a French bistro. The wife is out front, the husband is back in the kitchen. But they're from England, you know."

"I *am* interested. In your family, I mean. I want to know all about you. You did go to law school. You did do something."

She laid her menu flat, carefully avoiding the roses in the slender crystal flute. "Yes, I went to law school. Not to Harvard Law, like my brother. I went to B.U. and then to Mass. School of Law. Have you ever heard of it? No, I thought not. It's a little dump over behind the State House that takes whatever is left over from the good schools. I couldn't afford anything better. My father is a wealthy man by his standards, but he wouldn't put his daughter through law school because it wasn't right for a woman to be a lawyer. A woman was supposed to cook and keep house and have babies. Like my mother," she said snapping the menu upright.

"And my mother."

"Well, I wasn't having any of it. I put myself through Boston University, and through law school. Myself."

"How did you do it?"

"Are you ready?" asked the waiter.

"I don't want to talk about it."

"Well, I'll come back."

"No, no," said Owen. "We'll order. Are there any specials? Anything you want to tell us first?"

"The menu is written out each day. This is not a fern restaurant. Everything is special."

"I'll have the asparagus vinaigrette to start, and the scallops *provençale*," Demetria said.

"I'll have the same. And please bring us a bottle of . . . ," he glanced down the wine list, "ah, what do you recommend?"

"A bottle of Sancerre," said Demetria, "well chilled, please." She handed her menu to the waiter. "Thank you." She favored him with a thousand megawatt smile and he stepped back, blinded. "I hope you don't mind my choosing the wine. It's an interest of mine."

"How did you do it?"

"I subscribe to a few of the magazines. I go to tastings. I know people in the business. Quite a few of them, as a matter of fact." She laughed. "But I never, repeat, never accept presents. Not cases, not bottles, not splits, not nips. Not nothing," she finished flatly, as she tore a piece of French bread in half.

"So that means I can't give you a bottle of wine, either."

"Why this obsession with presents? No, you can't, as a matter of fact."

"What I meant was, how did you put yourself through law school?"

"Oh," she flashed the smile on him and it turned his guts to water. "I worked as a cocktail waitress. That gave my father something to think about."

"Was he angry?"

"He disowned me. That's what Greek fathers do. I haven't spoken to him in years."

"What prompted you to choose the Sancerre? I don't know much about wines." The scallops had vanished in a splendor of garlic. They were finishing the bottle over coffee and *crème caramel*.

"First, it's very good. Second, it's not expensive. Third, it's consistent, the vintage is not critical. Fourth, it's from Provence, so it matched our choice of *entrée*. Fifth, I like it a lot if it's really chilled."

"If I teach you to ride will you teach me about wine?"

"I'll teach you about wine if you promise not ever to take me near a horse."

"No, I won't promise you that."

"Madame would like to offer you an after-dinner drink. A liqueur? A cognac?" As he stood at Owen's side, the waiter bounced a little on the balls of his feet like a dancer warming up.

"Thank you."

"No, thank you." Demetria turned to Owen. "I told you, I don't accept presents. Please tell her we had a lovely dinner." The waiter vanished. "Shall we?" she smiled. As they were putting on their coats she explained. "The important things about learning wine are to read and to taste. I'll loan you Hugh Johnson. Good night," she waved at the proprietress.

"Do you know her? I didn't think you'd been here before."

"I haven't. We renewed her last month. There was a hearing, a brief one. Several neighbors appeared for her. It's a good operation. A real addition to the South End. Where can you taste wines?"

"At my club. I never think about ordering it." She looked at him curiously. The door opened and chill air cut through the warm melange of odors. "Shall we take a cab, or walk a little?"

"What club are you talking about, Owen?"

"The Charles Club."

She stepped back inside the door and it slammed, causing the hostess to frown. "Please call me a cab," said Demetria in her direction. "Who do you think you are?" to Owen.

Owen smiled. "That's better than what do you do, and where do you live." She didn't laugh. "I think," he cast a doubtful glance at her face on which a shadow had fallen. "I think I am a solitary person in need of the friendship of a good woman. That is who I think I am."

"Who do you think I am?"

"I think you are the woman I have always wanted to meet."

"I am the Chairperson of the Massachusetts Licensing Board, did you know that?"

"No, I didn't."

"I don't believe you, and I think this is one of the most blatant, most insolent . . . *attempts* I have ever seen in my life. I should have known. That bug Seymour Gland set this up, didn't he? The question isn't who you think you are. You can play Gary Cooper all you want. The question is, what do you take me for?" A cab pulled up, the front door slammed again and she was gone.

Owen stood looking at the empty street framed in the frosted glass of the door. Gary Cooper? Why did people keep bringing up Gary Cooper? His mouth had been injected with Novocain. He couldn't feel his teeth or his tongue. What the hell was Seymour thinking of? Why hadn't he said anything? Owen decided to walk home. He smelled Poison.

Chapter 10

The Long Table occupied the center of the Dining Room which was half again as large as the Other Dining Room and, next to the bar in the Lobby, the busiest in the club. No seats were reserved at the Long Table. Members sat wherever there was an empty chair. Four bottles of wine, two red and two white, stood open. The conversation, as always, was brisk and a good deal louder than that which emanated from the other tables.

"Architecture is the opiate of the masses."

"Really. I should have thought opium was the current opiate of choice," said Dormant thoughtfully.

"Cocoa, surely," put in Gland. The Long Table was almost full.

"Not religion, in any case." DePalma sounded acerbic.

"The developers use architecture to foist their loathsome schemes on a gullible public and the ant-brained bureaucrats who are supposed to regulate such things." The Architectural Critic might have had a second drink before lunch.

"Foist?"

"I said foist. I stand on foist. They spread their ideas of architecture, which seem, by the by, to have been developed watching prewar movies whose sets were doubtless concocted by bisexual set designers and other European second-raters who came to Hollywood because their standards of taste were unacceptable in their country, as we say, of origin, like peanut butter . . . "

"Peanut butter?"

"Precisely. Peanut butter. They spread it over those huge stacks of condominiums and offices like a sticky peanut glaze, circa 1935. Every new building erected in Boston in the past five years looks like the old Jordan Marsh store or something left over from the New York World's Fair of 1939."

"I am in real estate myself in a small way," Gland said modestly.

"Architecture is supposed to create living space, working space, designed for the needs of humans. The developers seem bent on creating a movie location, a—what do they call it—photo opportunity. All this pseudo-, this quasi-architecture is being slathered on the outside. And what, allow me to ask you, is on the inside?" The Architectural Critic raised his brows in question.

"Oh, well . . . " Dormant looked around for another conversational avenue, but they all seemed closed.

"*Ficus trees.* Atriums filled with ficus trees. A maze of sterile corridors and tiny cells. Windows that won't open. Climate control. Ninety dollars a square foot. Humanity is sacrificed. The only ones who benefit are the builders and those benighted cinema crews who are always loafing around town blocking traffic and dishing out overtime pay to police who should be out on the firing line in Mattapan or Blue Hill Avenue."

"Or directing traffic," said DePalma.

"No self-respecting Boston police officer willingly directs traffic, although they may condescend to step in and correct the situation if traffic is flowing smoothly."

"Would you pass me the white, please?"

"People stand dumbly by and watch these monstrosities erected where perfectly serviceable business blocks once stood; and as long as they see red brick and a mansard roof they feel the town is not being prostituted."

"I rather like some of the restoration that is going on around the city," said Roger with a view to stemming the flow.

"Restoration, you call it? When they gut some inoffensive structure, eviscerate it to the very footings, prop up one or two facades to establish the fiction of a historic preservation to capture the tax advantage, then puff some sickening glass soap bubble up out of the wreckage: is that your idea of restoration?''

"Actually . . ."

"You walk into the lobby of what used to be the beautiful old Mercantile Exchange with its N.C. Wyeth murals and what do you find? Twenty elevators surrounded by a pestilential swamp of ficus trees and little carts selling French bread. God in heaven.''

At the Long Table Owen took the last remaining seat between Roger Dormant and Seymour Gland. Roger turned to him more eagerly than Owen's rather dour expression might have warranted. Recent urban development quaked beneath the hammer-blows of the Architectural Critic holding forth directly across from him, a face unknown to Owen.

"What'll you have?" asked Old Jane with customary disregard of ceremony.

"Consommé, please," said Owen, "and the scrod."

"How about those Celtics?" she replied reasonably.

"No dessert and black coffee," said Owen, handing her the slip on which he had carefully transcribed his planned luncheon.

"Old Jane is becoming impossible," remarked Gland, patting his lips with the Charles Club linen. Owen looked at him, somewhat reassured to see the old, familiar, critical Seymour.

"I see no change," Dormant said.

"Clam chowder," said Jane setting a cup in front of Owen.

"Probably out of the consommé," said Owen as he tasted the chowder, which was, as always, excellent.

"No, but really," expostulated Gland, "the club is slipping. Quite slipping. In many ways."

"Perhaps women won't want to join. Did you read today's pronouncement by the Massachusetts Licensing Board?" asked Dormant.

"Crab cakes."

"Jane, I ordered the scrod," Owen said to her departing back.

"I understand we have until the first of the year to resolve the issue."

"Resolve! We are not being ordered to resolve anything. Capitulate is what is required."

"Scrod," said Jane handing a plate to the Architectural Critic, who seemed to have run out of steam. He and Owen silently exchanged plates.

"Damned unfortunate," said the Critic, shovelling lightly breaded crab into his florid face.

"Is everything all right?" asked Jane without pausing in her rounds.

"No, I mean about this membership thing." The Critic sounded almost plaintive. "The heart of a club is its membership. How can a bureaucratic body which deals with bars and restaurants take it upon themselves to tell the private clubs of the city whom to choose as members?"

"It's part of something that began in the sixties," said Dormant into his shrimps.

"Feminism?"

"Good God, no. Feminism began long before that. My mother was a flaming feminist before the First World War."

"How did she feel about clubs?"

"She was a charter member of the Pilgrim Club when they were organized in 1912. She was right out of Goucher and red hot for women's suffrage."

"And she joined a women's club?"

"Of course. The Pilgrim was quite the radical organization in those days. It was what today they would call a support group, I suppose."

"What have the sixties to do with the Licensing Board?" asked Owen.

"That's when politicians learned that irrelevant issues can produce votes. Pick an unpopular minority and legislate against them. That's the way to make a name for yourself."

"Such as?"

"Cigarette smokers. Or motorcycle riders. Can you think of any group of people less popular with the public than motorcycle riders—short of drug dealers?"

"Drug dealers must be pretty popular or they wouldn't be as busy as they are," said DePalma, "or as rich"

"Motorcycle riders," Dormant said firmly. "What outrages them will please the body politic, so you propose legislation that forces the cyclists, the, ah, bikers to wear helmets," he paused, "for their own good, of course."

"I wouldn't care if the noisy idiots all dashed their brains out," said the Architectural Critic.

"Of course, but that's not socially responsible. Or popular with voters. It's important to force minorities to do what the majority decides is good for them. And if the minority resists, like the motorbikers who hate their helmets, or black families who don't like their children bussed ten miles to school every day, so much the better. The sixties taught the politicos that resistance to a socially popular idea only makes it more popular."

"Roger, you surprise me," said the Critic.

"Well, I've thought a lot about this. The sixties were tragic years, tragic. For the first time authority and tradition, two of the entities I respect the most, were publicly reviled."

"The Licensing Board seems to have assumed the authority in this situation," said Gland.

"Yes, and if they were investigating the clubs to see if we were serving alcohol to minors, or ignoring complaints from the neighborhood, I would respect them for it."

"The poker evening in September got a little out of hand. I heard we got several calls about that. Did you stay to the end, Owen?" DePalma was finishing his coffee, ready to leave for court.

"No, I went home early. I could hear it from across the street, as a matter of fact."

"But you see, that's the point. We deserve to be criticized if we are drunk and disorderly."

"But that's not the issue here." Gland turned to Owen. "It's politics. The Licensing Board, especially the termagant who runs it, are doing all this for selfish political gain."

"Is there any other kind?"

"You think she really believes that clubs should be integrated, if that's the correct word?" Gland smiled at them all.

"Perhaps she does," said Roger, "but what kind of an issue is that in the face of homeless derelicts wandering the streets in an alcoholic haze, or the remnants of the Combat Zone dispersing across the city as the developers move in on their real estate, or the gay bars and the sports bars and the college bars that stay open all night?" Dormant paused for breath and drained his glass of Vouvray. For once no one spoke. An unexpected silence spread across the room for ten seconds.

"Are you still working on that?" asked Old Jane, indicating Dormant's half-eaten shrimp casserole Before he could answer she was gone, the plate added to the stack on her arm.

50]

"Well, Roger, I must confess that this is one of the few instances in which we are in agreement," said Gland. "It *is* a political issue, the kind the people at City Hall call a win-win."

"What exactly is a win-win?" asked the Architectural Critic, as he folded his napkin.

"If they win, they win. And if they don't win, they still win."

"Why shouldn't women be admitted as members?" Owen was surprised to hear himself ask.

"Why not, indeed? But let us debate the issue in a dignified manner," said Gland turning to his colleagues on either hand, "not with a gun to our heads."

"Perhaps she, Constantine, I mean, feels the issue has been debated too long," said Owen.

"Perhaps she wants to run for the Legislature," said DePalma.

"But why trample us in the process?"

"Because, as you so succinctly pointed out, Roger, next to South Africa, she could hardly have chosen a safer group to attack than private clubs." The Critic looked down the Long Table.

"Are we such pariahs, then?" asked Roger.

"Indeed, we are," said the Critic. "And if we admit women, we will be no less unpopular. We will just be, as you put it, integrated pariahs."

Owen pushed back his chair and walked through the dim, cream-colored lobby to the coat rack by the foyer door. "Speaking of City Hall," he said to the red-faced Critic, who was pulling on his hat, "what do you think of it? Architecturally, I mean. I'm sure you saw the piece in the *Sphere*, uh, that called such a sixties modernist statement out of context in Boston."

"I'm rather fond of it."

"I would have thought the opposite," said Owen, shrugging on his old raincoat.

"Not a bit. It's quite genuine. It is what it is. No pretense, simply the ugliest building in New England. We should value it for that." Smiling, he stamped out of the door, on firm ground again.

Chapter 11

Getting to work was the biggest problem of Roger Dormant's day. Usually, it involved at least one telephone call and a series of troubling decisions which challenged his self-esteem, never robust in the morning. He had several transportation choices. Over a solitary breakfast of cornflakes and coffee he would try to match these to the level of his spirits, the state of his digestive tract, the absence or more likely presence of throbbing in the frontal lobes, the degree of revulsion evoked by the prospect of social conversation, and his need for a drink away from home. This matching process, not unlike a child selecting Legos and connecting a random series of sizes and colors, eventually produced a construct which if it did not collapse of its own weight would cause Roger to rise from the Chippendale dining table and begin his journey.

The problem was created by the fact that Roger did not drive. He could drive, but having once been admonished by the Commonwealth for DWI—he could never recall exactly what the initials stood for but remembered well the consequences—he chose not to. He lived in a Georgian house in Dover. It was comfortable even by Dover standards, in that it had approximately twenty rooms—although no one had counted them since his mother had died and left it to him a decade earlier. It was known as the Cushing House since his mother had inherited it from her mother, who was married to a Cushing. Tucked away on forty acres of woodland and rolling pasture, it afforded a generous vista of the Charles River. The garage/carriage house contained three automobiles—a Mercedes, a Volvo station wagon, and a Range Rover—which were used by his wife and daughter. Roger had often considered hiring a chauffeur, but he was uncertain how to go about it. In addition, he was reluctant to raise the subject with his wife and was sure it would be talked about at the Charles Club. Thus, he could ask Celia, his wife, or Ann, his daughter, for a ride into Boston if and when they might be going in. He could call Tom Appleyard, a neighbor and fellow club member, assuming he was not already on the road to his law office or to court. He could walk a half mile down the lane and wait for a bus. He could call Earl Loud, who charged him a special rate of thirty dollars each way in the single Dover taxi.

Or he could reconsider the chauffeur idea which must, he now determined, include a nondescript, *unmarked* car, which would let him off two blocks from the club. Perhaps, Roger thought as he paused in the sunny entrance hall at the foot of a graceful cascade of stairs, I could ride in front. The problem of finding a deaf-mute chauffeur in Dover was no less daunting this morning, so Roger began the search for an alternative.

One of the complications which made the Legos hard to fit was that Roger had no work. When his lawyer, Tom Appleyard, told him several years earlier that he must declare an occupation for the benefit of the IRS they settled on consultant. Roger was not comfortable with any of the alternatives which alluded to investments or real estate. He harbored fears that someone might ask his opinion on the market or real estate investment trusts. He had spent much of his life since graduating from Harvard College avoiding any discussion of real estate investment trusts. Consultant was a horse of another color. Roger knew well that none of his acquaintances would consult him on any question more vexing than a good hangover cure. This limited his consulting practice to the Charles Club, which had long since become his daily destination. He was about to enter the library to pick up the telephone when his daughter appeared at the head of the stairs. "Daddy," she said with no evidence of surprise.

"Ann," he replied, the relief audible in his voice since she was not wearing any clothing associated with horses. "Are you by any chance . . . ?"

"By any chance I am. Let me get a cup of coffee and we'll take the Volvo." She descended the carpeted stairway, tall, too heavy-boned to be called leggy, too often frowning to be called pretty, too abrasive to have many friends, too lazy to be a college graduate, but an undeniably excellent driver. Roger smiled gratefully at his only child.

Owen stopped at the Newbury entrance to the Ritz-Carlton, the one which was designated an Accredited Egress. He slipped the loop of the leash over a wrought-iron curl on the planting box under the marquee and shoved the revolving door. He was in a hurry. He had hurried home to give the dog a quick walk and he had to be back to the office in twenty minutes. He was sweating. In November. This thing about a dog in the city which everyone derided as such a pain was actually good for you. It kept you in shape no matter what the weather. He had been thinking, while he hurried along, about his basic lack of business knowledge which in an office full of venture capitalists was more than a little conspicuous and so he decided to get a copy of the *Wall Street Journal* to read at his desk in the afternoon. He handed a bill to the woman behind the marble pulpit in the Ritz newsstand. "Nice day," he ventured.

"Cold," she said, "and gusty," as she handed him two quarters. He smiled, pocketed his change and reached for the paper. "But no snow yet," she said. He nodded. "We should be glad for that." He nodded again and took hold of the paper but it was not relinquished. A column head said, "Real Estate Investment Trusts Rebound." "They say snow this weekend. If," she added.

"If what?" he said reluctantly.

"If the jetstream swings a little down. You know and lets in the large high-pressure area that's up there." Owen gave the *Journal* a little tug. "They say these things are set up in the Pacific Ocean. By the El Neeno. I wish sometimes you didn't know, you know? When you know like all that can happen, they show you these maps with the flashing stuff on them, then there's no way you're gonna be surprised, you know what I'm saying? Not that I want to see snow before Thanksgiving, believe me, but if it happens it won't be a surprise to anyone, will it, since they tell you so much stuff?" Owen nodded and she gave him the paper. He ducked out of her cubicle as another supplicant entered. As he unhooked the leash he glanced apprehensively at the sky, pristine above the Victorian rooftops. Snow? He hurried his dog down the street.

After Ann dropped her father at the steps of the Charles Club on what they agreed was a surprisingly mild and sunny November day, she reversed direction on Commonwealth, turned right up Exeter sliding by on a yellow light, and left the Volvo in the most expensive parking lot in Boston. The attendant, a tall man of impressively forbidding countenance, greeted her. "Yo, mama," he said as she handed him the keys.

"What can I say?" said Ann, completing their ritual. She strode quickly through the sunlight to Lord and Taylor. After a strenuous swing which included Saks, two shops on the second floor of Copley Place, and an emergency run to Bonwit's, she stood on the corner of Boylston and Clarendon, brushed back her mink sleeve and checked the time. "Shit," she said, wondering where the time goes. She was late, so she hurried to the Ritz, where her friend Leslie Sample, perhaps her only friend, she thought, as they embraced carefully in the lobby, was waiting.

"Ann, you look fabulous. Where are the packages?"

"Yo, mama," said Ann. They went in to the Cafe where the maitre d' seated them at the table in the center of the bow window where everyone could get a good look. "I don't carry anymore," said Ann after they had ordered wine and water respectively. "It's a basic mistake. It slows you down, you can't cover the ground. And it gives one time to think about what one has bought if they send it out. On the way home, I sort of try it all on again."

"And?" Leslie stared at this creature from another world with rapt attention.

"And by the time UPS arrives I can send half of it back without even opening the box."

"Don't the stores mind?"

"Are you kidding? They just want to see the stuff move around. That's retailing. Actual purchase is not as important as movement."

"It's a little different in my business."

"Don't believe it. How do you keep your clients, your boss happy? Movement, a steady stream of johns moving through the, what do you call it, inventory. As long as someone is inspecting the inventory, everyone is happy."

"Not me," said Leslie. "I have to close. If I don't close, I starve."

"Well, I suppose there's that. I was talking more about business principles." They ordered salads and Ann devoured the pita toast until they came.

Leslie had been silent for a few minutes. "Are you a happy person, Ann?" she asked after a second round of drinks was presented. "I don't mean to pry, but I have a reason for asking."

Her friend smiled under arched eyebrows. "What a question. You do ask the questions, don't you? Of course I'm almost always quite deliriously happy, aren't you?"

"Well, no. But working keeps me busy so I don't think about it."

"So?"

"So, I thought you might want, well, want a job, perhaps. I thought you might want something to do."

"Do?"

"Yes. You know, like a business career and stuff. It might, well, keep you busy."

"My dear child, I am one of the busiest people you know. My life is a dizzy whirl of this and that and the other. What kind of job?"

"Well, you could sell real estate like I do. I'm good at it, everyone says so, and if I can do it, you can with how you look, and how you talk . . . "

"I'm speechless."

"You could be great."

"Let's talk about something else." Ann caught a glimpse of a tall young man dragging a white dog down Newbury Street. "How's your sex life?"

"Like nonexistent. I'm too busy. I have to work every weekend."

"Then there you are. How could I give up all that?"

"All what?"

"None of your business."

"Is there someone?"

"No. Not anyone you would know."

"How do you know, Ann? Who is it? Maybe I've shown them something."

"If you had, I'd have nothing to keep secret."

"Don't you like to talk about secrets?"

"No. I've got to hold on to what I've got. Let's have dessert. I couldn't sell real estate. I don't have the head for it."

"You have more brains than anyone I know."

"Don't worry your pretty head about my brains. Let's split a dessert." They divided a napoleon and then parted, one feeling full and one feeling empty.

Chapter 12

Owen could not believe the awful symmetry of his luck. To discover the girl—the woman, why did he always say girl—who could quicken life again for him and then to lose her ten days later was almost beyond luck. Perhaps luck had nothing to do with it. But if there were no luck he was dealing with a vengeful God whose intent seemed clear. Demi's face as she slammed the door of the restaurant was the image before him as he walked down the Mall heading for Gland, Hollings Ventures.

The November day shone deceptively bright and mild. The next-to-last red and yellow leaves drifted in front of him as he paused, waiting for a crease to open in the traffic on Arlington Street. He dodged across and glanced up at the belly of Washington's horse at the Garden entrance, his eye automatically checking the tightness of the cinch. Two birds perched on the brim of the General's hat. Washington beamed at the scene of civic order and prosperity that flowed beneath him. The Garden's beds of chrysanthemums were threaded by streams of men and women many of whom had ventured out into a morning three weeks short of the first day of winter without coats. The men carried shopping bags, small knapsacks, newspapers. The women strode along in charcoal skirts and white sneakers, swinging their briefcases. Except for the bald and the gray, most wore tiny earphones connected by wire to a plastic case whose electronics poured a steady stream of sound into each ear. Owen, who had most of his hair although a few strands were lately gray, remembered Seymour Gland's lecture about the earwear of the young. "It's the Japs' revenge, they've discovered a way to turn off the American mind for most of the day and we *buy* these poisonous devices, along with the software, if you can call hard rock software. In an elevator it sounds like you are riding with a swarm of bees. It leaks out of their heads, the music, I mean, it just dribbles out."

Owen wondered about Gland. Had Seymour set him up as a pawn in some devious plot on behalf of the Charles Club? Had his old friend and new boss tried to get something started between Demi and himself? If he had, he had almost succeeded. But why had Seymour not told him who Demi was? Gland was nothing if

[57

not devious. But his motives aside, what was to be done now? Owen walked quickly across the bridge over the Swan Boat lagoon, now empty of its flock, in something like misery. He noticed they were beginning to drain it. Who drained lagoons? The nameless, faceless They, he supposed. Could he ever again get Demi to speak to him on the phone? Their evening a week ago had gone so well. The feeling of life renewed that had filled his gut along with the scallops *provençale* returned now as heartburn. He had to talk to Demi again. As he paused, waiting for the chance to cross Charles Street between the Garden and the Common by the statue of Edward Everett Hale, he decided to call her as soon as he reached his desk. He would dial her every five minutes through the day until she took the call. Who the hell was Edward Everett Hale anyway, he wondered angrily, staring at the bronze beard and the wide slouch hat.

"One of the great egos of history," said the last balloon vendor of the season, as if reading his mind.

"Oh?"

"Yeah. He kept Lincoln sitting in the rain for two hours while he read a speech which was a lot of horsecrap anyway. You know, at Gettysburg. He was the one who introduced Lincoln."

"No," said a Park Ranger, "that was Edward Everett, his uncle. This one wrote *The Man Without a Country*."

"Is that why they built a statue to him?" asked Owen in spite of himself.

"Who knows why they build statues?" said the first historian, snapping a balloon off the valve of his air cylinder. The light changed and Owen moved quickly with the crowd. The nameless, faceless They put statuary around the city as well as draining lagoons and naming perfumes. He thought he caught a whiff of Poison as he crossed the Common heading for Milk Street.

It proved to be amazingly easy with the grudging assistance of Gland's secretary, the icy Ms. James. Usually unapproachable, she had yielded to Owen's explanation that he had been asked by Seymour to return some plans to Constantine. As she checked her Rolodex, Owen noticed that the card was filed under M for Massachusetts Licensing Board, rather than C for Constantine. He entered his office and without sitting down reached over, punched the speaker phone button and dialed Demi's office number. He listened to the electronic music of the dialer and to his astonishment Demi's voice came booming through his office like an announcement at Fenway Park. "Hello," it echoed. "Constantine," then, "Who is this?"

Owen snatched up the receiver and found he could not speak into it.

"Hello. Who *is* this?"

"Ah, Demi . . . "

"Oh. I might have guessed. I'd rather not talk to you."

"Why?"

"I am likely to say something very rude."

"I can't imagine you saying anything rude."

"That's only because you know nothing about me. I can be exceedingly rude. Rude as hell, as a matter of fact, when the circumstances warrant it."

This speech had a calming effect on Owen if only because it was so long. "Demi, I'm sure you must think I'm either a conniving bastard, or a fool . . . "

"That's rather well put."

" . . . but I want to assure you I am not a conniving bastard."

"I don't know which is worse."

"It's much worse to be thought a conniving bastard than a fool. I've been a fool often enough to be sure of that."

"Are you trying to tell me that you did not deliberately seek me out to try to sell me a bill of goods about the Charles Club?"

"That is what I am trying to tell you."

"That you had no idea I was Chairperson of the MLB?"

"Right. I'm trying to tell you that."

"That this is all coincidence and misunderstanding?"

"Yep. That's it."

"Don't pull Gary Cooper on me again."

"Nope."

"Stop it."

"Can I see you? I'm really anxious to see you."

"It's very much against my better judgment."

"Look, Ms. Chairperson . . . "

"Watch your ass, Owen Lawrence. I was—am—really furious."

"Sincerely furious?"

"Furious in a way a few people around town have learned to appreciate."

"Look, you had every right to jump to the wrong conclusion. But clubs and licenses are the last things I want to talk you about. I'm not very good at this."

"What?"

"Begging. I'm out of practice. Can I please buy you a drink after work? Then I'll try to persuade you to have dinner with me."

"All right. A drink, I mean."

"Where would you like to meet?"

"Your apartment. One look around and I'll know whether you're a conniving bastard or a fool."

"I'd rather we went somewhere else."

"I'm already getting a signal."

Owen walked quickly past Ms. James' beige desk and smiled at her back as he pushed Gland's office door open. He knew Seymour was in because his office, perched on a small mezzanine, was enclosed by glass panels the size of department store windows. From his eminence at the top of the curving stairway Gland had a commanding view of all the other offices, the two conference rooms, the tangle of computers, the mailroom, and the reception area with its plants and imitation leather couch, all of which—with the exception of the plants—were beige. His employees, in turn, had full view of their leader whose every movement could be seen through the large panes. Gland clung to the theory that the chief executive of a company should set a visible, virtually uninterrupted example to his subordinates. The only exception occurred when he disappeared into his private bathroom. Otherwise he was on stage for his associates throughout the day. It was Ms. James' duty, however, to limit access to the glass box only to those who had been summoned. Owen waited until she was occupied with the telephone before running up the stairway on her blind side as she poked among the twenty-four buttons on the phone keyboard.

The offices of Gland, Hollings had been remodelled from the second floor of a bank. Gland had acquired the building five years earlier when the Old Currency Bank had moved to its new home, One Currency Place, next to the reincarnated Mercantile Exchange. Gland caught the crest of Boston's avid demand for office space. He refurbished the old marble lobby, reserved the second floor for his own beige suite, installed new elevators, leased the bank vault to a restaurateur more interested in atmosphere than ventilation, and signed lucrative long-term leases on all the remaining office space within six weeks. Since that epic period his coworkers could watch him hard at work crafting deals on the telephone every day. They did not, however, realize that many had little to do with the investment of venture capital in technology.

As Owen stepped in the door he found his friend talking with a strange mixture of fury and sincerity into a beige telephone. "Lester, that is not the parcel we are talking about. I specified the old Walton block, the one with the bookstores and the peepshows on the Washington Street side and, I believe it is called, Pussy's Lounge on the corner. Owen, excuse me, please, I'm on a call. Can you come back . . . no, Lester, can you hold for a minute?" Gland punched a button on the elaborate telephone console that occupied the center of his leather-covered desk, "Owen, this is quite important. I'll buzz you when I'm finished on the . . ." he searched the buttons in front of him ". . . intercom, yes, here it is I think, when I'm through."

"Seymour, remember when I bailed you out of the Cambridge Jail? When I lent you taxi fare to Northampton? From downtown Boston? When I helped you look for your car for two hours when it wasn't even there and then you puked on your patent leather dancing pumps?"

"Please get out. This is important." He pushed the button to reestablish contact, but was assaulted by a dial tone. "God damn it! Why does this idiot system never work the way it is supposed to?"

"Have you read the instruction book?"

"Of course I haven't. It's sixty-four pages long, for Christ's sake." Gland's voice had risen both in pitch and decibels. "Why should I have to read an instruction book to complete a simple telephone call?"

"Technology, I suppose."

"Technology? What do you know about technology? You're only an engineer. I've invested more money in technology . . ."

"Be quiet for a moment, Seymour. I want you to answer a question. It has nothing to do with technology. Why didn't you tell me Demetria Constantine was the Chairman, or whatever, of the Massachusetts Licensing Board? Why did you send me to meet her at the Parker House? You could have sent the office boy for those plans."

"Ah-ha! Did you listen to yourself? That's two questions and a declarative statement. I choose to answer the statement. I did send the office boy."

Owen studied Seymour Gland. "I can't decide whether you set me up or not." He thought about office boy for a moment. "Don't involve yourself with my private life, Seymour. It's been enough of a disaster so far without your help. I am going to say this just once. I like Demi and I don't want anything of a, uh, political nature to spoil our relationship. I hope you understand me."

"Your 'relationship'! You sound like the cover of *Cosmopolitan*! And as to your two questions, you don't want me to 'involve myself.' More psychobabble, but if it hadn't been for me you would never have met the estimable Ms. Constantine, who, by the way, could easily grace the cover of *Cosmopolitan*, or even . . . "

"Can it, Seymour." Owen turned to go.

"Just because I didn't give you the complete *curriculum vitae* of the lady, you come, blustering and complaining, into my office, interrupting an important, no, a crucial conversation that could well change the face of one of Boston's most blighted neighborhoods. Really, Owen, I don't understand you. I had no ulterior motive in arranging that you and Demetria become acquainted. I am delighted to hear you like her. I hope you get to know her better. The lady is what they call a comer in political circles, a potential political superstar in my opinion. Her friendship could be worth a great deal some day. Now, could you please see your way clear to allow me to return to my work?"

Owen walked across the beige carpet and opened the beige door. He stopped and glanced at the now smiling Gland behind his beige desk. "If you mess me up with Demi, or fool around with my private life, Seymour, I'll sic my dog on you."

Chapter 13

The dog barked. The doorbell rang., Owen tipped the dustpan, spilling the ashes he had just swept up with a clothes brush back onto the tiny hearth. He had never heard the doorbell before, never realized there was a doorbell. The sound momentarily paralyzed

most of his functions. His thoughts wandered, visualizing the outside frame of his front door at the foot of the three damp stone
steps with its mossy stone doorstep. He was sure there was no bell
by the door. His mind's eye wandered up the facade of the building,
the exuberant neo-Gothic pillars, the massive arch over the main
entrance, the hideous red sandstone carved in a variety of wreaths,
pediments, circular window frames and beetling cornices. The bell
rang again and he realized the sound was emanating from the door
itself, not an electric bell somewhere in the kitchen since there was
none, but from an old twist bell set in the center of the door. Shaped
like a half a bagel without the hole, it was encrusted with many
coats of paint, the last a purplish brown, all of which layered the
door itself. Tasha barked again, staring at the door with fascination,
intent on performing her watchdog duties, though the tone of her
bark suggesting the situation was not life-threatening.

"Owen, I know you are in there. I can see you through the
window. Are you going to let me in, or not?"

He leaped like a fish and threw the door open. Demetria col-
lapsed her umbrella and with a questioning glance edged past him
leaving a damp trail behind her. Tasha sniffed the hem of her
raincoat appreciatively. The room, ordinarily unobtrusive and even
welcoming in Owen's eyes, withered to the cell it had appeared
when the real estate agent first showed it to him. "I'm sorry. Let
me take your coat," he said, shoving the dustpan and brush under
a chair with his foot.

"What were you doing? It looked like you were praying in front
of the fireplace." She turned slowly, absorbing the apartment in its
entirety. She seemed to be searching for something to say. "What a
wonderful old rug."

"Oh, you mean that?" Owen glanced at the Navajo weaving
thrown across his—for once—carefully made bed.

"Yes, it's superb." She walked into the bedroom, a distance of
three steps. "A Ganado, and an old one, isn't it?" She lifted the
frayed edge, felt the close weave of the red wool, examined the
pattern of two encased crosses surrounded by a heavy black border
and a frame of stepped terraces. It smelled of dust and lanolin,
baked for a long time in the sun.

"I don't know. That is, I know it's old. I used to have it on my
bed at home. I'm not sure where it came from. Or if it's superb."

"Didn't you tell me you came from New Mexico?"

"Yes, but that doesn't make me an expert on Indian blankets."

"Rugs. Aren't you going to offer me a drink?"

Owen collected himself and looked around for the ice.

"It's from Hubbell's Trading Post in the Navajo Nation in Arizona," Demi continued, looking at it again, feeling the weave. "Probably worth five thousand dollars. Aren't you going to ask me how I know?"

"How do you know so much about Indian rugs?" he asked as he began to put ice in the two glasses set out on a tray on the birch log table. "At least I know what you drink." He poured a healthy dollop of Jack Daniel's in each glass from a small bottle and pitched the plastic ice holder into the sink.

"My father, the insurance agent who sold policies to all the Greeks in Newton, collected Indian things."

Owen, feeling a trifle silly, offered her the tray and Demi took one of the glasses. She smiled a little smile. "He had pots, rugs, chief's blankets, beadwork, silver. It was a lovely collection."

"Did he travel out West a lot?"

She laughed, a derisive little snort that brought Tasha's ears up as the dog lay in the Sphinx position studying this new being with an unwavering black-eyed gaze. "He and my mother never went west of Springfield. The longest trip he ever took was last year when he went back for a visit to his village in Greece."

"How did he do his collecting?"

"He read books and he went to estate auctions, the two things in life he loved to do the most, as a matter of fact. He discovered that many of the old New England families had travelled to the West in the twenties and thirties. There were beautiful Indian pieces sitting in attics for years until they turned up in the auctions. And, of course, everyone else was interested in furniture, or flatware, or a Colonial musket to hang over their fireplace."

"How big was it?"

"He had almost two hundred pieces. My brother has it all now. I was the only one in the family who ever showed an interest, but my father gave it all to my brother when Father bought the condo in Florida. God knows what Stephan has done with it now."

"I meant his village. The village he went back to visit in Greece. How big was it?"

"About six hundred, I guess."

"That's about the size of my village."

"But this village has been a village for a thousand years."

"So has Tesuque Pueblo, although I lived in another part of town."

Demi looked at him for a silent moment as she sipped her bourbon. The glass had a band of blue anchors and whales around it. The inscription read: NEW BEDFORD WHALING MUSEUM. "What are you doing here?" she asked, finally.

"I'm not sure."

"You're a bright person."

"I wonder sometimes."

"You're not unattractive. An engineer with an MIT degree, for God's sake. Why haven't you made a million dollars? It's not that hard to make a million dollars in Boston these days. Why are you living in this, this . . . "

"Yes, I know. Except, I don't really know. I guess I never set out to make a million dollars." He seemed to be out of words. The telephone rang, startling him again. It had rung only a few times before, the New England Telephone Company checking to see if the line was functioning, a wrong number or two. This time it was Abbie.

"Owen? I wanted to let you know that I gave the key to the safe deposit box to my lawyer. She's going to mail it to your lawyer, who will give it to you. I think it's the safe deposit box. It may be the key to the Post Office box in Mattapoisett. There's a problem with the Mattapoisett closing, too. You know it's been under agreement for six months. Now, at the last possible moment, it's been delayed because there is some stupid question about the title. Do you know anything about . . . am I interrupting anything?"

"Hello, Abbie. No, that's all right." He instantly regretted uttering her name.

"An easement across the property for a water line that goes next door . . . do you have someone there?"

Owen's mind went blank again. He looked at Demi, who was scratching Tasha's ears. Demi looked back at him and he again wondered what color her eyes were.

"This isn't exactly the best time for me to talk."

"No problem," said Demi. "I've got to be going. I've got a long day tomorrow."

"Owen, if you have someone there, why don't you just say so? Oh, and have you seen my passport? I can't seem to find it anywhere."

"Why don't you call your lawyer about the easement?"

"She's a divorce lawyer, not a real estate lawyer. I think you know that. This is something that isn't in our title, and the bank didn't spot it when they did a, what do they call it, search, but the buyer's lawyer did and now everything is tied . . . "

"Could I call you back? I haven't seen your passport."

"Owen, you surprise me. I didn't think you had it in you. It's only been seven months and twelve days."

"Abbie . . . "

"You are a fast worker. Not world class, but at least faster than you used to be. What's her name?"

Owen took the phone from his ear. "Demi, hold on a second."

"What? Sammy? Now you have me confused."

"Please sit down. Finish your drink. Tasha, don't let her out the door. Goodbye, Abbie." He hung up the phone, pulled Demi's coat off her right arm, pushed her into a birch log chair, lit a fire, poured two more drinks, pulled the shades, sat down opposite her. "Sorry. That was my wife."

"Your ex-wife, I suppose you mean."

"Right." Silence rose like moisture from the floor. The fire crackled merrily. From behind the kitchen wall came a throaty rumble like the purr of an enormous cat.

"Does she call often?"

"Nope."

"Some problems with the settlement?"

"Yep."

Tasha lay by the door, head between her heavy paws, not only to prevent egress but also because it was the coolest place in the apartment. Her coat absorbed like a white sponge the wet November emanations that gusted under the door. Her eyes remained on Demi, as did Owen's.

"Would you like to take me to dinner?"

"I'd like to take you to bed."

She looked at him with that appraising stare that seemed to be weighing all the evidence. Then she smiled. "First things first, I suppose. Don't move the Ganado."

Chapter 14

The sun was setting as Leonard Lapstrake's American flight from San Francisco via Chicago landed at Logan Airport. It had been a pleasant flight, both legs on time, no undue delays at O'Hare. He had used a little gold sticker given to him by a stewardess friend to accomplish an upgrade from coach to first class on the first and longest segment. Unfortunately, there had been no empty first class seat on the flight out of Chicago, but the back of the plane was surprisingly light. He found he had two seats to himself, was at least as comfortable as in first class, and celebrated his luck with a third martini. The combination of two airline meals and three drinks induced a spurious sense of well-being as the plane touched down amid a handsome sunset that illuminated the harbor islands from beneath lowering rain clouds. This mild euphoria dissipated quickly, however, as he walked out onto the chilly jetway.

Lapstrake was a short, well-fed man in his forties who had in the past ten years found a niche in the granite headwall of San Francisco journalism, leaping from City Desk assignments on the *Clarion*, to byline features, to a four-a-week column with the agility of a chamois. In a city of better than average columnists he had attracted a following that ranked him somewhat below Herb Caen but ahead of most of the rest. His specialty was a wry look at the most recent foible, and his word processor had a rich and inventive invective disk. His admirers felt he was equally adept at spearing social as political fish. Seymour Gland, on a trip to the Bay Area in September to visit Iguana Computer in Sunnyvale, had read three of his columns, including one he particularly enjoyed which skewered a gay city councilman for his retrograde views on prison reform. Gland, on his return, wrote Lapstrake urging him to come to Boston, promising him a story worth two weeks of columns. In a burst of uncharacteristic financial optimism Gland offered to pay expenses under the assumption the Charles Club would make good when he presented his plan.

It was sultry in Baggage Claim as Lapstrake waited for his two-suiter to arrive on the conveyor. He was curious about Boston. This was his first visit and as long as he had lived in San Francisco he had heard the two cities compared as coastal outposts of culture in contrast to the twin capitals of sophistication and sleaze that lay to the south of them. His head throbbed. He noted the time, seven-thirty, checked his pocket watch, and realized he had been travelling since eight that morning. The very act of setting the watch three hours forward caused a dull ache to detach itself from the general discomfort behind his eyes. It spread rapidly from the bridge of his nose back until it found a place to settle and expand at the base of his skull. He was reminded that his stewardess friend warned him to ignore time when he travelled east. She claimed to do so mitigated jetlag. Gin certainly wasn't helping.

Bursts of chill air swept into the hall as the doors slid open and shut like the shutter of a camera aimed at the street. He glimpsed a long impatient line waiting outside for taxicabs. Something in their body language told the columnist that Bostonians were not stoic queuers. It had been a beautiful crisp morning in San Francisco, he recalled, as he shrugged into his trench coat. Rain hissed under the tires of the traffic passing the door, moving, it seemed to him, too fast for the congested airport roadway. He grabbed at his soft leather bag, missed it because he hadn't been paying attention, and excited some derisive applause as he trotted through the crowd trying to catch it at the next corner. He trudged out to the cabstand and stood amid chaos until the starter shoved him in the direction of a distant vehicle bearing the markings: GYPSI TAXI, INC. As he dropped into the back seat he was surprised to discover that he was separated from the driver by a wall of sheetmetal topped with a thick, evidently bulletproof, plexiglass window. A hand-lettered sign taped to the glass exhorted:

NO SMOKIN
TALK LOUD

"The Charles Club," he said with as much force as he could muster. The driver, a swarthy lascar, turned from adjusting his radio and answered in a voice as inaudible as it was incomprehensible. But since they pulled quickly away from the curb, Lapstrake felt the message had been conveyed. He tried to adjust his legs to the cramped space and glanced outside to reassure himself that Bostonians were not routinely shorter than himself. Finding that with his back pressed against the seatback both his knees and his toes were jammed against the armor, he briefly tried sitting cross-wise on the seat, leaning against his bag. It was more comfortable but he felt silly and resumed his penitential position as the cab raced over the potholes.

Gland had recommended he stay at the Charles Club. Lapstrake, who belonged only to a loosely organized writers' drinking and poker club, thought it would give him some of the Boston flavor. Also he knew there was some sort of a story about clubs brewing and wanted to get in on it. He had done half a column already about problems that had recently arisen at the Bohemian Club. "You'll find it quite comfortable," Gland had assured him, and did not mention that it eliminated half the expense of the trip.

The cab paused briefly at the Charles Hotel in Cambridge, which turned out to be a totally different city on the other side of a river; the doorman invited Lapstrake to look up the address of the Charles Club in the telephone book. Lapstrake gave the driver the information, carefully inscribed on a small piece of paper, just as he had once done with cabbies in Tokyo. Thirty minutes later he stepped out into a puddle at the corner of Commonwealth Avenue and Hereford Street. The meter indicated sixteen dollars, actually less than he had paid to get from his apartment on Russian Hill to the San Francisco airport. He handed a twenty through the open window and watched the cab whistle away. This stretch of city street was lit by a file of archaic-looking light posts each supporting a cluster of four bare bulbs enclosed in a lantern of plate glass. The light cast by these fixtures barely exceeded the gaslights they were supposed to resemble. A Disney movie set, thought Lapstrake.

Head throbbing, he glanced up at the dark building, dimly perceived in the mist. Its Georgian facade was a mixture of brick and granite. Broad steps led to a wide black lacquer door embellished in brass hardware, crowned with a fanlight tiara, flanked by Doric pillars and narrow leaded windows. No nameplate on the door, noticed the columnist as he hefted his bag and with leaden tread surmounted the steep steps. No bell either, he noted. He tried the knob and found the door locked. Suspended in the center of the door panel was a giant brass hand, forefinger pointing down. He lifted the finger and let it drop on the plate, sending a crash echoing through the bowels of the building. Water dripped from his rather sparse yellow hair, trickled over the ache at the base of his skull, and found its way down the back of his neck. He lifted the knocker again and loosed another volley. Dimly he heard movement within, but no light showed.

Just as he was about to pick up his bag and begin the search for a hotel, the doorknob turned. A nose and a pair of eyes appeared in the crack as the door opened to the length of a chain. "Good evening. I am Leonard Lapstrake. I believe you are expecting me?" Try as he might, he could not prevent ending the sentence as a question. Somehow he knew a Boston clubman would have simply stated it as a fact. The door closed. "Is this the Charles Club?" he shouted at the glistening panel. A chain rattled and the door opened again. Lapstrake stared at the blackness within. "The Charles Club?" he repeated. Hesitantly he entered, the desire to get out of the freshening rain overcoming his trepidation. The door swung silently behind him revealing a glimpse of a bent figure in the light from the street. Nilson secured the chainlock, scuttled past, opened the foyer door and led the way to a small desk by the elevator shaft. There a single brass banker's lamp illuminated a large cat sitting on the open pages of a book. Lapstrake, who harbored feelings for cats which ranged from dislike to allergic revulsion, noted with a measure of alarm that it had an inordinate number of toes on each paw. The cat seemed to smile at the visitor but did not move from the pages of the register.

Nilson struck it a swift blow and handed Lapstrake a pen. His impassive face watched as the writer entered his name and address and the name of the man who had brought him to this pass. When he finished he returned the pen to Nilson who spoke for the first time. "You'll have to walk."

"Where? Why?"

"The elevator is temporarily broke. You'll have to walk up. It's on the fourth floor. Switch on the lights at the head of each landing."

Lapstrake stared at the man, hoping for additional information. The cat jumped back on the desk and in the yellow radiance of the lamp its calico bulk seemed to glow from within. It licked a forepaw, carefully extending one claw after another from a seemingly inexhaustible supply. Lapstrake sneezed and started for the stairway.

"It's a Boston Cat," said Nilson. This announcement halted Lapstrake's passage upward.

"I didn't think it was from London."

"Might have been! See its feet?" He grabbed a hind-quarter of the unresisting animal and held it up for inspection. "See all those toes? Any cat with extra toes is descended from the one tom who came over on the Mayflower."

"I find that hard to believe," said Lapstrake, who had reached the first landing and was looking for the light switch.

"Call them Boston Cats." Nilson watched him grope along the wainscoting. "Room six," Nilson added as an afterthought.

Lapstrake found the switch, an old-fashioned ceramic cylinder with a serrated black knob which, when turned, lighted a single receptacle hanging above the next landing. As he picked up his bag—which was becoming heavier with each step—he thought he heard a faint ticking noise. Nilson had switched off the light in the lobby and disappeared into the darkness. The club was quiet but not silent. Each stair tread breathed as Lapstrake made his hesitant way upward. A metallic noise sounded far off and somewhere a shutter slapped the side of the house. He was certain that he and Nilson were the only inhabitants of the place. Or perhaps Nilson left for the night. Lapstrake, now filled with deep misgiving, longed for a shower. His clothes hung on him like damp towels. Of course the room would have a bath. Until this moment it had not occurred to him to question such a thing. It had been years since he had spent a night in a room without adjoining bath. It had, in fact, been a country house in Ireland which reminded him a great deal of . . .

The light went out above him with a click. Something brushed against his foot. Lapstrake conquered an almost overwhelming desire to scream.

He gripped the leather handle of his bag and strove to orient himself. He was only about six steps away from the next landing. The light switch there would undoubtedly be in the same place as the last one. There was a sturdy banister that would protect him from, well, that would protect him. He stretched a tentative hand to his left and was relieved to touch the smooth oak banister that followed the curve of the stairs. He gave it a little shake to demonstrate its sturdiness. "Oh, Christ!" he whispered as it sagged outward under his hand.

It was important not to make noise. Lapstrake was buffeted by the conflicting notions that he might be the only human in this black cavern or, if he was not, that he did not want anyone else to know he was here. Slowly he raised his foot to the next step. He hit a stair rod that rattled and the tread gave a squeak that sounded reassuringly like the previous one. He took another step, another, and another. The last pitched him forward into stygian emptiness. After a moment he caught his breath. He was soaked with perspiration, but he realized he had gained the second landing. Setting down his bag, he took off his raincoat and the jacket of his tweed suit—which in another time he had felt appropriate for Boston—both of which he dropped on the bag. His heart rate began to slow as he loosened his tie and unbuttoned the cuffs of his clammy shirt. Damn Seymour Gland. It he had stayed at the Ritz or the Copley he would have showered by now and be enjoying a nightcap. Instead his life was in jeopardy.

The blackness was disorienting him so he moved cautiously, sliding his feet along the carpet as if testing the ice on a pond. This skating motion propelled him sideways until his right foot met the wall. With a sigh of relief he spread both palms against the wall and began to search for the switch. Had he come too far forward? He moved back a step or two until suddenly one foot slipped into deep space. He clawed his way forward and caressed the wall like a man making frantic love to an elephant. His fingers grazed the hard nipple of the switch and panting he gave it a vicious twist. Light poured down from the landing above. Lapstrake heard a ticking sound emanating from the switch. So that was the deal! A timer, one of those old European timer switches that shut off the lights behind you. Well he was up to it! Lapstrake ran for the next flight and, taking the steps two at a time, was halfway up before, with a sob of frustration, he realized he had left bag and coats behind. He raced down, scooped them up and regained the first step when the switch shut itself off with a click as final as the snap of a bone.

The stairs between the third and fourth landing exhibited a sickening reverse camber slanting off in the direction of the stairwell due no doubt to settling of the house over the years. Lapstrake knew the elevator enclosure was there but the knowledge did not comfort him. A vision of himself spreadeagled on it, clinging like a human fly to the brass rods, flashed before his eyes. A rustling noise above him froze Lapstrake in midstep. He stood like a Balinese dancer, one foot in the air, his face contorted in a mask of violent emotion. The house was alive with tiny sounds. It ticked and creaked and groaned and popped and rubbed its surfaces together. Somewhere he could hear rain being driven against a windowpane. "Fuck this!" he roared, and stamped heavily upward drowning the gentle obbligato.

The fourth floor had no carpet, he discovered, as his shoe hit wood. He was sure he knew where the switch was and indeed after pounding the panelling for less than a minute he found it. He switched it on and the light revealed a hallway with three doors on each side, an armoire with one door hanging open and finally a sight which broke his fighting spirit. Dimly through a half-open door at the far end of the hall he glimpsed a washstand and a clawfoot tub.

Number six, the gnome had said. The light switch ticked like the mechanism of an infernal device. The doors had no numbers. Wait, yes, a small brass plate beside the doorknob. Number one. Across from it, number six. As Lapstrake pushed open the door of his room the hall light went out again. He kicked a table, threw his bag and the coats on the floor and flailed about until his clutching hands caught a bedside lamp and strangled it into life. A fit of sneezing took him. The room was stifling hot. I will settle with you, Gland, he thought as he picked up his soggy clothes from the floor. He sneezed again as he hung his raincoat on a wooden hanger inscribed Dependable Cleansers and his suit jacket on a more elegant model from the Miramar Hotel in Palm Beach. It was only as he emerged from the closet that he saw the Boston Cat smiling at him from the middle of his bed.

Chapter 15

"Have you met Gland's journalist?" Walter Junior and a man named Blankinship were standing in front of the bank of American Standard urinals.

"No, I haven't. I didn't know Gland had his own journalist," said Blankinship.

"He says the Club agreed to import one from San Francisco."

"Odd. I don't recall anything about that, either." He pronounced the word eyethah.

"Yes. Nor do I. One would think Boston was oversupplied with journalists."

"I knew he had a Luders 32, but I didn't know he had a journalist."

"The *Sphere* has written a dozen stories mentioning the Charles Club in the past month and each one of them was signed with a different name."

"I think he keeps her at Hyannis."

"No, it's a man, and he is reputed to be staying here."

They moved to the basins, dried their hands on snowy towels monogrammed with two ornate C's back to back and dropped them into a white wicker basket. Walter Junior began to comb his hair while the other looked on with a trace of envy. "Why would the Club bring a scribbler to Boston?"

"Exactly. Quite coals to Newcastle. The only infestation worse than journalists in this town is politicians." He took a last lingering look at his white locks and the two men strolled to the door, parting the swinging louvered panels, heading for the bar. As they gave their pre-luncheon order to Abel, each patted his own head in an unconscious gesture.

"Where is he, Gland?"

"Actually, I don't know. We were to meet for breakfast this morning, but he wasn't here when I arrived. Abel told me he signed the book last night, so he is in residence in any case."

"I'm not certain I understand the point of all this."

"Yes, Roger, well, I'm sure you recall that at the meeting of the Strategy Committee last month it was agreed that we should strike back on all fronts."

"What are the fronts, again?"

"The legal, the political," Gland paused to take a sip of his drink, "and the pee-ah," he said.

"Quite."

"DePalma is handling the legal. Another of our many distinguished lawyers, Tom Appleyard, is handling the political. He has excellent connections on the Hill."

"Beacon?"

"No, Capitol. But I think he can deal with the local pols without much difficulty. And I volunteered to supervise pee-ah."

"And this man from California?"

"First of all, the expense, which everyone seems to be carping about, is negligible. Bear in mind that Lapstrake is one of America's leading newspaper writers. I persuaded him to come here for expenses only. We are not paying him a fee to help us tell our story. And the fact that he is from out of town derives to the greatest advantage. He won't be influenced by anything the *Sphere* has already regurgitated.''

"I suppose not.''

"And we agreed, the entire Strategy Committee agreed, that we must spend what is necessary to win the battle. Even if it means a special assessment. We are fighting for the continued existence of the Club, you know.'' Dormant started to speak. "But there's more,'' said Gland in a gleeful whisper. "I've set them up.''

"The Strategy Committee?''

"No! The *Sphere*. They've agreed to print Lapstrake's columns while he's here in Boston.''

"However did you arrange that?''

"It *is* a masterstroke, if I do say so.''

"No doubt.''

"My secretary, Rachel James, has been, ah, seeing the assistant editor of the *Sphere*'s Metro Region section. They know Lapstrake by reputation. He's syndicated in something like fifty newspapers, you know. They have agreed to run up to four of his columns on Boston. I, or rather Ms. James, has the agreement in a letter,'' said Gland positively chortling, "an agreement in writing!''

"And you think these pieces will help the cause?''

"Of course. That's what pee-ah is all about. Lapstrake is not a typical liberal, left-wing toady like most of the *Sphere* reporters. He'll write what he thinks. We can't always be on the defensive, Roger. Each time another *Sphere* writer calls Pinhead, they ask him questions he can't answer. He dithers, and equivocates, and contradicts himself, and they put it all in the story.''

"Really, Gland, I don't like the practice of calling Walter Junior . . . ''

"Successful pee-ah has to be offensive. You have to create the story yourself. I have studied this extensively. It's more or less a science. You take the fight to the enemy. The newspaper editor is a lazy scut. Write the story for him, that's the ticket. Get your own hired gun. Take the offensive and you can win the war. Sit back and react to each attack and they cut you to ribbons!'' As they were talking they moved, glasses in hand, into the Library, where Gland's dissertation was forced to compete with the Eldest Member, whose hearing disability caused him to speak louder than most of the others. Gland fell silent until the patriarch subsided. Then he leaned down and shouted in his withered ear, "Sir, your voice fills the room.''

"AND YOURS EMPTIES IT," snapped the Eldest Member as he struggled to his feet.

When he hung up the phone the night man on the Metro Region Desk picked up the copy that had been dropped in front of him. "The fuck is this?" he snapped at the pretty brunette standing by his desk.

"Why do you feel it necessary to talk like a character in a George Higgins novel?"

"Well, I graduated from the University of Oregon, not Harvard, as you did, so I have to compensate the best I can."

"Is that why you wear untied Reebok hightops and red suspenders?"

"Yes. And I don't wear pyjama tops."

"Neither do I. I think you'll like this stuff. It's from Leonard Lapstrake, a syndicated columnist for the San Francisco *Clarion*. He's visiting Boston for a week and we have a release to use what he does here. I took a chance and told him, told a friend who knows him, that we might use a couple, as many as four, if we decide we want to."

"You did take a chance. Is he any good?" His phone started to ring.

"I think so. We don't have anyone around here who can do this. I can see why his column is syndicated in ten papers. Do you want to get that?"

"Wouldn't that be a deal? Ten papers. He probably does three or four a week. Say they pay a thousand, less, say, twenty-five percent for the syndicator, that's, what is that?"

"He does four a week with two weeks off a year, so his column runs two hundred times a year." The phone continued to ring. "But he probably doesn't get a thousand a column. More like six hundred. So his gross is a hundred and twenty thousand, but his net is maybe two-thirds, say eighty thousand above salary." The phone stopped ringing as they thought about eighty thousand above salary. "It sounds great," she said, "but you're on camera every day, and it better be good or you're in the archives."

"And you think he's good?"

"Decide for yourself."

"Why don't you wear pyjama tops?"

"Because I don't wear pyjama bottoms."

TALES OF TWO CITIES

by Leonard Lapstrake

BOSTON. Special to the Boston *Sphere*. Copyright San Francisco *Clarion*, 1987.

NOTES ON THE BACK OF A BOARDING PASS: They call it the City on the Hill. Jack Kennedy said it, and he was quoting old John Winthrop, and now it's Boston chitchat.

But where are the hills? The local bumps and knobs are to *real* hills what New Hampshire "mountains" are to the Sierra.

The expatriate longs for the visceral tug when you crest the top of a real hill, the moment of truth when you are staring over your car's hood at the sky, wondering what's happening in front of you in the next second. Will it be a little old lady, a fire truck, Steve McQueen in "Bullitt"? Or maybe just the top of the hill almost wide enough to let you catch your breath before you shoot down the other side. Beacon Hill? It is to laugh. A blister. A Dr. Scholl's Corn Pad.

The few locals who have ventured as far as the Pacific come back with horror stories about San Francisco hills and the dangers of motoring thereon. Those who journey from the Bay Area to the Bay State return with a genuine horror of driving anywhere in Boston. The automobile is not used merely for transportation here. It is a weapon in a class war that rages on many fronts.

The drive to work and back are but the first and last skirmishes of the day. In between the real bloodletting takes place. Ever been to Filene's Basement? But, to begin the day with a Search and Destroy mission at least gets the adrenaline pumping.

Warning: Don't look the enemy in the eye. That's right, the enemy, your opponent, the guy ahead of you. Whether he's afoot or behind the wheel, he's going to get you if you don't get him first. How do you score? Cut him off. Move him over. Leave him at the light while you sneak through on the last of the yellow. Press him. Make him jump. Pass him, then slow down yourself. You know, all those nasty moves you learned as a teenager.

If the driver is a woman, score yourself an extra point. But watch out. She may be more road warrior than you are. Remember, don't look them in the eye. The head fake and the quick lane change. Peripheral vision is everything in this game. That, and a healthy contempt for drivers not as good as you are.

Another warning: Bostonians play these street games because there is no enforcement. Don't try them in nearby states like Connecticut or New Hampshire where they write a lot of tickets, especially for Massachusetts drivers.

No, this isn't California, and Boston ain't San Francisco. I've only been away three days and I'm already homesick for a glimpse of the Bay Bridge from the corner of Hyde and O'Farrell. The Tobin Bridge just doesn't cut it. I will never complain about San Francisco weather again. God is punishing Boston for calling itself the Hub of the Universe. But more about the weather later.

Sure, Boston has architecture, but the seafood is boring and it all comes from somewhere else. The shrimp come from India, the salmon from Norway, the swordfish from the Bahamas, and the lobster from Canada. No edible creature swims or crawls in the toilet that surrounds this city. The water is brown and thick and lumpy. Ships leave ghastly, grey wakes behind them as they plow through the muck of Boston Harbor. I miss the fishing fleet from the window of Tarantino's. I'll have the Rex sole and a very cold bottle of Montelena Chardonnay.

Did I say class war? Yes, that's what I said. Boston is not a friendly city. It is not only rude to its visitors (who are so dumb they can't find their way around a town that was laid out by wandering cows), it saves its worst manners for its own. There are more class divisions in Boston than in your old junior high. A neighborhood is not a place to grow out of, it's a place to keep those people out of. No melting pot, this. No glorious racial and ethnic and cultural stew that makes Baghdad by the Bay such an exciting place to live. Boston is a series of sealed compartments. The best game in town is trying to pry open someone else's. More fun than lions and Christians.

The latest civic circus is tormenting a rather pitiful prey. Boston is prising open the private clubs, which for a hundred years have been the hidey holes for men who can't find any other place to hide.

The local rag called the Boston clubmen "dinosaurs," but that's the wrong slant.

These are not the movers and shakers of this world. These are the small fuzzy ones crouching under a leaf. Comets, glaciers, cataclysmic collisions won't kill them. But open up their burrow and let the sun and the strange creatures in and they are doomed. In this case the strange creatures are women. The whole town is laughing because, if the men's clubs don't admit women members early next year, their liquor supply is turned off. From the fuzzy ones' point of view, the only thing worse than seeing a woman standing at the bar of the club is no bar at all.

Stay tuned for late-breaking developments. But, you women, think carefully about what you're getting into. An evening at the Charles Club is like waiting tenth in line to take off from Logan. When the air traffic controllers are on strike. And the plane's air conditioning doesn't work. It's at least as much fun as a hijacking. Makes you wonder why you ever made the trip in the first place.

"That's outrageous," said Roger Dormant to Owen, gesturing at a copy of the *Sphere* that lay open on the library table. "Did you read what he said about the seafood?"

Chapter 16

Owen sat by what he had come to call The Window. The Charles
Club had forty-three windows, nineteen facing Commonwealth Avenue, ten on the Hereford Street side, fourteen on the alley. Of
these, the four front curved-glass windows on the first floor formed
the salient grouping around which the facade of the building arranged itself. Two looked out from the Parlor, where female guests
were entertained. The other pair were in the Library, which was
reserved for the members. The thick glass bowed in a gentle arc,
its faintly purple depths framed in hard pine, an occasional dimple,
the odd ripple, adding character to the view. In all seasons these
windows afforded a pleasing picture of that portion of the world
that included one hundred yards of the avenue and the Mall.

The small front yard of the club was protected by a black
wrought-iron fence whose corners and gate posts were bundles of
bars and spears. The yard itself contained two mature tulip magno-
lia trees. For ten days in April they burst into sensuous glories of
pink and cream if the last snowstorm of the winter did not frost the
fragile exhibition, snow melting from petals which in an hour would
turn brown and fall. Under the magnolias an indifferent patch of
grass and ivy stitched the building to the earth. Beyond the iron
palings a dark forest of oaks, sycamores and an occasional ancient
elm scarred by the plague stretched in each direction. The two
highways of Commonwealth Avenue are separated by a strip of
grass one hundred and twenty feet wide, itself divided by an asphalt
walk down the middle. In this linear wood between Hereford and
Gloucester lurks the somber figure of Domingo Sarmiento, an Ar-
gentinian statesman of the nineteenth century. His presence on the
Mall in the company of Hamilton, Glover and the other North
Americans puzzled Owen. He imagined a room full of brave Argen-
tine immigrants passing a hat into which money was being stuffed.
"Por Sarmiento!" and "Viva Sarmiento!" they cried as they parted
with their life savings. Now the profoundly melancholy figure
loomed just within sight of the curved plate glass of the club windows. The local artist had written BORGO across Sarmiento's pediment, the smooth surface encouraging unusually broad, flowing
strokes of the paint can.

The trees even in December muffled traffic sound. The Charles Club was situated on the Sunny Side of Commonwealth Avenue where it received the morning rays of God's glory. Addresses on the Sunny Side, deemed the superior location, bore odd street numbers. The tulip magnolias grew only on the Sunny Side. Even-numbered residents pointed out, however, when as was sometimes the case they were patronized by their neighbors across the street, that they in fact had the view of the magnolias which the owners did not. Nevertheless *tout* Boston—from meter maid to matron—knew the Sunny Side of Commonwealth was the good side, just as the Water Side of Beacon Street, the next street over but one which paralleled the Charles River, was the good side of Beacon because the back windows of the buildings faced upon the Charles River Basin.

Of the four bay windows of the Charles Club, Owen preferred the library window farthest from the entrance. It looked out upon the corner of Hereford, included a glimpse of Sarmiento, and viewed the retreating traffic of the westbound lane of Commonwealth. In front of The Window was a black leather chair, much worn but often oiled and polished. It was precisely the chair Owen had always known men's clubs would have. He first saw the chair in a cartoon in a *New Yorker* magazine one summer when he was working during school vacation in the stacks of the Santa Fe Public Library. It was his first job away from chores at the ranch. He found wheeling carts of books back into the stacks where they were painstakingly returned to their holes an unexpectedly rewarding activity. It satisfied a sense of order which, at sixteen, he had only begun to recognize. No one in the stacks ever told him to stand up straight. The level of activity at the Carnegie Library rarely exceeded six carts of books in a day. When he had replaced them all he was free to wander and sample. After he had located the key to the locked cage and leafed through the meagre collection of sex and anatomy he found the bound periodicals occupying most of his attention. Unfamiliar worlds sifted like luminous sand from the pages of the old *Vanity Fair*, from *Blackwood's*, from *Scientific American*, from the *Boston Evening Transcript*. He wasn't sure why he found Peter Arno's choleric men-about-town so pleasing but a 1938 *New Yorker* supplied his first knowledge of proper men's club chairs. To discover, twenty years later, how closely life mirrored art was balm to that sense of order lately so severely damaged.

He balanced a cup of black coffee on his knee and tried in vain to suppress a sense of well-being rising from the pit of his stomach. He was more than a little concerned about Seymour. Something was not right. Office boy still rankled. It was like those moments in New Mexico before a heavy thunderstorm when the body felt what the mind did not know or the eye could not see. Seymour was up to something and Owen somehow was part of it. The vision of Demi in a black slip on the Indian rug passed unbidden in front of his eyes and another organ stirred. His early dinner had been excellent, as usual, and since there had been only one other diner—a short, rotund man in a salt-and-pepper suit whom Owen did not recognize—he ate in peaceful, pungent silence. When Anton Pesht stepped outside the kitchen Owen complimented him on the fragrant curry and was rewarded with a grave nod. Owen had been tempted to order a half bottle but settled instead for a glass of Graves with his perfect *crème brûlée*. He was dutifully exploring the wine list and Abel had proved a cheerful guide, willing to advance the research by opening various bottles for sampling. The Graves and the *crème brûlée* said something nice to each other.

Owen was running up a considerable bill at the Charles. He rarely missed dinner there although he knew he should be eating more often at home. Meals and wine at the club were much less expensive than at local restaurants and the cuisine superior, if not always the service. But his budget was stressed to the point of collapse between the all too occasional dates with Demi and his club expenses. He watched the last evening light disappear into the meager incandescence of the nighttime avenue. The problem is, he thought, these are such new experiences. First finding Demetria. Then discovering food.

Food had never been a significant part of Owen's life. For thirty-eight years he had eaten because he was told to by his mother, his dormitory master, his wife. The association of food with pleasure was as foreign to him as religion. It was a necessary interruption—like shaving or cleaning a rifle—of more important activities. Now to his surprise it produced such pleasure that he continually sought to prolong it, repeat it. He was not unaware that this was the definition of addiction. He would become addicted to Demi too as soon as she would let him. For some time, since his courtship of Abbie in fact, he had not associated pleasure with the company of a woman. Now he was wondering if he would seem a fatuous idiot to call Demi before he went to bed. Or when he was in bed. The telephone was in easy reach from almost anywhere in the apartment. The introduction to pleasure, like any conversion, produced unfamiliar doubts, guilt, ecstasies, and visions. He found himself thinking of Demi as a glorious dessert. If only he could afford to live this way. The legal fees from the divorce, the Volvo payments which seemed never to end, the initiation fee for the club prorated over his first year of membership, all stretched his new salary to the limit. Seymour had offered him $50,000. It was less than he had been making at Portman and Sells but it sounded adequate for a quiet, celibate existence. Now he was neither quiet nor celibate. Where was the money going?

Everything about his current life seemed tentative. He was spending more than he earned. In addition, he was not at all sure he was cut out to be a venture capitalist. The pace at Gland, Hollings seemed painfully slow. A new fund was being assembled, thirty million dollars, from a group of investors including insurance companies, corporate pension funds, a few individuals. The total was almost twice that of the firm's previous capital pool, now fully invested. The formation of the new fund had put all the current projects on hold—including Owen's recommendation that they invest in the freight forwarding company and as yet uncompleted studies of the desktop publisher and two other ventures. In the three months he had been there very little of substance seemed to have transpired at Gland, Hollings. He received his salary check. He had health insurance again. Perhaps he should stop worrying.

In contrast, his personal life was crammed with incident, pleasure, pain, and upheaval. Not his least concern was that he needed a new suit. Not only had Demi characterized his best suit as a joke, but now his trousers no longer hung on his flanks as they had throughout his life. Owen stood up, balancing his cup and saucer. His pants seemed suspended on a bulge at his midsection. He looked down at the roll of shirtfront that stuck out over his belt. God damn, I'm getting fat, he thought with pride. I'm in love and I'm getting fat! Life can't be all bad.

"May I join you?" The person Owen had noticed at the other side of the dining room stood in the doorway cradling a pony of brandy. Without waiting for permission he sat in the chair opposite. "Are you a member?"

Owen sat down as well. "Yes. I'm Owen Lawrence." He looked the question at his companion.

"A guest. Just staying for one more day. Then heading back to the lefthand coast."

"Enjoying your stay?" Owen felt the proprietary urge to make the guest welcome.

"It's quite different than I imagined," he waved his glass in a sweeping gesture that encompassed the room, the club, the dark city on the other side of The Window, "Boston, I mean."

"Really? I'm not a native myself. I'd be interested in hearing your impressions." Is this me talking, Owen wondered.

"Well, perhaps you will. Where are you from?"

"New Mexico, originally."

"How long have you been a member? You look younger than most of the others."

"About three months. I'm what they refer to as new blood."

"Not to your face, I hope. How do you feel about this business of admitting women as members?"

Owen started to reply then shut his mouth. "You're the journalist."

"I confess I am. Leonard Lapstrake." They leaned forward and shook hands, Owen with some slight hesitation. The other man's grip was surprisingly strong. "I'm afraid I've ruffled some feathers."

"Especially about the seafood. The local lobsters are from Maine, not Canada."

"Just so long as they're not from Nahant or Winthrop. There are plenty of pots still out there in the shit, so I'm told."

"You've learned a lot about Boston in a short time."

Lapstrake took a sip of his Rémy. "I think I may have been a little more negative than I intended. Or even than circumstances warrant. I was in a vile mood when I arrived."

"Do famous columnists let their moods influence their writing?"

"Of course. That's what we're paid for."

"Tough on your subject matter if you get up on the wrong side of the bed."

"Absolutely. Life is not fair. Neither is journalism."

"So much for 'all the news that's fit to print.' "

"Even that is not fair. Most papers, including mine, modify the phrase to 'all the news that fits, we print.' "

"What about television?"

"Television has nothing to do with news. Sometimes it does a good job of recording visual events. The rest is entertainment."

"And what do you call what you do?"

"*Touché*. I'm a talk show for people who can read. God knows there are few enough left. But you didn't answer my question."

"Would you like another? I'll join you." Owen rang the bell on the wall beside the black leather chair. He found he wanted to talk about it. "It's hard for me to sort the membership thing out. I'd hate to see the Club change much. I enjoy it a lot. It's been a lifesaver to me, as a matter of fact. But I can't see why it wouldn't be just as pleasant a place with women as members. There are wives and daughters and female guests here all the time. No one minds that. It's membership, not their presence, that is the sticking point."

"What do you enjoy about the Club?"

"It's funny, I was just thinking about that. This chair, for one thing. Sitting in front of this window." He gripped the leather arms and leaned back. "I decided it fulfills a teenage fantasy. I can sit here by the window and pretend I am a Boston clubman." The lanky frame leaned forward and he stuck out his jaw in a reasonable imitation of Walter Junior.

"But you are a Boston clubman."

"I suppose in a technical sense I am, but I don't feel like one. I feel like a kid pretending to be one."

"What else do you enjoy? Besides your chair fantasy, I mean."

"The food. It keeps me alive. More than that in fact. I live alone now. I never could cook. The restaurants around here are expensive. For the first time in my life, I look forward to dinner. Did you try the curry?"

"I had the sweetbreads. Quite good. Have you ever been to San Francisco?"

"There are a lot of places I haven't been."

"So, the fantasy of the clubman, the food, and . . . ?"

"The conversation. The companionship. I suppose some of these men may look a little ridiculous to you . . . "

"Major Hoople does come to mind."

"But by and large they are good, sincere, well-meaning . . . "

"I notice you don't include hard-working."

"Some of them have worked hard at some point in their lives."

"Or brilliant."

"Not brilliant, perhaps, but the conversation is several cuts above the Harvard Faculty Club. Let alone MIT," he added.

"Are you sure?"

"I've been both places. We could probably add the newsroom at the *Clarion*."

Lapstrake shuddered slightly, sniffed his cognac and took a bite. "Well, you make a good case. Why is it you seem to be in the minority?"

"I'm not sure. Some of the members feel very strongly about the whole mess. It *is* a mess, and it's getting worse. Some are not so adamant, but they resent being forced to change by an outsider. The rest don't say much on the subject, but if it comes to a vote . . . I don't know."

"And this outsider, the Wicked Witch of the East?"

"What about her?"

"What indeed? What's her motivation in all this?"

"I assume she feels it is her duty."

Lapstrake smiled. "Do your fellow members share that particular fantasy?"

"No, they don't. It's become very polarized. But they don't know her." He bit his tongue.

"And you do?"

"I've met her."

Lapstrake rose. "I've enjoyed talking to you, Owen, but I think I shall be off to my hotel."

They shook hands again. "I thought you were staying with us," said the Boston clubman.

"No. There was a problem with the room. I've moved down the street to the Ritz. But I have been dropping in here once or twice each day. Call me and we'll have a drink tomorrow. Suite 14A."

A nice man. I think they misjudged him, Owen reflected, as he watched the short figure descend the steps and disappear from the screen of The Window.

I think I'll stay a little longer, Lapstrake thought as he walked down the Sunny Side in the dark. He sniffed the woodsmoke of the first winter fires drifting down from the chimneypots. Maybe the Boston cowboy is worth another day.

Chapter 17

Newbury Street radiated self-satisfied evening energy. Galleries splashed pools of color on the sidewalk. Couples strolled perusing Banana Republic, Carroll Reed, Betsy, Esprit. Italian windows sported excitingly ugly clothes. Singles walked more quickly, ignoring windows, heading for DeLuca's Market, a restaurant, the hardware store before it closed. Owen enjoyed Newbury Street in the evening. Except for the scruffy chaos of Harvard Square he had little experience of cities at night. The infrequent forays into Boston with Abbie from Weston had been carefully plotted excursions from the parking garage to the Shubert or the Pops or a movie theater and return. She had worried, hence he had worried, about being mugged. It was well known in the suburban towns that Boston was an international capital of crime and violence. Most suburbanites had at one time or another driven down the mean streets of the old Combat Zone as they escaped the city. Weston hearts raced at the thought of the sickening depravity that existed behind those dark doors and neon windows.

Owen and Abbie had known no one who actually lived in Boston. When friends or neighbors left Weston they moved to the Cape or to Maine, not to the city. If they were transferred they seemed to fall off the edge of the earth never to be heard from again. A tickle of guilt at being alone in the city at night in the midst of yuppie tumult increased Owen's pleasure. Occasionally, he wondered if he would ever grow out of adolescence. Occasionally, particularly of late, he wondered if it made any difference.

Tasha was pulling tonight, head down, the leash weighted like an iron pipe. Owen carried a plastic sack of largely liquid groceries from DeLuca's: orange juice, milk, a bottle of soap, a plastic jug of carbonated chemicals with an avowed lemon taste, a package of English muffins neither English nor muffin, six cans of Alpo Beef Chunks, and four cardboard packets of assorted food scraps intended to be heated in a microwave oven. Owen did not have a microwave but assumed the oven of his small Roper gas range would suffice. He had not experimented with these products but his club bill delivered in yesterday's post had encouraged him to learn to cook. It had occurred to him, as he set his selection in front of the cash register, that the Alpo might contain more food value than anything else he had chosen.

Tasha parted oncoming traffic with her nose, stopping every twenty feet or so to investigate a shrub or the stairs to the converted basement shops known on Newbury Street as digouts. As they passed the most elegant digout, Davio's, Owen glimpsed napery, silver, crystal, and Demi with her back to him. Before he could be sure or, more important, see her companion, Tasha pulled him along, the tension between man and dog increasing to the breaking point. Shit, he said, not quite out loud as he looked over his shoulder. Perhaps it was out loud since two young women jogging in sweat suits advertising a footrace in benefit of a popular disease turned to glare at him. The combination of the heavy bag and the relentless dog prevented him from stopping and returning to Davio's. "Shit," he said again, quite audibly.

Of course Demi had other dates. She must have lots of men calling her, inviting her to dinner. But why did they have to come to his neighborhood? There were plenty of good restaurants downtown, in the North End, in Cambridge. Why didn't he take her to Michela's? Then Owen wouldn't have to know about it. He pulled Tasha to a stop with the thought of turning around, when a brown rat streaked out of the shrubbery decorating a newly completed digout. Owen had only an instant to set his feet. Tasha hit the end of the leash and the choke chain cut into her thick ruff. The rat disappeared down the sidewalk causing a ripple of small shrieks. The two of them stood for a moment both on their hind legs, Tasha's forepaws waving in air, pointing at the target. Then they turned right down the dark block of Gloucester, away from the music of Newbury Street, such as it was.

He did not hear them coming. The street was quiet but the noise of the bicycle tires was overlaid by city hum. One hit him on the right side and sent the bag of groceries flying into an orange BMW parked at the curb. The other came by him on the left, applied the brakes, and in a stylish kickout flipped the back wheel of his mountain bike around and blocked the sidewalk. Owen went down to his knees and felt his trousers tear on the cement. Now I *have* to get a new suit, he thought. There was no one else on the block.

Parked cars screened them from the traffic that hurried by, windows closed against the chill. Tasha barked once and stood still, her tail waving. "Gimme your plastic, man," said the tall one blocking the sidewalk. He wore bleached jeans and a leather jacket that said Flying Tigers on the front and had the Chinese Nationalist flag on the back. He straddled the bike easily, hightops planted on either side, a knife held between two fingers of his right hand.

The short one leaned his bike against the BMW and smiled. "Nice dog, mista. What's he name?" Owen did not answer. His knees hurt and his right shoulder was numb.

"Gimme the wallet, man, or I cut you. Got a Rolex? Gimme that, too." He looked at the short one. "Git it."

Owen felt hands in his pockets. The short one pulled up the sleeve of his coat and snorted. "Just a shit Timex. How much your dog cost, mista?" he asked politely.

"You can have her," said Owen hoarsely. He crawled forward and unsnapped the leash, the end of which he still held in his hand.

"Thanks, mista," said the short one. Owen fumbled in the plastic bag of groceries. Dishwashing soap, no. Sprite, no. Milk, no. Alpo. He withdrew a large can of Alpo Beef Chunks and threw it at the head of the tall one, who dodged it easily and laughed. It smashed the windshield of a Mercedes parked behind the BMW.

"Hey, shithead," said the tall one, "you bust that guy's window. I'm gon call a cop." He leaned over and looked inside the car. "Git the radio."

"It's gone. They took it out. Prolly in the trunk."

"Let's go. So long, shithead."

Owen staggered to his feet and put his shoe through the spokes of the mountain bike leaning against the BMW. They were beautiful bikes. About four hundred dollars apiece, Owen guessed, short straight handlebars with thick grips, wide knobby tires, lots of gears. Who was she with, he wondered.

"Hey, mothafucka, get away from my bike." The short one grabbed the handlebars and heaved. Owen fell again, his foot stuck in the front wheel. The tall one whipped his bike around and was gone in a flash of chrome. Tasha waved her curly tail.

"Go," said Owen. The dog shot away into the darkness of the street under the trees.

"Doan fuck with my bike, sucka," said the short one, adopting a more belligerent tone. Owen decided he was about fourteen years old as he reached for another can of Alpo. His foot hurt now almost as much as his knees and his shoulder. As the boy jerked the bike Owen hit him in the knee with the edge of the can. He fell down next to Owen and his face began to work. Owen struggled upright again and extricated his loafer from the spokes of the bike. Then he bent down and grabbed the short one by the belt. He held his skinny butt aloft while he went through his pockets, producing his own wallet, another wallet of expensive pigskin, a gold chain, several keys and a wristwatch which may or may not have been a Rolex. Owen dropped him and heard him yell as his kneecap hit the pavement. Unsnapping a black U-lock from the frame of the bike, Owen tried the keys until he found one that unlocked it. Then he dragged the bike to a parking meter and shackled the frame to the meter post. Three notes, each in a different hand, begged the metermaid to notice that the meter was inoperative. The car beside it bore a Day-Glo orange ticket tucked under the nearside wiper. He limped back to the short one, who was curled up on the sidewalk watching. Owen showed him the key. The liquid eyes locked on his. He held the key above a sewer grate. He dropped the key. Then he retrieved his grocery bag and hobbled up the street to the commotion on the corner.

The other bike was sprawled half under a mailbox. Tasha had selected the right leg of the tall one's jeans and locked immutable teeth just above the hightops. She had no flesh but enough denim to pull her prey down. Now she was braced, head flat, legs outspread, while he tried to tear himself away from her. The black eyes watched his spasms impassively. Several young people surveyed the scene with interest. An old lady threatened the dog with her umbrella.

"Don't," said Owen. A Jaguar stopped at the light. The right front window whispered down and the driver leaned across the leather seat. "What's the trouble?"

"Call the police for me."

"Sorry, I'm on a call and I've got a call waiting." The light changed and he disappeared.

A cab pulled up and a man emerged, hurrying with his briefcase away from involvement. Owen leaned inside the cab. "Can you call the police on your radio?"

"Sure. I'll get the dispatch. Whaddaya got?"

"A couple of kids with a bunch of wallets."

"Lorraine, call nine one one and ask 'em put a blue and white on the corner Gloucester, Comm Ave. We gotta couple bushwhackers here. No, this is a good one. Some guy nailed 'em with his dog. Like a big white wuff. Yeah, it's eatin wunna the kids right now. Tell them get their ass in gear or there won't be nothin left but scraps.''

Demi called him at work. He could hardly believe his good fortune. "Owen, did you see the piece in the *Sphere* this morning about the dog? I'll read it to you: 'Inner city child mauled by dog in Back Bay.' Well, it goes on to say a large dog pulled a juvenile off his bicycle and attacked him. The police arrived and saved him from serious injury, but the dog escaped. A witness said a homeless man in torn clothing ran away with the dog. The child told witnesses he is afraid to ride the streets in Back Bay anymore. It's just that I wondered if you had seen it. It happened only a few blocks from your apartment. Keep your eyes open. I wouldn't want you or Tasha to be hurt . . . No, I can't . . . I'm busy. Call me later in the week. I have a meeting now. Please . . . Owen. I have to run . . . Yes . . . So do I.''

Thomas Appleyard's voice quavered with unaccustomed emotion. "Really outrageous. My wife had just stopped that evening to go into Conran's to pick up a towel rack. She found a spot on a side street a few blocks away. Only gone about fifteen minutes, and when she got back she found the windshield of the car smashed with a can of *dog* food. No, she had lost the radio the month before. This was just *sense*less vandalism. Someone saw a homeless throw it at the car. They get dog food to eat, you know. It's cheap and nutritious, I suppose. It was a protest. Just *fired* it at the first 300 SEL he saw. Shall we go into the dining room? Listen to the hubbub. No, my wife put me on one of those low cholesterol things. I can't eat much of anything anymore, spoils everything. A bore.''

ON THE SHANK OF THE HUB

by Leonard Lapstrake

BOSTON. Special to the Boston *Sphere*. Copyright San Francisco *Clarion*, 1987.

NIGHT THOUGHTS: It's a tough city and a mean city. Sometimes the stories can break your heart. Two kids out in the evening on their bikes. Okay, so they should have been at home doing homework. How many times did you sneak away for a quick look at the night when the books got to be too much?

Out of their neighborhood, pedalling down the quiet streets of Boston. Quiet, did I say? A berserk homeless leaps out in front of them and both kids are down. He has a dog who is at their throats. He shouts incoherently. One kid's knee is smashed. The other, savaged by the dog. The beloved bikes, wrecked. And—bizarre even for this City of Contrasts—the homeless takes cans of dog food from the pockets of his tattered coat and throws them at the passing cars. A cry of hopeless rage in a city where affordable housing has never been much more than election rhetoric. Where crazed men must eat dog food to survive. Where tooth and claw rule the night.

Nice note: The city *does* have a heart. The local rag is raising a fund to replace the two bikes. A buck will make you feel the world is not a totally rotten place for a couple of kids.

Local forecast: I want to say a word about Boston's weather. Problem is, they won't print this particular word in the family fishwrap. No other city in America suffers weather like this benighted town. Not only is the weather uncomfortable, frightening, noisy, dangerous, boring, shocking, and unhealthy. It is also plentiful. Abundant. Fulsome. Copious. In oversupply. A redundance. Altogether, a bad joke.

Late update: Remember the one about the Boston men's clubs? Well, the latest rumor heard in the Members' Bar is that one enterprising club has sent one of their better-looking young bucks to plead their case, out of court so to speak, with the beauteous official who is forcing them to choose between gender integration or alcoholic extinction. The smart money says Prohibition is just around the corner with no hope of Repeal.

But I don't want you to think I haven't enjoyed my stay. It's been interesting. Boston *is* different. The natives pride themselves on the fact they never have to travel. They have diversity here. If one more New Englander asks me, "Isn't it boring to have sunshine all year round?" I'm going to clout him with a snow shovel.

"What about the foliage?" they bleat. It's true, New England has collected more dead leaves than any region in the U.S. of A. Maybe in the world, if you don't count what's going on in the rain forests of Brazil.

"Do you really eat flowers in California?" someone asked me at dinner the other night, while he scooped up something called Indian Pudding.

Anyone who has tried it knows it is the ultimate slur on the Native American. Give me a nasturtium anytime.

"You know, Gland," said Walter Junior, "I thought he was way out of line on seafood. But I have to admit he's right about crime in the city. There was a shocking outbreak the other night, just a few blocks away from the club. A very expensive car was almost destroyed. And, I must confess, I sometimes share his impatience with the weather. We've had almost three inches of rain since just before noon. I didn't like him at first, but he grows on you. I suppose that's what pee-ah is all about."

Chapter 18

Avery Coupon had moved that summer from New York to accept a position with the Old Currency Bank. He was accustomed to the mantle and trappings of authority, which lately, due to his relocation, seemed to have diminished. A new member of the Charles, his views on the Central Topic had not been sought until he rather curtly offered his services to the Strategy Committee. "Please join us by all means," said Walter Junior. "We are in point of fact meeting tonight for coffee, about eight o'clock. We have just re-filled the humidor with some," he tittered, "contraband, which you may enjoy." Coupon, who indulged himself in every pleasure of the flesh save tobacco, nevertheless accepted with alacrity.

That evening, in the Small Reception Room on the second floor where the lesser of the two Sargents hung above the fireplace, he viewed through an aromatic haze the array of brainpower—largely self-appointed—which had been massed to defeat the Forces of Evil. Included in the gathering were Walter St. Henry Thomas Junior; the Eldest Member; Roger Dormant; Seymour Gland; Edu-ardo DePalma; Thomas Appleyard; Owen Lawrence, also new to the group; the Distinguished Poet; and himself. He poured a cup of black coffee wishing the while for a drop of something, noticed a decanter at Dormant's elbow, and employing a series of discreet nudges and gestures soon found a glass of port in his other hand as he sank carefully into the last unoccupied chair. Most of the group were talking. Only Coupon and Owen, the two new mem-bers, sat silent. Umbrage vied with outrage.

"WHAT DID YOU SAY?" The Eldest Member as usual rose effortlessly above the din.

"I said it has been a complete failure, a waste of money, and worse yet, has blackened the club's reputation." DePalma, who sometimes referred to himself as the club's commitment to Affirma-tive Action or more simply as the Resident Spic, seldom raised his baritone voice. A successful litigator, when he so chose, his words penetrated. The room fell silent.

Before the conversation broke out again Roger Dormant has-tened to speak. "Shouldn't we appoint someone to run this meet-ing? This is the third time we have met. Each time the group is different and we all talk at once."

Gland removed from his mouth the Cuban panatela, a gross of which—in his capacity as head of the Cigar Committee—he had triumphantly procured from an enterprising travel agent. "Our need is not for Roberts, it is for a concerted plan." He described an oval trail of smoke in the air into which such a plan might fit. "I believe," he emphasized his personal pronoun, "as a matter of fact, we are well advanced with our campaign."

Before he could proceed Dormant pressed his point. "I suggest we ask Walter Junior to serve as *de facto* chair—I believe the correct term these days is—person."

"Well, is that not *precisely* the problem?" cried the Distinguished Poet. Chair*person*, indeed! Why we, or any other group of civilized humans should have to abandon the ancient traditions of the language to mollify a militant . . . " he searched his lexicon for the word—"micro-fringe" was the best he could summon—"is beyond my ken. I will gladly give my assent to Walter Junior, as chair*man*, but no pandering solecisms, please."

Without further dissent Walter Junior called the group to a still noisy order. "We, of course, are not the only organization caught up in this dilemma," he said when he felt he could be heard. "I speak of it as a dilemma because I believe we are all," he glanced around the room and seemed about to modify his last words, but went on, "men of goodwill. Perhaps the world has changed around us more rapidly than we realize, but we are not, I feel, *chauvinistes*, nor bigots, nor misanthropes, nor misogynists. However, the Club has always defined its own membership, hence has always defined itself. Now we are being told that our traditional definition is no longer acceptable to, ah, others in our society."

At this the room burst into an emotional characterization of their principal tormentor. Owen's cheeks burned.

Walter Junior, after a moment, continued. "Many of us belong to other clubs, have other associations which have been subjected to, which have had to face this, ah, new, ah, how shall I put it, trend. Perhaps it would be instructive to hear of some other situations. Please raise your hand to be recognized," he added hastily.

Avery Coupon was gratified to be called upon first. He sipped his port until the room was quiet. This paltry club at least has a decent cellar, he thought. "I belonged, still belong in fact, to the Garden Country Club in Garden Village." Noting blank stares where he expected appreciative nods, he added, "on Long Island." Still no reaction. "We have male members only. A single locker room. No social events which include women. With one exception. Once a year, on the day after Christmas, we have a tailgate picnic for wives and female friends." He sipped his port appreciatively. "In the parking lot."

The chair did not need to call the group to order. Silence swirled in the Cuban fumes above the room as they contemplated this concept. "The parking lot?" asked Gland.

"Yes."

"On the day after . . . ?"

"Yes."

"Do many attend?" Appleyard inquired.

"Some do. Some don't. Seems to depend a lot on the weather." Coupon paused, conscious of the rapt attention of his audience. "My wife doesn't care much for it. Says it's too cold. And there's usually too much to do after Christmas."

"Are any special efforts made for the comfort of the guests? A tent, perhaps?"

"No tent. A fire. In an oil drum."

"Is the club going to change its membership?"

"No."

The monosyllable lay in their laps like a flat stone from the parking lot at Garden Village, a more interesting community than they had imagined even though it was somewhere to the south.

Roger Dormant raised a tentative hand. "I have never understood what has been happening to the schools and colleges." Since his friends and acquaintances were cognizant of many things he did not understand this pronouncement did not cause a stir. Walter Junior, however, encouraged him to go on. "It would seem," Dormant said with emotion adding an uncharacteristic vibrato to his voice, "that childhood is so brief, youth so short, that young people might be able to choose how they wish to spend it. I went off to Exeter when I was fourteen. It was a wonderful period in my life. I remember the Headmaster as vividly as I remember my father. He stood for authority. Responsibility. Tradition. It was a boys' school then, of course, had been for more than a hundred years when I arrived. Now it is, ah," he looked around for assistance in finding the correct word.

"Integrated."

"Co-educational."

"Ruined."

"Well, it has girl students, and now a female is Headmaster. I mean," he said, "Head. Of the school. I don't know of any private school that is still of but one gender. Why has this all changed so suddenly, so completely? Do people no longer want a choice? Was my experience so unusual? Hasn't something been lost?"

The hubbub broke out again as member after member attempted to give testimony. Appleyard stood up. "I have a son who is going to Vassar." He sat down with the air of someone who has just got something off his chest.

DePalma spoke without raising his well-manicured hand. "My sister is an alumna of Wheaton. As you probably know, the college is about to admit men for the first time. They just completed a major capital campaign. Somehow, the board neglected to tell the alumnae of their decision to change the composition, the personality, if you will, of the college until the campaign was successfully concluded. My sister is angry. She, and some others, have demanded their gifts be returned. She thought of her years at Wheaton as rather idyllic. She is very angry with her college."

"Why?" asked Owen.

"She says she has had to live with men all her life. Four years of feminine society was to her, as I said, an idyll."

"So that's the end of her association with Wheaton."

"Actually not. Her daughter has applied for early admission next year."

"Holderness was a boys' school when Seymour and I first attended," said Owen. "I enjoyed it thoroughly. It was almost home to me. I was what they called a lifer, I spent four years there. Before we left they began admitting girls. I can't see that it has hurt the school. Quite the contrary. And the academics are up."

"Holderness is very sports-oriented, is it not?" asked Dormant.

"Very. Skiing, ice hockey, football, baseball, lacrosse."

"What sports do the girls play?"

"All of them, I believe."

"Hockey? I mean, ice hockey? Football?"

"I'm not sure about football. I am sure about lacrosse. The girls' team won the conference championship last year. They demolished Exeter."

"It would seem that the school has retained a rather masculine personality," said DePalma, glancing at Appleyard.

"Perhaps those sports are no longer considered the sole property of the boys," Owen answered.

"Perhaps the girls are becoming more masculine than I remember," Gland interjected in a stage whisper that carried across the room.

Owen was about to reply when Walter Junior held up his hand. "I think we are straying a bit afield, interesting though these subjects are. I would like to return to the club scene, if we may."

"I also belong to the Union League," said Coupon. He did not have to elaborate. The Union League Club was known even in Boston. "We are awaiting the Supreme Court ruling. We will not cave in."

"The New York situation, however, is quite different from ours," explained Appleyard, pleased to regain a legal footing.

"The city has passed a statute, Local Law 63, if I am not mistaken, which bars discrimination on the basis of, ah, race, religion, sex, sexual orientation, and other grounds in private clubs with a membership of four hundred or more." He was about to proceed, when Gland interrupted.

"What do you mean by sexual orientation?"

"What I suppose the wording of the statute to mean is sexual preference."

"You mean queers?" Gland's voice rose. "The clubs in New York have to admit queers?"

"I don't mean anything. I'm simply trying to explain the legal issue in New York."

"I'll be damned."

"New York is quite another kettle of fish," said Dormant. This statement provoked no dissent, not even from Coupon.

Appleyard continued. "Clubs of over four hundred members, as I said. They are deemed to play an important role in business and professional life. They receive a good deal of income for meal service, luncheons and dinners, which may include business meetings. The New York City Human Rights Commission is the body which is involved here . . . "

"Is it a right of all humans to join the Union League?" asked Coupon rhetorically to the cloud above his head.

" . . . some of the local clubs have already achieved compliance by changing their admissions policies. They will periodically report to the Commission on the number of women applicants, as well as the number of women admitted."

"And queers? The number of queers admitted as well?" Owen suspected Gland had been punishing the decanter. "Is there a quota?" A bit of cigar adhered to the corner of his mouth.

"The Union League will stand firm."

"Other clubs are opposing the law. The New York Athletic Club, for one. They have a membership of over ten thousand, I believe," continued Appleyard.

"All close friends, no doubt," remarked the Eldest Member, who had been enjoying the emotional currents if not all the details of the discussion.

"The suit against several clubs will be heard sometime next year by the Supreme Court."

"How does this affect us?" asked the Distinguished Poet.

"It doesn't appear to affect us at all," said DePalma smoothly before Appleyard could continue his dissertation. "A, we have fewer than four hundred members. B, we have a prohibition against the display of business papers in the common areas of the club as specified by our bylaws. C, and most important, we are not ruled by the laws of New York City.''

"I beg to differ," said Appleyard hotly. "If the New York law is upheld, other cities will rush to follow suit."

"And, in the meantime, our problem is not created by law," said the Distinguished Poet from his corner, "but by a simple ruling, promulgated by an individual, affecting only one aspect of club life.''

"Pass the port," whispered Dormant.

Gland leaped to his feet. A rush of emotion seemed to give his words wing. "So, *here* it is, the new age, the age of *compliance*, in which we cannot choose our associates, we must admit one and all: women, queers, paroled criminals, used car salesmen, to our clubhouse, to our table, to our councils, to our innocent revels, and, mark you, not only admit them, but report regularly to some loathsome, self-important, self-righteous, ego-inflated, do-good, state functionary, ensconced behind an expensive desk, smoking ten-cent . . . " Gland glanced at the instrument with which he was emphasizing each point, jabbing it as it were into the face of the enemy, " . . . sucking snuff, and filling spittoons like some New Hampshire farmer, surrounded by the tawdry trappings of political power, never having turned a hand to attempt an honest day's labor . . . " As he soared, Owen relaxed to some extent. It didn't sound as though Gland were describing the woman he loved. Perhaps he was referring to someone in New York. But Gland was in full spate.

"I say no. We cannot become a party to this egregious," he smiled for an instant, savoring the word, "invasion of a life we have created for ourselves, harming no one, denying business opportunity to no one, conceived in fact, and built in fact, for *one hundred and twenty-five years*, on the now apparently reprehensible notion that men might enjoy each other's company without resorting to the dross of commercial conversation. *There must be a way*.'' He delivered these last words with unexpected force and intensity then, spent, sat down to smoky, thoughtful silence.

Passion largely expended, the fourth meeting of the Strategy Committee ended twenty minutes later. Other clubs in other cities were mentioned: Cosmos, Bohemian, Metropolitan. Fellow sufferers in Boston were reported on: St. Botolph, Tavern, Somerset, Pilgrim. It was suggested that the Charles try to discover their intentions. A traveler recently returned from London reported that he believed the issue would not arise during Mrs. Thatcher's reign. No plan of action was proposed let alone agreed upon.

As they walked down the broad stairway, Dormant leading the way, Owen limping painfully, Gland said over his shoulder, "Holderness girls must look damned attractive in their hockey uniforms."

"Yes, very cute, I imagine." Owen stared at him, the phrase office boy in the back of his mind.

"Those baggy padded shorts and suspenders."

"I haven't actually seen them play a game."

"At least their generation has rediscovered the garter belt."

Owen had no reply. He felt, as he often had before, that Seymour had carried the evening.

Chapter 19

Owen yawned as he buttoned a Saturday shirt. It had been a frustrating week. The question of whether a job as an analyst was work for a real person lodged in the back of his thoughts. Seymour added regularly to the pile of business plans on Owen's desk. He was sorting them into two stacks. The short stack would get a second reading. Despite several calls each day he had not been able to speak to Demi. Over a cup of instant coffee he sat flipping Friday's bills into a basket on the table. There were fewer of them than there had been in Weston and for lesser amounts. His telephone bill rarely rose above the minimum charge since he made most of his calls at work, while it had often exceeded two hundred dollars a month in Weston. Even with the fourteen thousand a year from Abbie's trust fund Weston had been a financial struggle. But incredibly he was still struggling. He had six payments to go on the

Volvo, and the monthly bill from the Charles Club was a shocker. He read the event sheet that accompanied the bill: a list of four names posted for membership and an invitation to meet the Candidates for sherry on the day after Thanksgiving; a game dinner on December 18th. Owen glanced at the list to see if he knew any of the nominees, was unsurprised to find he did not.

It was a depressingly bright morning for the weekend before Thanksgiving. Owen felt restless and unwilling to spend the day alone. He was not sure why the holiday was important to him since he had little history of festive Thanksgivings either when he was growing up or in Weston, where cocktail parties and dinner out had been the usual plan. The season's change, more subtle in New Mexico than the gaudy death of summer in New England, always seemed the emptiest moment of the year. When he called Demi he reached only her echo on the machine. She had not returned any of his calls. Maybe she was out of town. Without making a conscious decision he grabbed a scarf and a tweed jacket with a hole in one pocket and reached for the leash. Tasha was at the door before he picked it up, speaking in the Samoyed tongue which came out as a querulous, gargling, muted howl. All seasons were hers, the only emptiness indoor space.

They bolted from the badger hole and jogged down Fairfield, across Marlborough and Beacon, up Back Street—the alleyway that separates the garages and sheds of the Water Side of Beacon from the canyon of Storrow Drive—over the footbridge whose height above the speedway always gave Owen a twinge of agoraphobia. Tasha, immune to neuroses, smelled the river. Down the iron stairway they ran for the path along the shore. The riparian landscape was still green, the grass slick with moisture, the trees bare but alive and in motion against the sky. Traffic of another sort flowed around them as Owen unsnapped the leash and Tasha bolted after a careless squirrel. Bicyclists in the latest tour gear, roller skaters sailing by on wings of urethane, babies on wheels and in sacks, slow walkers, power walkers, weight walkers, Olympic walkers, and sonambulistic runners, dreaming through their pain of marathons to come: the pathway was filled with refugees from the city fleeing in both directions. Winter was coming.

They moved downriver toward the salt and pepper shaker towers of the Longfellow Bridge. A stiff breeze from Cambridge drove a little chop against the riverbank. Tasha, who relished all that was wet, cold, and unbounded, was tempted but Owen whistled her back. A Red Line train rumbled over the granite bridge and disappeared into the bowels of Cambridge as they turned right past the last softball game of the year, crossed a backwater on a footbridge decorated with gryphons and graffiti and stopped by General Patton. While Tasha was busy Owen studied Old Blood and Guts. Poised on the balls of his feet, booted, spurred and gloved with his tanker's goggles pulled up on his helmet, Patton radiated Washington's calm superiority with none of his benevolence. The grips of his twin revolvers were polished by the reverent hands of Boston's youth. "Move it or lose it," Patton said to him as they passed. I'd like to have seen him ride, thought Owen. A polo pony at Myopia or Santa Barbara, a Lippizaner from the Spanish Riding School, a tank in the Rhineland. Classy bastard, he thought. No paint on Patton's pedestal.

They re-crossed Storrow Drive at the Esplanade, trotted across Beacon, hurried down Commonwealth. Owen hungered for lunch and for someone to talk to. For Demi. For a Thanksgiving. He felt he was marking time, running in place. The thought made him run faster. What was he waiting for? Why wasn't he *doing* something? The question immediately rose: what precisely should he be doing? Making a million dollars in Boston? Something back home? What was home? It seemed hard to imagine his destiny was a two-bit spread in Santa Fe. Maybe he should get married again. Nothing seemed beyond consideration on a glorious day at the moment of summer's extinction. He tied the leash to a fence rod as Tasha settled down on the little patch of grass beside the club steps. No one was likely to reach a hand through the wrought iron no matter how inviting her white pelt. The eyes discouraged it.

Owen bounded up the steps, opened the wide door, and collided with the solid bulk of the Architectural Critic. "Sorry!"

"Quite all right. I was about to leave. Club's as empty as a tomb. An empty tomb, that is. Are you coming in for lunch? If you are, I'll join you, if I may. The only reason I came over here on a beautiful day like this was to find someone to jaw with. Hope you don't mind? Perhaps you weren't thinking of lunch. Have a drink then. What would you like? A bit early, I concede, but within hailing distance of noon. What is your pleasure?"

Owen hastily interjected his pleasure as they moved toward the little bar off the lobby. Abel nodded a greeting. Owen pinched the open throat of his shirt and raised a questioning eyebrow. Abel smiled and shook his head as he handed the drinks to his only guests. They moved into the Library and sank into chairs by The Window. Following Owen's glance his companion said with evident pleasure, "What a magnificent beast." Owen grinned. "So, you keep a dog in the city. An affirmation. Of course it is a bother, creates problems, but it is a statement. Worth all the effort and more. It says," he leaned forward and fixed Owen with his rather pop-eyed gaze, "that the city is liveable. Not merely habitable, *liveable*. A place to live and enjoy all that life has to offer, including that most satisfying and reinforcing relationship, the companionship of animals. How many do you have?"

"Animals? Just that one. At the moment."

"Had you more in another life?"

"Well, yes. When I was growing up I had quite a few dogs, sometimes two or three at a time. And about a dozen horses. A cow and usually a calf. A few barn cats. A kitten in the house if my mother could catch and tame one. Chickens."

"And did you live in Boston during that period?"

"No. A little town called Tesuque. I doubt you've heard of it."

"I know it well. I'm out there for the opera every August. I drop in on the sculpture gallery at Shidoni to see what atrocities are being committed in the name of architectural sculpture. I knock on Eliot Porter's door to see if he will show me any of his current photography. I stop by Felipe Archuleta's house next to El Nido to beg him to sell me a wooden pig. The galleries have pushed folk art prices beyond all reason, but I keep hoping he will take pity on me." He paused and tasted his drink. "Do you collect anything, besides animals, I mean?"

Owen's mouth dropped open at this recital of the cultural elite of his hometown. "Not folk art. I sort of took it for granted when I lived there."

"Well, do not lose Tesuque in Boston, my boy. When I get completely distracted by the abominations being committed by the builders in this city, I go back to Santa Fe to refresh my soul."

He was momentarily interrupted as Abel handed them menus and the order slip, which the Architectural Critic seized. Owen seized the moment. "I must say I don't think that Boston is being spoiled. It seems much more, ah, beautiful than I've ever seen it."

"Odd you should see it that way," said his companion studying the menu. "What I see is destruction. Devastation. Decay." A pause. "Duplicity." He seemed to have exhausted the list. "Dumb decisions," he said with finality. He scribbled their orders and they went into the empty dining room together.

"Well, I can't agree," said Owen. "I love Boston's architecture. It's what makes the city great. If it weren't for the architecture this would be just another state capital populated with less than friendly people, with a polluted harbor, and a bunch of bad drivers. Did you read . . . ?"

"Yes, indeed. Much of what he said was quite true. But we should examine your views about the cityscape. What do you like about it?"

"About the old buildings?"

"No, most of what has escaped the wrecker's ball by now will survive us, I suppose. It's the new ones that give the most pain." Before Owen could frame an answer, his host went on. "Let me cite two much-noticed examples within a few blocks of this very spot: the new Back Bay train station, and that building at the other end of Newbury Street that Frank Gehry has remodeled. Now, that's an interesting one. It was just a big forties business block when the developer bought it. Then this clever California—designer is what I would call him—turned it inside out. He covered the outer walls in a kind of chainmail of lead sheets, the sort of thing which might be used to line an elevator shaft. Then he hung a structure of platforms and supports, also clad in lead plates, over the street. It suggests the skeleton of the building protruding from the flesh. No real function, but admittedly a striking effect. Like nothing ever seen in Boston.

"Now then, ten blocks away in a direct line we have the Back Bay railroad station. Used to be an unoffending little terminal where you could catch the train to New York without having to go all the way downtown to South Station. Boston, of course, could never quite connect the northern lines with the southern lines so we've always had two major termini, North Station and South Station, two monuments to bad planning, venal politics, and, in the one case, hockey, circuses, and basketball. But to return to our little whistlestop station in Back Bay, a few years ago it was decreed that it must become a monument itself. So where did the architects turn? Why to Europe, to the great *gares* and *bahnhofs* of the nineteenth century with their grand arched roofs, sometimes a hundred feet high. Magnificent buildings of iron and glass, like giant greenhouses, through which trains and passengers and baggage trucks and armies and brass bands and crowds of folk moved like tiny toys, put into proper perspective by the soaring aspirations of the new age of steam transportation.

"But why, you might ask, did they build the great arched roofs? It is obvious, on a moment's reflection: to allow the steam and the coal smoke to rise above the busy platform. Perhaps the steam might condense and sprinkle a black little shower on the travellers below, but the stupendous roof shielded them from God's rain and snow which fell outside. So what is amiss with the new Back Bay station, caricature as it is of a *bahnhof*, with its tall laminated arches and its huge enclosed space? Nothing, except it encloses nothing. No trains. The trains creep beneath the floor of the station, ugly diesel cows pulling strings of mismatched cars. The station is just another stage set. No magnificent panorama of transportation. Just greeting cards and tee-shirts.

"They are both clever stage sets," he said sadly. "Better than most. But empty of meaning. That is, if you consider meaning to be the structure which underlies the surface. Boston's new architecture is all surface, no meaning. Or, I suppose, the surface *is* the meaning."

"Oh, for God's sake," said Owen, cutting off the flow, "my old town is more of a stage set than Boston. Every gas station in Santa Fe is built of fake adobe."

"Perhaps, but so beguiling to an Easterner."

"It's still cement block plastered over to look like adobe. The meaning of it all is that you can pump your own gas for a dollar-twenty a gallon."

The Critic gazed thoughtfully out the window, sighed, turned to Owen. He seemed about to speak of something which troubled him greatly. Old Jane came in, left lamb chops in front of Owen, shirred eggs with the Critic. As she departed, they exchanged plates and the Critic asked sadly, "Have you ever looked closely at the trunks of the young trees planted in front of all these new hotels and condominiums?" Owen's answer went unheard as his companion began to pick up momentum again. "Yes, those little trees that get stuck in the sidewalk like pins in a board. Which is what they are, of course, to the current crop of *poseurs* who think they are architects. Not living things, just matchsticks with a bit of sponge at one end, jabbed into a model."

"The trunks?" Owen managed.

"Yes, that's the significant thing. That's what shows you the architect's true intentions. That's what characterizes the Boston of the," he almost whispered the word, "eighties."

"I don't follow you."

"It's the electrical boxes, of course. No one can plant a tree anymore without an electrician. Just consider the thousands of innocent maples and locusts and plane trees with one hundred and ten volts strapped to their trunks, draped with little twinkling Christmas lights THE YEAR 'ROUND!" With his eyes rolled back he seemed to be appealing to the gilt octagon in the ceiling.

"I see," said Owen, who did not see at all.

"One must ask what dramas they think they are playing, these erstwhile rebuilders of the city, in front of their self-created stage sets." He paused to munch a chop bone, then dropped it on his plate. "I fear, dear boy, it is a little Molière farce whose themes are greed, vanity, and the inability to recognize the portents."

"Portents?"

"Yes. I stand on portents. All fads in architecture forecast the future. Think of the buildings of the twenties. Mannered, European, ornate, fussy with decorations and cosmetics. Consider what followed." He took breath. "The fact that mere leaves are not sufficient embellishment for a Boston tree tells me what is coming. We no longer build to *use*. No building has a lifetime of more than a few years now. Real estate development has become our leading industry. They will as happily dynamite a glass tower as a warehouse to get at the land. Buildings are all temporary. Construction is no longer the means, it has become the end. Actually, financing is the most creative architectural function left. Living in a new building is simply a brief interruption of the true real estate cycle. But," he smiled sadly at Owen, "all that is about to come to an end."

As they rose and walked into the hall the Architectural Critic placed an avuncular hand on Owen's shoulder. "Are you heavily invested in real estate?" he asked. "In the stock market?" Owen shook his head. "Good. Then you won't be hurt too badly. It's coming soon, you know." They opened the front door and stepped out into the unexpectedly warm light. Tasha looked up at them, perhaps worried about the expression on her master's face. Owen wanted to ask what exactly was coming, but it was not necessary. "I think it overly dramatic to call it an economic Armageddon, don't you? That makes people think in terms of the end of the world. Of course, it is not going to be the end of the world, just the end of a brief economic cycle, say forty or fifty years in length, which by chance has coincided with our lives. Change is not only the end, it is the beginning as well. The important thing about change is to anticipate it, to prepare for it, to benefit from it . . . ''

"And the lights in the trees say to you that another crash is coming?''

"But when it comes it is going to seem horrendous to those who were not prepared. All that debt tumbling, crashing down, defaulting.'' He nodded happily. "You're aware, I'm sure, that the ratio of debt to the gross national product is greater than it has ever been in history, the entire history of our country, going back,'' he gestured at the statues in the Mall, "to the years in which they built this city. Banks rupturing. Companies turned inside out. The financial structure imploding. Treasure and worth evaporating. It will be,'' he said with relish, "something to watch.'' He bent down to scratch the dog's ears.

"This has been very, very pleasant, my boy. I'm so glad I ran into you. I was really feeling a little blue. Nothing like a good lunch and good conversation to lift the spirits. By the by, please come to the Club Friday night. We're introducing four new candidates for membership. I've been asked to stand sponsor for a friend of Roger Dormant's family by the name of,'' he searched his vast, echoing mind, so like a European train station in its grandeur and activity, "Leslie Sample.''

Chapter 20

Since it had been the way she had found her way into the Charles Club on her previous visit, Leslie walked around the corner from the spot where the cab deposited her at the foot of the front steps to the Ladies' Entrance which, with its tidy green awning extended to the curb, was much more welcoming than the huge, unsheltered front door. She couldn't remember if you were supposed to ring or knock. She tried the bell, but since it brought no response she rapped on the door with gloved knuckles. I'm a little zoned out, she thought. It had been a long and, she was beginning to realize, unproductive day showing a Japanese couple expensive condominiums. In addition to the impatience she felt when clients failed to recognize value when she took the trouble to point it out to them, the language barrier had been exhausting. Mr. Sekido had refused to admit by opening his mouth even once that his mastery of English was imperfect, hence the fiction accepted by the three of them that he spoke and understood only Japanese. Mrs. Sekido did most of the talking in both languages, painstakingly translating Leslie's every comment, including what she said about the delivery truck driver who backed out of an alley in front of her BMW. Mr. Sekido's questions to his wife, always in Japanese, quickly revealed, however, that he understood most of what was being said in English. Leslie had to remind herself through the course of the afternoon not to address him directly. By the time she dropped them at the Westin her head throbbed and her feet (in a new pair of Joan and David spiked pumps) as well.

After parking the BMW behind her South End apartment she showered and changed into a suit, not the Fiandaca but a black number which set off her new figure. She carefully took inventory, made certain adjustments, then indulged herself by calling a cab. The short ride helped her head and her feet but it was fifteen minutes later than seven o'clock when she knocked on the door. Since that proved as unproductive as the doorbell, she turned the knob and looked inside. It was dark and silent, the hallway attended by a haughty Victorian coatrack and a little loveseat, its silk stained by generations of umbrellas. Leslie entered this ambiguous space warily. She shrugged out of her fox and glanced around for someone to accept it. Finding no one, she settled for a hanger dangling from the almost empty coatrack. As she inserted its wire shoulders in her heavy fur ones she noticed by the paper jacket that it belonged to the New Ocean House in Swampscott, an immense wooden hostelry which had burned to the cellar hole when she was ten years old. It had been featured in the *Sphere*, she remembered, as the greatest conflagration north of Boston in modern times. The relic of this historic event sagged but held and she walked up a small flight of steps, past a yellowed mirror which reflected her dubious expression, a crease between the symmetrical brows above the beautiful dark eyes. What *is* this, she asked the mirror and stepped through a padded door into the, by contrast, brightly lit lobby of the Club.

Abel, standing behind the bar, was not too busy to smile at her. "Good evening," he said as he handed drinks to a group of men trying unsuccessfully not to rush the growler. "May I help you?"

"I'm looking for the . . . " Leslie searched her tiny beaded clutch for the invitation, "reception?"

"Ah," said Abel. "May I offer you something to drink? There are two receptions this evening. One for the Billiards. One for the Candidates."

"Thank you. I'd like a Perrier and lime. I'm not for the Billiards, so I'm quite sure I must be for the Candidates."

Abel deftly poured water, added fruit. "I'm sorry, we do not stock Perrier. Most of the members prefer Evian. I hope that will please you. I would like to think you were for the Candidates, but I doubt so."

"Well, I doubt that I'm for the Billiards, and I'm certainly for something."

"In any case, both receptions are on the second floor. I recommend that you walk up the flight of stairs. You can enjoy the paintings; and the elevator is not in a current state."

With a smile of gratitude, Leslie took a sip and started up the grand staircase. A scene of cheerful New England alcoholic activity extended below. Some forty people milled, drinks in hand, around a large table laden with cheeses, fruit, and small objects pierced with slivers of wood and nestled in grease on a Spode platter. The men spoke boldly to each other of sailboats, skiing trips, the vicissitudes of air travel. Places were dropped more often than names, since they all seemed to know the same people. "Longboat Key," offered one; "Jackson Hole," answered another. Leslie was pleased to see there were several women present, none within twenty years of her age, most dressed from a catalog that probably included garden shears and rubber boots. The hum of conversation suggested they saw each other often, had little need to produce the shriller variety of cocktail talk that serves to establish space and status. It sounded comfortable, even friendly. Reassured that these were indeed her customers, she continued upward, glancing at the canvases which punctuated the wall whose occupants stared back with disinterest, if not disdain. She wondered which reception room she was looking for. Ann had been so vague.

Roger Dormant occupied his customary corner. In each room of this club to which he had given his heartfelt allegiance—as well as the best years of his life since Harvard—he had a favorite spot. He was, he knew, a corner sort of person. In the Small Reception Room he enjoyed the northwest corner near the tall windows which faced the alley. No one had ever seen the alley from this room since heavy brocade drapes and dusty interior curtains sealed the room against undesirable drafts and views. From his corner Roger could stand gazing at the fire in the grate without roasting his legs. He could watch his friends, acquaintances, and the occasional stranger as they entered the room. Best of all, he could steal a proprietary glance at the lesser Sargent, magnificent above the mantel, glowing more from the muted radiance of its color than the reflections of the sconces or the hearth. It was one of the master's family groups, two boys arranged with their mother on a sofa in a dark, high-ceilinged room, a young girl standing in the doorway as if awaiting permission to enter. He loved the painting. It spoke of a life whose elegance and peaceful gentility was as desirable as it was unattainable. From the moment he first saw it, the Sargent had been his room within a room. On a comfortable evening like this, when his only responsibility was to ensure in some small way the continuity of the Club, he tried to enter Sargent's room, stand quietly in the corner admiring the beauty of the boys, the strength of the mother, the timid grace of the young woman.

Roger caught his breath. There at the door stood a girl, almost *the* girl, hesitant, uncertain if she should take a step, looking for a sign of welcome, a signal. Before he knew it, he had pushed past the tiresome friend of Avery Coupon and stood in front of her. He could think of nothing to say so he smiled shyly and touched her elbow. Her bones were tiny, her scent disturbingly evident over the wood smoke, the cigars, the vapors of expensive spirits which filled the room. "May I help you?" he said with effort. Her black dress accentuated her color, complemented the dark eyes.

They're all so helpful, Leslie thought. "Is this the Billiards? I'm quite sure I'm not for the Billiards."

"This is a small reception for candidates who have been proposed for membership, my dear." As this surprising phrase passed his lips Roger realized he had never in his life called anyone his dear, not his wife, not his daughter, certainly not his mother. He began to tremble slightly and gripped Leslie's elbow more tightly for support.

Hoo, boy, she thought. "Then I am in the right place," she said brightly, transferring her glass of water to the other hand since it was slopping slightly from Roger's tremors.

"I would like to think you are, but these are candidates for membership in the Charles Club. I'm awaiting one myself, a friend of my daughter's."

"Oh, is your daughter by any chance Ann Dormant? I'm . . . "

"His name is . . . "

As they spoke her name in unison, Leslie smiled her warmest, brightest smile, the smile that had moved three million of largely residential product in the previous calendar year. Roger's knees wobbled. At that moment she caught the eye of Avery Coupon's odious Italian friend. Excusing herself and gently disengaging, she walked across the threadbare Oriental carpet toward him. In company with most of the other men in the room, Roger followed her progress, seized as he was in the grip of several emotions not experienced since his undergraduate days, and one with which he was very familiar.

Avery Coupon's friend was holding forth on the relationships between American automobile manufacturers and the Italian design houses, a subject which had not engaged his listeners beyond the lowest threshold of Charles Club civility. As he turned in mid-sentence to greet Leslie, his audience evanesced and they were left standing alone, undeniably the two most handsome specimens in the room.

"What are you doing here?"

"I think I am going to be asked to join the Charles Club, can you believe it?"

"No, I'm afraid I can't, but will you have dinner with me after we escape this," he glanced around, "*tumulte*? You look positively smashing," he added with unaccustomed sincerity.

"You haven't said what you're doing here."

"Actually, I *have* been asked to join the Charles Club, or will be after I've done the rounds here tonight."

"So will I"

"No, *bella*, they have no women members here And all candidates must have a sponsor. Avery is mine," he gestured with his glass of scotch at a group in front of the fire. "He owes me."

"Roger Dormant, the father of a dear friend of mine, is my sponsor. And I spoke on the phone with the head of the Membership Committee, or something," said Leslie warmly. She turned and speared Roger with a smile. Reeling him in, she took his arm again. "Have you two met?"

Dormant, who had been fingering a blackball in his mind like a duelist about to load his pistol, smiled nervously. Avery Coupon's friend grabbed his free hand and pumped it twice in the European manner "Yes, I have met Mr. Norman, and it is a very great pleasure to see him once again. Leslie tells me she wishes you to sponsor her as a member. What a charming idea. I only wish it could be true. What a delicious addition to the otherwise rather austere amenities of the club." He offered his perfect white teeth for universal inspection.

"Of course it's true." Leslie felt her composure, not entirely secure since she arrived, slipping. She looked at Roger. "Ann set this up." The arm vibrated in her grip but she would not let it go. "What's the story?"

As Owen entered the room, tired after another in a succession of boring, unproductive days, he noticed Roger Dormant entwined with a stunning woman who looked like she could be Owen's ex-wife's younger sister He smiled at the expression on his friend's face which reminded him of nothing so much as a horse with a stone embedded in its hoof. "Evening," Owen said as he joined them.

"Leslie Sample, Owen Lawrence. And this is . . . ," Roger could not admit he did not remember the man's name.

"Subito. Paul Subito. I'm a friend of Avery Coupon's. Very happy to meet you indeed." He launched into a detailed description of his feelings about Boston, the Charles Club, and the early work of Pininfarina. Owen found himself studying Leslie.

Dormant drew her to one side. Before he could begin, she spoke urgently into his ear, her fragrant breath the most potent stimulant he had felt in years. "Isn't he a horrible *man*? I certainly hope you don't make *him* a member. Won't you introduce me to some of the others? I must say, I'm surprised to discover such an attractive group," she glanced over her shoulder then looked deep into Dormant's soul. "I thought you all might be sort of . . . like . . . old." The trembling increased, setting up a harmonic in Roger's right leg. He took a carelessly large swig of undiluted gin.

"Miss Sample," he croaked.

"Oh, please, Leslie."

"Yes. Leslie. That, I'm afraid, is precisely the point." He was about to attempt another sentence when he became aware of Seymour Gland's baleful gaze. Gland stood in front of the fireplace, dancing flames rimming the kewpie figure with luminescence, wispy hair alight on the top of his head like a candle. Dormant studied the features of the club's leading advocate of inalienable rights, personal freedom, and single-sex enjoyment of cigars and alcohol. Gland was staring intently at Leslie Sample. She retained Dormant's sleeve firmly in her grasp. Gland gestured at Roger with a curious swivel of his head. Dormant stared back in stubborn defiance.

"Roger," Gland hissed. Dormant set his receding but genetically sound jaw.

"Can I meet him?" asked Leslie, following Dormant's gaze. As if in answer, the glowing figure detached itself from the flames and marched towards them, a small Churchill prepared, as Roger well knew, to fight on the beaches, in the fields and in the streets.

"Please introduce me."

"Seymour Gland, Leslie Sample. I mean, Leslie Sample, Seymour Gland."

"Did I see your name on the list of candidates?"

"Oh, I hope so. Mr. Dormant has offered to be my sponsor. His daughter and I are good friends."

"I do not wish to cause you any embarrassment, Miss, Mrs.? *Miz* Sample, but I am afraid Mr. Dormant is participating in a rather uncharacteristically cruel joke at your expense."

"Oh, no, not," said Roger vehemently.

"Not uncharacteristic?" asked Gland with eyebrows raised.

"Not cruel?" asked Owen.

"Not at *my* expense," said Leslie flatly. They looked at Dormant.

"Not a joke," said he bravely, now completely out of his corner.

Chapter 21

"Damme," cried Gland.

Owen looked at him sourly. Over the length of their acquaintance, Owen had become increasingly aware of his friend's tendency under social stress to assume rather stagey English airs. To the best of Owen's knowledge Seymour had been to London on three occasions only. The first time had been during their last year at Harvard when an English uncle had invited Seymour to spend Christmas. Since Gland's parents had been divorced for years and his mother spent most of her time in Palm Beach, holidays were often as much of a trial for him as for Owen. They sometimes spent Thanksgiving or spring break wandering the city of Boston together arguing about whether or not to see a movie, dining well, occasionally, on Seymour's mother's credit at a few good restaurants like Locke-Ober. Owen remembered that particular Christmas as one of the loneliest he had ever spent. Seymour was away, as he was at pains to put it later, a fortnight. It snowed most of the fortnight and Owen spent the time walking beside the Charles River until he caught cold. Gland discovered him in bed in his Cambridge rooming house reading old issues of the *National Geographic* magazine borrowed from the landlady. Seymour was wearing a double-breasted waistcoat. Owen had not found him amusing then nor in the present instance.

Seymour was holding forth at an emergency meeting of the Strategy Committee which had been called the afternoon following the candidates' evening. The reception itself had ended abruptly as word spread among the attending members that Leslie Sample was *the* Leslie Sample. Most of them disappeared from the scene, anxious to avoid a speaking part, in rapid, silent succession. The candidates were left in the hands of Gland, Owen and Roger Dormant. After a tense few minutes Leslie and Paul Subito departed to have dinner together. The others followed their lead with a few mumbled words. Most felt the need for reflection and counsel.

The following afternoon, the Strategy Committee was convened by Gland's secretary. Dormant was not invited.

He had spent the morning at home trying to track down his daughter on the telephone. She proved to have erased her footprints and forded several streams. Roger could not decide whether to discuss the matter with Celia or not. He made a tentative appointment with her for dinner by calling her acupuncturist, where she was expected later in the day, then cancelled by telling her podiatrist that he could not make it because of an engagement at the Club and would she please inform his wife.

Thus, while the recalcitrant member sat taking rapid small sips of his second martini in the Library, an eye on the clock and the memory of Leslie's elbow in his hand, the Strategy Committee met upstairs.

"If you're going to swear at us do it in American," said Owen. He was, in fact, in a rotten mood, not entirely sure why.

Gland looked at him in surprise. "I'm not swearing at anyone in this room," he said, "it's just a damnably awkward, needlessly difficult, poorly timed, utterly inexplicable, completely unexpected . . . " He would have continued but was overridden.

"WHERE'S DORMANT?" asked the Eldest Member.

"He's hiding in the Library," replied DePalma.

"POOR PLACE TO HIDE," said the patriarch. "WE'LL ALL BE DOWN THERE AS SOON AS WE CAN GET THIS PALAVER DONE WITH."

"Well, the Club is faced with a disastrously dangerous . . . "

"Why did he put the girl up for membership?" asked Appleyard.

No one answered. Then Owen spoke. "I was talking with them. I got the impression that he hadn't planned to do just that. He seemed a little confused."

"A little confused! Of all the incredibly stupid, unbelievably obtuse . . . "

Walter Junior, who had not even attempted control of the meeting, spoke up. "As you know, I have been acting as the *pro tempore* Chair of the Nominating Committee. When Roger Dormant spoke to me last month about this Leslie Sample, whom he identified as a, uh, friend of his daughter, I offered to call him, her, I offered to call, to, uh, extend an invitation to meet the Club membership."

"I knew Pinhead was involved somehow," said Gland to Owen in an aside.

"Dormant asked me to stand as a sponsor, as well," volunteered the Architectural Critic, his eyes bulging, "which I readily agreed to do, little dreaming . . . "

"When I made that call, it was to a real estate firm on Commonwealth Avenue," continued Walter Junior. "I asked for Leslie

Sample and was promptly connected to a person who seemed very much aware of the situation. This, uh, person had a rather low, husky voice, but, uh, I recall thinking at the time, a somewhat effeminate manner. Of course, I do not feel that automatically must exclude potential members. We do, after all, have . . . '' He faltered under the ferocious glare of Gland, who leaped from his chair and began pacing.

"Well, here we are again! I, for one, am not aware that we have admitted so many effeminate members over the years. I assure you that, were I aware, they would not have been admitted. Now, it seems, we are presented, through the good offices of Mr. Roger Dormant, with a *completely* effeminate candidate."

"She's not effeminate," said Owen reasonably, "she's female."

"Let us not bandy words," said Seymour, a finger held admonishingly aloft.

This was too much for the Eldest Member. "OH, WHY IS HE LECTURING US? MY GREAT-UNCLE WAS AS LIGHT AS A FEATHER. RAN A DANCING SCHOOL IN DUXBURY FOR YEARS. WOUNDED HIS MAN IN A DUEL. WAS A MEMBER HERE LONG BEFORE WHAT'S HIS NAME WAS BORN. RING THE BELL." This last was addressed to Appleyard, who hastily summoned aid from below.

"As I was saying," said Walter Junior, "the combination of the, uh, person's name and the unusually low pitch of, uh, her voice led me to believe that I was speaking to a, uh, male. He, that is, uh, Sample, expressed great interest at the prospect of becoming a member of the Charles Club. In the spirit of our agreed-upon goal to strengthen the Club by injecting new, uh, blood, I invited, uh, I invited, I invited her to come last evening. And she came," he finished lamely.

The silence was broken by Abel, who swiftly collected drink orders from around the room and departed. After a moment Appleyard spoke. "There's really no problem here. Yes, admittedly it is embarrassing, but it was an honest mistake on the Club's part. Our bylaws are explicit on the gender question. We have made and, as far as I know, contemplate, no change in those bylaws. An apology, perhaps, is in order to the young lady. But nothing has changed."

"Nothing has changed?" DePalma's brows shot to their peak. "I see the situation in quite another light. We have, by our own stu . . . '' Abel's return gave him a moment to reflect. "We have, by our own errors and misunderstandings, provided our nemesis at the Licensing Board and, most particularly, the *Sphere* and the other media ghouls, a perfect opportunity to attack us again. Now there is a division in our ranks. Now there is a woman, a very attractive, I might add photogenic, woman, who, *rightly or wrongly*, has been proposed for membership. We must face this fact and we must deal with this fact in a timely fashion."

"How would the *Sphere* hear about it?" asked the Architectural Critic. A buzz around the room supplied the many possible avenues of information transfer.

"Well, what is Dormant going to do?" demanded Gland.

"I think he may stick to his guns," said Owen.

"I really can't believe that," said Appleyard.

"WELL, WHY DON'T YOU ASK HIM?"

The room fell silent as Roger entered, a third martini resolutely in hand. He gazed at his favorite corner, glanced at the cold fireplace, looked up for a moment at Sargent's improbably beautiful family. Then he eyed his erstwhile friends. "Yes," he said, "why don't you ask me, instead of hiding away up here?"

Leslie grabbed the receiver and gave the lighted button on the console a jab, breaking a dark red nail. The click of computers, the buzz of phones, the prattle of printers faded as she shoved the earpiece under her heavy hair. "Ann, where are you?"

"I don't want to say."

"*Ann.*"

"If I tell you, torture may force you to reveal my whereabouts."

"No, really, where are you?"

"I'm in Santa Barbara, if you must know. At El Encantado. Or, as they put it on this coast, *the* El Encantado. But since it is raining here, I'm thinking of taking an Air Plastic flight to San Diego, maybe stay at the Coronado for a few days."

"Ann, I'm in the most ghastly mess."

"Mess?"

"Yes, mess. The Charles Club thing. They called me and invited me to come to a party to meet the members, and then just went *out of their way* to embarrass me and make me feel cheap. I'm furious."

"Tell me more."

"Well, the only ones that showed even a little bit of friendliness and politeness were your father, who I must say is a rather confused person, he didn't seem to fully understand that he was my sponsor, I suppose you know that every candidate needs a sponsor? Yes, you told me that, didn't you? Well, I have two in fact, the other one is in real estate, I believe, but I didn't even get to meet him in all the confusion, and then there was a sweet one named Lawrence.''

''Owen Lawrence? He was the other one who was nice?''

''I thought it was Lawrence Owen, but whatever, yes, he was. And, can you believe this? Another one of the candidates was that *odious* friend of Avery Coupon's.''

''The Italian hunk?''

''Yes, and he was exactly what I expected, just the sleaziest. Manipulative? I can't begin to tell you.''

''Tell me.''

''I don't want to talk about it.''

''Did you go out with him?''

''Well, sort of. I was so *devastated* by the way those old farts treated me.''

''I hate to say I told you so.''

''Well, don't then. *Ann*, you got me into this!''

''Not quite true. I helped you into this. You wanted a ride in the car. I opened the door for you.''

The jetstream howled faintly on the transcontinental connection.

''Has the *Sphere* called you?''

''Yes. That's why I was so desperate to talk to you.'' Leslie sucked for a moment on her fractured nail. ''I don't know what to say to them. I'm so glad you called, Ann. How could they hear about all this? It only happened last night. I wish you were here. I need help. A reporter is coming to see me in an hour. What am I supposed to say?''

''What was the Italian hunk like, really?''

''Oh, he was no problem. I just let him run on and played the smiling little listener.''

''Was that all you played?''

''Ann, get real. Are you coming back here, or what?''

''Probably not. For a while, at least. When the *Sphere* reporter, male or female, you don't know, when he shows up tell him, her, everything. Everything. But if there's no photographer along, don't talk to them at all. You are going to have your picture on the front page, remember.''

''I've decided I don't want that.''

"Yes, you do."

"I'm not at all sure I want to be interviewed either. In fact, I know I don't want to."

"It's too late."

"What do you mean?"

"You are going to be famous, as I promised."

"What if I don't want to be famous?" Leslie wailed.

"That has nothing to do with it. You will see your beautiful puss smiling out of tomorrow's paper."

"Oh, God."

"Look at it this way. It will be good for business." The disconnect echoed across the intervening miles.

It could hardly be called an argument since there was no exchange of views, simply a simultaneous volley of all the emotional ammunition the Strategy Committee members had with them. The room echoed, then gradually quieted, as first one and then another fell back, magazines exhausted. Gland was the last one firing. He faltered on the word "quagmire" as he noticed the room was silent again. The target of the fusillade stood in the doorway apparently unwounded, his glass held delicately to his lips.

"Well," demanded Gland.

"Well, what?" responded the criminal Dormant.

"Well, what do you propose to do to get us out of this, uh, quagmire?"

"Nothing."

"Nothing at all?"

"Nothing." He seemed unperturbed at the vacuity of the exchange.

"Perhaps, Roger, if you explained to the girl," began Walter Junior.

"I think we should invite her to join. I have already mentioned that to her," said Dormant. The room was stony.

"But, we can't, Roger," said Appleyard, as if explaining matters to a particularly obtuse client, "because our laws don't allow it."

"I have come to the conclusion that we should change our laws. We may as well do it before we are forced to do it."

"But why make an issue of this woman?" asked De Palma. "She's not at all like any of the," he hesitated, "well, any of the wives."

"That's true," said the Architectural Critic, "not exactly the Charles Club sort, perhaps."

"CERTAINLY WOULD CATCH THE WIVES' ATTENTION," said the Eldest Member.

"What is our sort?" asked Owen. The room exploded again.

Roger turned to Owen as the noise clattered around them. "Yes, that's a question we should think about, I suppose. We never have to ask. We always seem to know. But I would like Leslie to be able to come to lunch here, and have a drink in the Library if she wants to. She's not at all our sort. That's why it would be so pleasant."

"Are you going to press the issue?"

"Yes, I think I am. They can all shout at me, but I don't think they can throw me out."

"What will your wife think about this, if you don't mind my asking?"

"I really don't know," said Roger. "Celia is an unusual woman. In some ways, that is. In other ways she's extremely predictable."

"Which will she be about, ah, Miss Sample?"

"Hard to predict," said Roger glumly. Then he looked at Owen. "But you haven't said what you think about all this." He ducked his head and said into the remnant of the martini, "Are you fer me? Or agin' me?"

Owen smiled and touched his glass to Roger's. In his best Gary Cooper voice he said, "Pardner, I'll back your play."

Chapter 22

This Monday began as many Mondays before it. Anton Pesht leaned into the entrance of the refrigerator room surveying the devastation within. His shoulders bulged under his spotless white shirt. The naked head thrust forward, the fencer's legs spread apart, the wild eyes veiled, the mouth under its awning of black moustache twisted in a grimace of ennui and disgust: Hercules venturing his first glance into the Augean stables. The normally well-organized refrigerator was in a state of disarray. The Annual Game Dinner the evening before had required four pheasants to be hung dripping for several days in one corner. A suckling pig had occupied one complete shelf. Twelve complicated courses had placed unusual strain on the resources and staff of Pesht's domain. Before it was concluded with applause, singing, ribald toasts, and a triumphant if reluctant appearance by the chef to accept the gratitude of the table, the delicate balance of the kitchen, the pantry, the larder, and the walk-in refrigerator had been upset. Chaos met Pesht's eye wherever he turned. The zinc counters were stacked with clean but unhoused plates and cups. A pile of mixing bowls tottered on a stool. The stove had been hastily cleaned. The oak cabinets above the counters gaped at him, their glass doors hanging open. He kicked a dish towel that lay on the floor and sent it fluttering. His staff had all been exhausted when they left the club around midnight.

"Fool, fool," cried the great man. He pronounced it full, echoing in the cavernous cooler. Pesht addressed the empty kitchen. "Where you are?" he demanded. "Come out, to be dealt with."

The door of the pantry opened slightly. Pesht's eye pounced upon the crack. "Come here. Come in. Face me, I demand you."

"How dare you speak to me like that?" said a small voice from behind the pantry door.

"What?" Pesht asked, his deep voice rattling the copper pans which hung above the central worktable like bunches of overripe fruit. "Speak like what? I speak to you like I wish. You and your box destroy my icebox, my kitzen, my life." Slamming the heavy door, he strode across the room. The pantry door quivered but did not open. Pesht stood, arms akimbo, his eyes like augers. "You don't face me," he said accusingly.

"Yes, I can."

"No, you don't. You and your little green stupid box. You cannot face."

"Yes, I can." The door, however, only trembled.

"Come out, or I kill it." He grabbed a tablecloth that was draped over one corner of a counter under the spice cupboard and jerked the cloth into the air. Beneath it, like a memorial group unveiled, was a small computer with keyboard and printer huddling close to the blind monitor. Pesht glanced around his disheveled kitchen for an appropriate weapon. He lifted a heavy wooden pestle used to force meat through the grinder, glanced at an array of carving knives stuck like quills in a wooden porcupine, then seized a large pastry roller. With a thin smile of satisfaction at the balance and heft of the long tapered pin he waggled it in the manner of a golfer focussing his concentration before a drive.

"Don't dare," snapped Miss Ontos as she stepped from behind the door. Black curls radiated from her agitated face like a thousand little springs. Her eyes were wide with alarm and arousal. She pressed her five-foot frame against the door that had shielded her, then staggered a little as it swung out as well as back, giving her a familiar pat. Regaining her stance she faced the ogre, her courage held tightly in clenched fists. "It is so *typical* of you to blame the computer, when it is clearly your own lack of foresight which creates the problems in this kitchen."

Pesht slashed the roller in widening, waist-high sabre strokes. It was evident he enjoyed the sound of the tip ripping through the stale air of the kitchen. He lunged forward in a sudden extension and with a powerful backhand stroke which carried the full force of his wrist and forearm cracked the weapon into the corner of the cupboard inches from the computer screen. The pastry roller splintered, the oak of the ancient cupboard groaned. Miss Ontos screamed in satisfactory fashion. Pesht grinned at her as she removed hands from her eyes to survey the damage which proved to be a small dent in the leading edge of the cupboard and the broken pin. "I feel like kill, but I am merciful man."

"You are *bestial*."

"I am artist, not accountsman."

"You are a *throwback*."

"I accept bestial. I accept throwback. I am proud to be artist of food, who creates with the senses. Nose, hands, eyes." He leered at her and opened his mouth, from which curled an enormous tongue. He extended it to an impossible length and then touched it to the tip of his nose. "And tongue," he finished proudly.

Miss Ontos recoiled in horror, her plump bust heaving. "No artist would behave as you do."

"Fah. You know no artists. Only Cambridge pretty boys. Art is bestial. I am proud to be bestial throwback and I don't want *this*," he lunged again with the point of the splintered rolling pin aimed at, but just short of, the computer screen, "in my kitzen."

This time Miss Ontos forbore to scream. She marched to the counter, drew up a wooden chair in front of her workstation and switched on the power supply. "I think that is quite enough." Her slender fingers rattled the keys, sending a shower of file commands down the serene green screen. "Shall we begin?" she asked icily, in control of her voice if not her respiration. "We will start with the menus for the week. Then we will make up the orders." She stressed the plural pronoun. "I shall call them in by telephone before noon. You will have all of your deliveries by five o'clock except from the Hingham fruit man, who, as you know, delivers on Tuesday morning."

Pesht threw his broken rolling pin into the copious gray plastic barrel in the center of the room. With a heroic sigh he began to pace about the room. As he walked he muttered to himself, occasionally casting glances at Miss Ontos' straight back in its pale blue silk blouse with a row of buttons from nape to waist. "A desolation," said Pesht. "Empty. Look, nothing left. For Monday dinner, sole *meunière*, pot roast with vegetable garnish, scrod creole, duckling with raspberries, leg of lamb, sweetbreads. I am only one man. Cobb salad, endive salad, hearts of palm, Waldorf salad for Mr. Dormant. I need more help. No man can do this all." As he moved slowly about the large, high-ceilinged old kitchen his voice grew softer. Absently he rearranged the knives in their slotted block, hung the family of mixing bowls in graduated order on their proper hooks. The dishes for the week to come rolled from his tongue wrapped in little puffs of self-pity.

Miss Ontos' fingers raced over the keyboard. She was an expert typist whose computer skills had been developed from earliest childhood, honed at Buckingham and Wellesley until at twenty-nine she was as facile with a personal computer as any expensively educated liberal arts major with a specialty in musicology in Boston. Her instrument was an Iguana, one of two obsolete demonstration models Gland had, with much fanfare, given the club two years before when Iguana, one of the crown jewels of Gland, Hollings Ventures, went into Chapter Eleven for the second time only to emerge six months later with new financing and the now famous Iguana II. The computers had been indoctrinated by Miss Ontos with the Club's accounts payable, its accounts receivable (including a special file for members overdue in various degrees), its payroll, its events calendar, miscellaneous accounting programs, and menus.

Within an hour Pesht had planned the offerings for seven dinners and five luncheons. Together they prepared the provision orders, taking into account breakfast needs for guests who might occupy the upper rooms. As they worked, Nilson padded in and with a grunt—perhaps intended as a greeting—helped himself to a cup of black coffee. In all, Miss Ontos entered twelve different orders to suppliers of meat, fish, shellfish, lobsters, game, fruit, spices and herbs, bakery goods, bottled water and other items, as well as one large general grocery order to S.S. Pierce. The liquor order would be prepared with Abel in a lighthearted session free of the baser emotions such as fear, lust and shame, which usually colored the Monday mornings with Pesht. The wine order was assembled once a month in a meeting between Miss Ontos and DePalma, the Chairman of the Wine Committee. She did not anticipate these encounters with pleasure. DePalma's condescension galled her. He sometimes stumbled over her name, never stayed a second longer in her little office below the stairs than was strictly necessary. There the second Iguana was set up on a proper computer table with a special computer chair like a prie-dieu, which allowed her to assume a very correct posture while entering information. This eased her back and enabled her to work without interruption for several hours if necessary. Since the two Iguanas were connected, information input from the kitchen was stored on the basement office disk. A large impact printer of antiquated design produced the order sheets, the bills, the checks, all the announcements issued by the club, and the menus. Miss Ontos, scrupulous in such matters, had chosen tasteful type fonts—a different one for each purpose. She did not mind the noise of the printer, which often clattered along for hours on end. To her it was the work of the world being accomplished. For all her romantic education she had a strong practical streak which required a daily regimen of physical and mental application. The printer sang progress to her. Miss Ontos believed in progress.

Pesht sank into his wooden throne in the corner of the kitchen which afforded an unobstructed view of the huge nickel and black gas range. The assistant chef, Rory Halloran, poked his sandy head through the door, assessed the tranquility of the scene, and ambled in to brew a pot of tea. A young Irishman without a green card, he was Pesht's most promising pupil in years. A sensitive touch, a sophisticated palate, boundless good humor, and a desire to absorb all he could from the master outweighed the fact that no one in the kitchen except Pesht could understand his Kerry brogue. The Boston Cat slipped in and curled up by an empty plate on the floor next to the stove. It was followed by three women who shared the preparation and serving duties, and a few minutes later by the young drudge, Earl, who did cleanup and washed the dishes. They tied on their whites, casting enquiring looks in Pesht's direction to gauge his emotional temperature. The kitchen began to hum quietly, then buzz as the disruption of the night before was finally put to rights. The air grew warmer and the first of the day's soup kettles gave off a spicy essence of simmering chicken stock. How long has she been here? Pesht asked himself, studying the buttons on the back of Miss Ontos' blouse. He watched her stroking the keyboard like an organist flying through an intricate partita. Occasionally she leaned her head back and searched for inspiration in the patterned garlands of the yellow tin ceiling. Her fingers, however, never slowed. Why do I devil her, he wondered. Pesht studied the graceful curve of her throat, the elegance of her wrists and forearms, the narrow span of her waist.

He had lived alone since the death of his wife, in a small apartment eleven blocks from the club. In the confusion and bitterness of his grief he had closed the little restaurant they had run together on the floor below. Now, when he returned late at night, the sight of the ugly convenience store that had so quickly replaced all that they had built ended each day with a taste of bile in his mouth. As he mounted the stairs the image of his wife was always vivid. She was Hungarian, as was he, beautiful, strong, with broad shoulders and powerful arms. She was born in Buda across the Danube from his home, well-educated, from a good family, intelligent and quick with figures. They had never met in their own country. He saw her first at a party given for Hungarian refugees in Boston in 1957. Within six months they were married and had opened the Magyar. For twenty years he had never given a thought to the past. Although no children came, they were busy and content with the creation of their new world. Life in America with Ava was a song for him until the day she was killed in the street in front of the Magyar by a truck which hit her and did not stop. Since there was no focus for his rage he retired into his room. He gave up the English classes he had begun at his wife's insistence, cut off communication with their friends, sold the Magyar. It took him almost a year to emerge, a man of black moods and wild moods, but a man who knew that if he did not work he would die. He found a job at the Charles

[125

Club under the legendary Marcel. When in two years Marcel retired, Anton Pesht stepped forward to assume his own greatness. Miss Ontos was one of the few at the club who realized he did not read English.

She sat back in the uncomfortable chair, her throat and cheeks flushed with exertion, her curls bouncing. "The brunch you have planned for Sunday sounds intriguing." She took a grateful sip of tea. "Thank you ever so much, Rory."

"*Argh la wurrie ta*?" asked Rory.

"No. Thank you," replied Pesht. To Miss Ontos he said, "Come back tonight after dinner if you still stay. If you can leave stupid box alone, I give you a sweet."

"I suppose you think that will erase the memory of your ugly and quite inexplicable behavior this morning."

"Come if you want."

"No one has ever called me a fool. Never in my life."

"I did not call you a fool."

"Well there were only the two of us within the range of your bellowing. Thank goodness," she added under her breath.

Anton did not answer, just stared at her with heavy-lidded eyes as, amid the quickening pace of the kitchen, she re-read him the menus for the week in her elegantly modulated little voice. I am the fool, he thought. I am a great fool.

Chapter 23

His first impression was that Demetria Constantine owned the room. Owen slipped inside the door just before the guard closed it. As he squeezed past this burly presence who was armed with a sinister black radio and a stick the length of a perpetrator's forearm Owen trod clumsily on the officer's foot. "Beg your pardon."

"Sit down and be quiet," she growled and Owen obeyed. The room reflected the spacious, shabbily utilitarian architecture of the State House Annex. The ceiling vanished in haze some twenty feet above them. The far wall of the room was panelled in tired wood, its surface innocent of moulding or decoration other than a large symmetrical waterstain which hung like a map behind the dais. The other three walls were decorated with framed officeholders of yore who were set off nicely by the light green plaster behind them. A carpet of the plastic fiber usually identified as indoor/outdoor absorbed some of the moisture brought in by the boots of the small audience. Owen counted a few more than thirty people occupying the metal stacking chairs that faced the bar. Several towers of unused chairs leaned in casual attendance at the walls and corners. The room could hold a hundred, he thought as he shrugged out of his trench coat, stuffed his plaid cashmere scarf, one of the last tangible reminders of his former life of, if not affluence at least comfort, into a side pocket, draped the coat on an empty chair and dropped down beside it. It was the day before Christmas.

The Licensing Board sat in its majesty on a riser that ran the width of the room. The five members or, as Owen saw it, the two pairs of men sitting on each side of Demi, faced the supplicants over a long oak counter furnished with five pitchers of water and five plastic glasses. Yellow legal pads and yellow pencils graced each place, the tools, Owen supposed, of the trade. In front and below the counter sat a man with a stenographer's machine before him on a small stand. He was at rest, possibly asleep, Owen thought, since his head hung forward and his eyes were not visible. As he breathed heavily, in and out, radiance from the industrial lighting fixtures danced on his bald pate. At the center of the counter and the center of everything in the room existed Demi. She looks as though she has a spotlight on her, Owen said to himself. He absorbed her image. She wore a red suit and no jewelry. Her blonde hair gleamed like a metal, neither copper nor gold, perhaps some improbable alloy. She held an object in her long red-tipped fingers as she counted the house. Then at the moment when the room paused fractionally in its gabble she whipped the wooden mallet smartly against the wooden block. The report shut all sound off like a switch. Demi smiled, her generous mouth conferring welcome, her eyes rescinding it. "This hearing of the Licensing Board of the Commonwealth of Massachusetts will come to order." As she spoke the stenographer moved his fingers over the mysterious keys of his machine. The connected pages began to fold like large tickets into the basket in front of him. "Please read today's agenda," Demi said staring straight ahead. Her voice was rich with a theatrical timbre which did not require a microphone to carry.

The light in the big chamber was patchy and Owen sat in a little pool of dim in a back row. He knew she had not seen him. It's her place, he thought. She is not only in charge here, this is her stage. He slouched down in the chair studying the scene with fascination. The secretary of the board began reading, in a toneless Boston drone, the cases to be heard. It was to be a busy morning. A bar called Nephews Three was called to respond to complaints registered by various individuals and the South End Neighborhood Association. The allegations included noise, serving after closing time, fights, excessive late night traffic, careless disposal of trash, and several lesser charges. The litany filled two pages. When the secretary finished he looked at Demi. She paused a moment then invited a representative of the establishment in question to speak in its defense. A short, stocky man in a blazer and turtleneck, presumably one of the Nephews, rose and refuted in uncompromising terms each of the charges. "We heard all of this before and we handled it. And besides it's a crock." His lawyer stood up, pushed his client back into his chair and in a more conciliatory tone asked exactly what steps were necessary to have the matter resolved.

"This is the third time in a year we have heard this story," said Demi in her effortless contralto as she sorted documents on the desk. "Both sides of it. It is evident that the problems have not been cured. Many credible sources have complained that this establishment is a constant and major focus of disturbance in a largely residential neighborhood." She looked down at the lawyer. He started to speak, then changed his mind. Perhaps it was something he saw in her eyes. Her expression suggested to Owen the professional gaze of a ranch hand honing his cutter on his boot before turning a bullcalf into a steer. Without consulting her colleagues she went on. "We will give you six months to clean up this situation." The lawyer smiled a sickly grin of relief and sat down. "Your license is suspended for six months," she added and snapped the gavel down again.

During the shouting which followed Demi turned to the board member on her left to discuss the next item on the agenda. Owen got up to stretch his legs. He followed a young man out into the hall. A short recess was declared while the aggrieved Nephew registered dissent at the top of his voice. The guard was moving purposefully towards him as the door swung shut. Owen walked to a window overlooking the back side of Beacon Hill, four floors beneath them. He knew he should be at work, that his desk had a pile of new business plans to be read, that a review meeting was scheduled in half an hour. Umbrellas slid along the sleet-slicked bricks like jellyfish on the surface of the water. "Isn't she a piece of work?"

Owen turned to the young man who stood under a no-smoking symbol taking a deeply relished drag. "Well, yes, I guess you could say that," said Owen.

"She's going to be a star. One of the bright new faces in this toxic waste repository." He inhaled mightily. "I like to drop by when she's holding court. She's good copy."

"Do you work for one of the papers?"

"The *Sphere*."

"She's a good picture, too."

"You noticed. There isn't anyone in what passes for government around here who comes within a country mile of her. Most of them are empty suits."

"What's the story in there today?"

"Well, she just stuck her pretty neck way out. That mouth, he's connected. He runs three bars around town and each one is sleazier than the next. He handles the cops who come around and the health inspectors. But no one seems to be able to handle Miz Constantine. Not that there aren't plenty of volunteers," he added thoughtfully.

"Is she going to have trouble because of this decision?"

"Probably. That's what politics is, trouble. But I wouldn't bet against her. When she goes after someone, she makes it stick. I'm not sure she can be turned. That prick will probably give it a try."

"Are you writing a story about it?"

"No. It's small potatoes so far. If it escalates to the next level, so to speak, then it might be something. I like to write about beautiful women anyway."

"Do you know her?"

"No one seems to know her." He stepped on his cigarette and Owen followed him into the hearing room again. The Nephew and his lawyer were gone. The morning droned on with discussion about licensees, leaseholds, rights of renewal and other technical matters. From his dark corner Owen watched Demi operating in her own patch. It was a much bigger territory than he had guessed. Larger by far than his own at Gland, Hollings, where they must be wondering about his absence. He decided he was sick. Sick of his job, among other things. Demi spoke and moved with the authority of command. She seemed to be more than the Chairlady. She seemed to be the Massachusetts Licensing Board.

He had not talked to her for two weeks. The sound of the message on her answering machine affected him like a breath of ether, instilling such deadly lassitude as took an hour to overcome. How many times have I been with her, he wondered. Watching the red and gold figure at the far end of the room he tallied the events of their, what should he call it? By the time he had re-screened their meetings, lunches, dinners, film dates, drinks, kisses, cab rides and arguments from the day in the Parker House lobby to the evening in his apartment he decided it seemed something like a love affair. But in the last two weeks it had been all telephone conversations and broken dates and recorded messages which began Hi I can't come to the telephone right now but. Owen devoured her from the back of the room. She was speaking to the owner of a failed restaurant in Dorchester who wanted to sell his liquor license for fifty-three thousand dollars to a Canadian hotel chain. Demi smiled at the man and bade him return in two weeks. Owen got to his feet and went out in search of coffee.

In ill-spaced letters the schedule board beside the hearing room door proclaimed that the Mass. Licensing Board session would break at 12:15 to resume at 2:30. Owen was coming up the stairs, a container of coffee in his hand, when he saw the door open, the spectators filing out followed by the board members, the stenographer, the clerk, the guard but, after a minute, he realized, not Demi. He waited a moment until the hallway cleared then pushed open the door.

Demi sat in her chair, still in the spotlight, playing not to the empty room but to a single person standing in front of her dais who was laughing at something she had just said. Owen stopped inside the door. He watched the two of them, both laughing now. The young man was tall and beautifully encased in a suit of soft glen plaid. It was, Owen realized, a suit he could never wear and would not even look at in a clothing store—supposing for the sake of argument he were ever in a clothing store being shown patterns from which to choose. All the suits he had ever worn were dark blue or gray, mostly gray, perhaps, the thought occurred to him, because he might be a little color-blind. He stared hard at the suit talking to the woman he loved. Try as he might, he could not tell in the uncertain light whether it was green or gray or blue-green or bluish-greenish-gray. The suit had gold cufflinks and a white collar that stood up higher on his neck than any collar that Owen owned. Owen unconsciously reached back and pulled his limp collar a little higher but felt it shrink back into the obscurity of his jacket where it was used to hiding. The suit had on a yellow power tie, Owen was sure of that; and it, they, were walking toward him.

"Owen. What are you doing here? Oh, this is Kevin Connors from the Governor's Office."

Owen realized he was holding a very hot cardboard cup of coffee so he did not attempt to shake the suit's muscular manicured hand.

"Demi, I've got to run," said the suit. "Remember what I said. It could be very important for you to be seen there. I know you've got a wild schedule but this is one of those opportunities you can't afford to miss."

"Thanks, Kevin. You're a darling. But you already know that."

The suit brushed past Owen and ran down the stairs waving one immaculate arm. It wore a gold chain-link bracelet.

"Owen. What a surprise. Look, I'm sorry but I've got a conference upstairs and I have to be back here by two-thirty."

"I want to talk to you."

"Call me tonight."

"Your answering machine is giving me a fatal disease."

"Well, this is not the time or the place."

She looked dazzling in red. He had never seen her in red before. He put his hand on her sleeve. "When can I see you?"

"I'll talk to you tonight." She was moving to the elevators.

"Instead of talking let's have dinner tonight."

"*Owen*. I can't. I have a meeting."

"Then how can we talk? I'm going to get that recorded message again and I'm going to do something ugly."

"Don't be silly."

"Too late for that," he said as the elevator door closed.

Chapter 24

Owen was late for a business lunch. He hurried up State Street through interminable January rain which aspired to sleet. He strode past the Colonial Bank, whose facade simulated with Disney-like attention to detail a humble roadside tavern complete with purple leaded panes and crumbling brickwork. Beyond it in an unbroken three-block rank came the drive-in entrance to the Bank of Bangladesh; Consolidated Fiduciary, a seventy-story glass showerstall; Commonwealth Specie, whose middle stories bulged above the street in the shape of a black marble bowling pin; and the Wampatuck Bank, whose symbol, a bust of Chief Wampatuck, glared out from every window, his expression of savage contempt daring Owen to come in and be scalped. Crossing Congress Street at the Old Currency, he splashed by the Mercantile Exchange, whose ficus forest nodded lazily in the empty atrium, and turned up Franklin Street.

He knew he would not find a cab in the rain which at that moment began to crystallize into something less than liquid. He was certain to arrive late under the best of chances since Seymour had kept him on the telephone past noon telling him to bring as quickly as possible the financial exhibits which he, Seymour, had forgotten when he left the office for the Charles Club at eleven-thirty. Seymour had reserved the Large Reception Room for a luncheon for fourteen. Owen had not originally been included, but since he was bringing the display cards around which the discussion would center he assumed he would be inserted at the table however awkwardly. Seymour did not often use the Charles for business meetings since there were other locations, the downtown Harvard Club or the Bay Tower Room for example, close by in the financial district. The choice meant to Owen that Seymour was worried about this deal and needed to apply some gloss to the proceedings, or that there were European investors in the group, or both. He headed for the T station at Park Street, portfolio flapping. Sick weather, he thought. By tomorrow half the people on this street will have a sore throat. He turned the corner past the Parker House and ran as best he could against the freshening wind toward the subway entrance rising like a granite tipple at the head of the shaft. As the wind blew him sideways along he pondered the two great enigmas of life: women and mezzanine financing.

He realized he knew little about the emotional or intellectual motivation of either. It had taken three calls to persuade Demi out to dinner again, three calls which were the result of half a dozen attempts to get past the machine. After each failed attempt he told himself he would not call again. Then an hour later or two hours later or a day later he called again. Suddenly the sun shone and she said yes.

"You mean you don't have a meeting?"

"Stop it, Owen. Where shall we go?"

"What about a movie?"

"Can we agree on a movie?"

They could and they did. It was Clint Eastwood but not "Dirty Harry" and by God's grace it was funny. Then after their leaving the theater in Copley Place hand in hand everything mysteriously began to turn sour. Walking through the crowded halls of the shopping mall they somehow could not agree on a restaurant. Demi wanted to sit at the bar at Durgin Park and eat strawberry shortcake. Owen did not think that was the best suggestion of the evening but he agreed. They had to stand in line and after fifteen minutes he persuaded her to go to a seafood restaurant across the way. She agreed, but before the meal was over they agreed it was a poor choice. That was the last thing they agreed on. That an evening which started with a pretty good movie ended in black disaster and despair was as surprising to him now as it had been when she slammed the cab door on his scarf and disappeared into traffic with only the departing flutter of the Burberry plaid as goodbye. The hell with it, he said to himself as he hurried down the treacherous steps of the oldest subway station in America. I haven't got a clue. Whatever I do or say seems to make her angry. I'm not the right person for her. She's not the right person for me. What has that got to do with anything, asked a voice which proved only to be the voice of reason. As he fumbled for a token in the chill steambath of the station he knew he was still as lost to reason as ever. The hell with it, he said again. I'll call her tonight and have a conversation with her answering machine. He ran for a trolley on the Green Line heading for Copley and points he had never visited farther down the line.

The riddle of mezzanine financing was as puzzling—if less painful. At times, and this was one of them, Owen felt that venture capital had a rhythm of its own to which he could not seem to dance. Why would a group of venture investors entrusted by individuals and corporations with millions of hard-earned dollars consider pouring money for the third time into a company which had clearly demonstrated a talent for self-destruction? He looked out the window of the Japanese-made lightrail car which rocked along through the tunnel. Occasional light bulbs popped into view revealing gravel roadbed, sagging cables, indentations in the concrete where workers could escape the clattering cars. Workers were not present, nor was enlightenment.

Metatarsal Technics, a manufacturer of cloth and rubber shoes, had sought oblivion on two previous occasions and almost achieved it each time. One of Gland's personal enthusiasms, MT had begun life appropriately enough in the gymnasium of an empty schoolhouse in Malden. There the inventor, Prescott Hensile, known to his cohorts as Pre, working at night on a trestle table littered with scraps of plastic and tubes of glue, fashioned the first Watershoe. Walking or running in a shoe whose sole was a cell filled with water produced a sensation hitherto unexperienced by the country's young athletes. A television commercial featuring a Celtics guard who likened wearing Watershoes to walking in bacon fat achieved instant national awareness. A Los Angeles Laker said it felt like his feet were inside a pumpkin. Despite or even because of these endorsements MT was an overnight success, selling all the Watershoes they could produce. The boom did not survive the winter, however, when shoes began to burst and Hensile was forced to initiate experiments with antifreeze compounds.

Gland, Hollings led a second round of investment with the infusion of another three million dollars. Metatarsal brought out the next generation of athletic footwear six months later, the Duckboot, which enclosed the entire foot and ankle in a cushion of liquid. Duckboots, although heavier than most sport shoes, were an immediate hit with the industry trendsetters, the pickup basketball players in New York, Boston, Philadelphia, and Los Angeles who spent their discretionary funds on gold, automatic firearms, and designer sneakers. When abrasion began to cause internal leakage and it became apparent that the glycol solution produced skin burns and blisters, Duckboots were recalled. Hensile left the factory in Derry, New Hampshire, for an extended trip on his forty-foot yawl to rebuild his shattered dream in the British Virgins.

In its four years of life Metatarsal Technics had consumed sixteen million dollars. Now Gland, Hollings was pulling together a third round of financing to re-invigorate the company. Hensile, tanned and refreshed, had come up with a revolutionary design. Eschewing liquid completely, he had attached two plastic strips to a molded sponge-rubber casing. The New Age Puttee was described by its inventor as the most versatile shoe design of the century. Iridescent turquoise on one strap, Day-Glo orange on the other, it could be wrapped and tied in an infinite number of ways. The prototype had been tested with focus groups in the South Bronx and at an Indiana high school. All that was lacking was more cash.

When Owen reached the Charles Club the sleet had turned gritty and he wished for any shoes other than his worn tassel loafers. He splashed up the steps, threw his coat on the rack and dashed the moisture from his hair. "The Gland group?"

Abel pointed upstairs. Owen pointed at the elevator. Abel shook his head. Owen, glancing at the clock behind the bar which indicated fifteen minutes past one, started up the staircase two steps at a time, the cards which allocated six millions in new funds to manufacturing, working capital, marketing, and a media campaign featuring a famous young Muslim from Houston under his arm. Before he reached the landing, however, a commotion in the foyer below arrested his progress. The Distinguished Poet was engaged in a heated exchange with an attractive woman in furs. They stood in a cloud of sleet at the open front door. "I most certainly will do nothing of the sort," she said and attempted to push past the shorter but equally determined Poet.

"I am terribly sorry indeed, but it is a rule of the Club," he managed to convey the capital, "that ladies must use the Ladies' Entrance."

"I am not one of your 'Ladies,' " she expressed the quotation marks nicely, "I am a vice president of the Old Currency. I am here for an investors meeting. I am late because I could not find a cab. I am freezing, and we are soaking this very nice Oriental runner."

"Madam . . . "

"I am not at the moment married . . . "

The Distinguished Poet clenched his teeth. He could not bring himself to utter the Ms. appellation.

" . . . if it is any business of yours, which it most certainly is not. You may address me as Vice President, if you wish. My friends, among whom you will never be numbered if you do not stand out of my way, call me Margo.'' With that she flung past him and stalked in her elegant black leather boots to Abel. ''Where is the Gland, Hollings investors meeting?''

''The Charles Club does not allow business meetings,'' said the Distinguished Poet heatedly and incorrectly from the doorway.

''In the Large Reception upstairs,'' said Abel.

''Follow me if you like,'' said Owen.

''I shall report this to the Committee,'' cried the Distinguished Poet, although it was unclear exactly whom he was addressing. He held onto the door as if he had caught it in a heinous act, sleet encrusting his overcoat like the Northwind's spittle. With something between a grunt and a sob, he forced the door closed against the gale. By that time Owen and Vice President Margo had reached the second floor and opened the door on dessert and Gland's speech.

''New England has for one hundred years been the shoe capital of America,'' he continued as he made flapping motions at Owen indicating his need for the financial cards. Owen extracted them from the portfolio and brought them to the easel by Seymour's chair. The investors made room for Margo and continued to munch on Anton's bread pudding. ''With Metatarsal Technics we have joined Route 128 technology with one of our great traditional industries. The result is an enterprise with tremendous potential. Admittedly MT has not realized that potential as yet. What it has done, however, is to press the envelope of podiod technology,'' Gland paused with a frown intended to convey the drama of the situation. ''In four short years MT has profoundly changed the footgear market. Never again will the consumer be satisfied with a hundred-dollar pair of sneakers. Now, with the introduction of the New Age Puttee which, by the way, the technical people are calling the NAP, we can expect MT to take off. Before I take you through the financials are there any questions? Glad to see you could make it, Margo.''

Owen had always wondered why businessmen spoke in initial caps. He assumed it reinforced the aura of reality but he knew this was not the moment to ask.

''Puttees went out with World War I,'' said a man at the foot of the table. It was not phrased as a question but Gland smiled at the man nonetheless.

"Most living American basketball players have never heard of World War I," he replied reasonably. "Four million dollars carefully spent on our target audience, and I am about to show you exactly how that will be done, will make the NAP the hottest item in foot sportwear."

"How does it stay on the foot?"

"High-adhesion Velcro."

Margo interjected, "A man attempted to prevent me from entering the front door of this building. What was that all about?"

Gland looked at Margo, then at Owen. Owen shrugged slightly and nodded his head.

"He told me to go around to the side door," she added. "It is sleeting and snowing and raining all at once. Perfectly dreadful. Of course I refused."

"I'm terribly sorry but it is a rule of the club." Gland smiled ingratiatingly. "Would you like some bread pudding?"

Margo looked around the room. "Am I the only woman in the group?" She ascertained that she was. "Then I shall have to walk out by myself. I am walking out of the deal as well as the front door. It's a ridiculous concept, by the way, any woman can see that." She left without having removed her coat.

"What ROI are you looking for?" the man at the foot of the table asked, as if nothing had happened.

Gland uncovered the first display card. "Excellent question. Let's take a look at the five-year projections." Coffee was served. The British investors were intrigued by the audacity of the vision. The venture arm of the Bank of Bangladesh nodded his head. By two forty-five Owen was pretty sure Seymour had made the sale. Owen's understanding of mezzanine financing had advanced no further. Nor had his understanding of women.

Chapter 25

"This is the Boston Garden. Not where the Celtics and the Bruins play, that's the real Boston Garden. This is the Public Garden, the site of the Boston World's Fair of 1895. See the pond over there? Where they're skating? It was dug out of the bedrock by Chinese laborers who were out of work after the railroads were built. They founded Boston's Chinatown which we will see later this afternoon. The Garden was laid out by the famous landscape designer, Frederick Homestead. It is a reproduction of the famous gardens at Buckingham Palace in London, England. That's the famous Ritz-Carlton Hotel, the most expensive hotel in the world. Howard Hughes once took an entire floor of this hotel for a year. He came to Boston in a private railroad car and no one saw him arrive or leave, but while he was here the elevators didn't stop on the twenty-second floor of the Ritz except for Room Service. It will cost you five thousand dollars a night to stay in the famous Presidential Suite by the way." The driver lifted the sponge-covered microphone for a moment and cleared his throat. He felt he was on today. It usually took him about ten blocks to warm up. A bigger load helped. They were light, as they often were in the winter. He ran his fingers through his curly black hair.

The vehicle, a jitney to the driver and a trolleycar to most of the passengers, was actually a bus powered by a gasoline engine concealed under the floor. Unencumbered by electrical pickups or cable grips, it circumnavigated Boston without restraint of tracks or wires. Its square shape parodied the streetcars of fifty years earlier with open sides and wide, uncomfortable seats. A round brass front light and a gong on the roof which the driver frequently rang by pulling a cord, completed a halfhearted gesture toward mechanical antiquity. Hubtour's Trolley Twelve carried three German businessmen travelling in pharmaceuticals from Mainz; a retired man and his wife a week out of Omaha with five weeks of sight-seeing ahead of them; a group of Japanese computer scientists attached to Tokyo University but on loan to MIT; four teenage girls from Bristol, Rhode Island, who were to sing that evening in the semifinals of a television talent show; a drug mule from Medellín who had never been to Boston before; and one passenger who boarded when the driver, to relieve himself, stopped at the Bull and Finch Pub. In the brief interval it took Gary, as he had introduced himself when he loaded at the Tourist Information Center on Tremont Street, to empty his bladder, an elderly man in an ankle-length quilted coat stepped inside and glared at the passengers. "Just checking," he said fiercely and walked to an unoccupied rear seat. Before Gary returned he was curled on the floor between seats near a heating duct.

With the clear plastic side curtains lowered the jitney was warm enough if drafty. Turning down Newbury Street the driver continued in his butterscotch radio announcer's baritone: "This is one of the three most expensive shopping streets in the world. The others are in Paris and Tokyo. I'm sure you know the ones I mean. That parking lot charges six dollars every half hour and if you leave your car there all day you might as well let the attendant keep it, ha, ha." A sedan stopped in front of them and a double-parked van blocked the other lane. Gary waited as an old lady began backing herself out of the front passenger door. "There are art galleries on this street that sell Picassos and Old Masters for millions of dollars. You can see one of them in the window above you on the right." He indicated a watercolor of a Mediterranean villa which brightened a second-floor display window. "That's an original Andy Warhol that was just bought by Larry Bird for a high six figures. Well, for shit's sake lady, please give me a break. All right everybody let's give her the old raspberry when she finally decides to let us by." The passengers dutifully saluted the woman as she negotiated the curb with the exception of the couple from Omaha, who were not sure what a raspberry was, the Colombian, who thought it impolite, and the man on the floor, who was asleep.

"These are some of the most exclusive boutiques in Boston," Gary reported as they rolled past Banana Republic. "This is real yuppie country. Most of these people are stockbrokers and investment bankers. They're the only ones who can afford to live in Back Bay. I certainly can't on what they pay me to drive you good people around, ha, ha. See the little market on the right? It doesn't look like much on the outside but oranges cost ten dollars a dozen there and they will deliver your caviar anytime of the day or night." Trolley Twelve turned right on Hereford and stopped at the light. "This is the famous Commonwealth Avenue, so named because only wealthy people have lived here since Colonial times. These all used to be single-family houses. Now they are all condos. Do you want to guess how much a condo in this block costs? Don't even try. They are all in the million dollar class. I guess they should call it Uncommonwealth Avenue, ha, ha.''

He turned left and stopped just past the corner. Three men stepped out of the Charles Club and paused to adjust their coats against the chill. ''This is one of Boston's oldest and snobbiest men's clubs,'' said Gary, his amplified words clearly audible through the side curtains. He didn't have much to work with for the next few blocks. Until he reached Kenmore Square and Fenway Park his load tended to get out of control, to talk among themselves, and to read their maps and guidebooks. ''You have to be a member of one of the old Boston families like the Kennedys or the Fitzgeralds to join a club like this. They do not allow Jews, blacks, Muslims, Iranians or women. No woman has ever set foot in this building. Including, I might add, the Queen of England on her royal visit here several years ago.''

''Whatever is the man talking about?'' asked Roger Dormant. ''I've never heard such nonsense in my life.''

''They come by all the time now,'' said Walter Junior.

The Architectural Critic hung his walking stick on his arm and pulled on his gloves. ''It's worse in the summertime when they have the curtains up. You can hear them blocks away.''

''See the fat one? The one with the cane? He's a Cabot. You remember the old song: The Cabots speak only to Lowells and the Lowells speak only to . . . I can't remember who the Lowells speak to but that's a real Cabot.''

''God,'' said the Architectural Critic, ''what a spiel. Imagine being trapped in there all afternoon.''

''Are you connected to the Cabots?''

''Only by marriage, thank heaven. My second wife. I was a Cabot for twenty-seven months.''

''Was she the one . . . ?''

''Yes. Devil of a time keeping it out of the *Sphere*, too.''

''The name of this club is the Somerset Club. The members are all graduates of Harvard. Once a year they put on a show and most of the actors dress up like women. You can bet they have some high old times, ha, ha. I guess it would be a few laughs at that to see those old duffers in drag.''

''He seems to have muddled us up with the Somerset, the Tavern, and the Hasty Pudding. Should I set him straight?''

"I didn't much care for the old duffer remark."

"Let's tell them what we think of their snobby old club." This time the entire group gave tongue since the Nebraska couple had learned how, the drug distributor did not care for the three men who looked to him like government officials, and the homeless man like a restless baby had been wakened by the cessation of movement. With a clang of the bell, Trolley Twelve headed for Fenway.

"Isn't that remarkable," said Walter Junior, as the trio started up the street together.

"Boston has always been an unruly city."

"As the British discovered."

"Still, it's a great old town." For whatever reason all three were smiling as they walked along past black wrought iron and hibernating magnolias.

"Of course it is," said Roger, "of course it is."

Chapter 26

Demi and Owen came back laughing about another terrible dinner, this one in Chinatown. Telephone communication had magically been re-established. They apologized to each other about their ill-fated movie date, she hadn't been feeling well, she said, and he threw himself on the mercy of the court. With a minimum of persuasion Demi had agreed to meet him for dinner. He had called her the next morning and she confirmed the time and place. She seemed warm, even eager, on the phone. Owen's day had crawled by, an eternity of anticipation. Kevin, the suit in the Governor's Office, had recommended the restaurant to Demi as serving the best Chinese food in the city. Owen was not completely unhappy to find the food mediocre. "I wish I had ordered spaghetti," Demi said as they were putting on their coats.

"I'm not sure we didn't."

She had insisted on paying, saying it was her suggestion, and her turn anyway. Then she asked him if he wanted to come to her place for a drink. Owen said yes if I can pay for the cab. It was snowing again and the snowplows were out. Something about the night in Chinatown and the soft snow and their destination made them silent in the taxi for a few minutes. Owen reached for her but she said wait till we get home, and they found things to laugh about again. The one thing they never talked about was the Charles Club. Every time Owen had been tempted to ask her about Seymour he had hesitated, afraid to rock the boat.

Her apartment, on the first floor of the house, was white and filled with soft leather furniture and soft rugs. They came out of the noisy street and the snow into a hush. She pulled off rubber boots and told Owen to take off his wet shoes. There were two glass tables: one a low coffee table, the other a dining table encircled with four white chairs. Flowers floated in the center of each sheet of glass. There was no mess of books and magazines; no disarray. Owen felt she must have prepared the room for his eyes. He hadn't imagined she lived this way. But, he reminded himself, there was a lot he didn't know about her. She waved a black bottle at him from the little white lacquer bar table and he nodded. He was absurdly happy to be there with her in her apartment where everything felt warm and pleasant to the touch. He dug his toes into the soft carpet. The leather of the couch and chairs was a shade she described as taupe. As she fixed the drinks he heard a plow scrape by outside. A week ago I couldn't talk to her, he thought. Now, with any luck, I won't be able to get a cab home. She switched on an audio deck and it produced soft bouzuki music, the only Greek flavor in the room. Demi offered him a heavy crystal glass—her own in her other hand. He stood up and kissed her and after a moment she pulled away. "Here, don't make me spill them."

They sat together on the wide couch and drank and then kissed again. "Don't you like my apartment?"

"Course I do."

"Well you haven't said anything. Usually that's the first thing people say when they walk in. I've worked hard on it."

"It's beautiful. I think it looks like you but I'm not sure. I don't want to say the things other people say when they see it."

"You haven't so far."

"Good."

He set his bourbon down on the glass table and kissed her again. Nothing but the kiss happened for a while. Then she said, "Let me show you the rest of it."

"I'm not interested in the kitchen."

"Then we'll skip the kitchen."

"What's left?"

"The bedroom and the bath and two closets."

"Let's look at them in that order." Her eyes are huge, he thought, and seem to change. Tonight they were almost black. Her white silk shirt with the long full sleeves seemed to absorb all the light in the room.

"I think I'll show you the kitchen after all." They finished their drinks while she told him the history of her kitchen and its appliances. She made them another Jack Daniel's and managed to keep the butcher block center island work area—made to order by Somerville Lumber—between them until the tour was completed. She led him back to the couch and they sat apart while she told him how she found the place and bought the lease from the woman who had lived there before. He reached up and turned out the lamp beside the couch. Only the light from the kitchen let him see the glow of her blouse. They listened to the music for a while. She finished the rest of her drink and looked at him. "Tie my hands," she whispered.

"What?"

"Do it. Dominate me." Owen looked at her. "*Do* it," she said urgently. He pulled off his necktie and looked at her again. She crossed her hands and held them out and he tied them with the necktie crossing first one way and then the other. It was a silk rep tie with narrow stripes of yellow, blue and green. She lay back against the smooth cushions her eyes studying him, the violet lids hooded and heavy, her mouth open a little. He kissed it and it opened more. He decided he was not going to see the bedroom. He fell on her. He had never tied a woman before. No one had ever asked him.

More than half the buttons of her fragile silk shirt were already open. Fumbling, but trying not to tear anything, he managed to get the rest undone. Then he realized it might have been a mistake to tie her hands first. He was determined to get the shirt off but he wasn't sure how to do it She had a delicious beige bra on underneath and two long gold chains. He'd deal with all that later. She was not helping at all lying across his lap, a heavy load of limp woman, smelling luscious, smelling, he remembered, of Poison. Her breathing was as harsh as his own, but she definitely was not helping. "Hurry," she said.

He sat her up and jerked the blouse out of her skirt and up over her head. Then backing away a little to get more room to work he pulled it down her beautiful slender arms and wadded it up in a ball at the junction of her wrists. "Hurry up," she panted, which did not help. He examined the brassiere and discovered it opened in back. Sliding around her he unclipped it, then realized that short of tearing the satin straps out it was not coming all the way off either. "Shit," he muttered. He pushed the bra down her arms and shoved it into the blouse. He had to kiss her again. Her breasts were soft and warm and loose but he found that due to the accumulated clothing in front it was difficult to get to them. He tried to kiss her mouth again but found that hard to do satisfactorily as well. I can't get *at* her, he said to himself in something close to frenzy. She's not helping at *all*.

"Hurry, goddamn it."

"Stop saying that. Let me untie you. This is ridiculous."

"*No*. Do it. Dominate me."

"I don't want to dominate you. I want to love you."

"I said dominate me and that's what I meant, you wimp, you . . . " She did not finish because Owen grabbed her and using a sort of fireman's carry hoisted her over his shoulder and went in search of the bedroom. "Not there," she hissed in his ear. "That's a closet."

He found the right door, flung it open and threw her on the white bed more or less face down. All the lights in the room were on. While she bucked and struggled he quickly removed shoes and skirt and skimmed off her panty hose. "Stop it goddamn it," she gasped into the eiderdown, "or at least turn out the lights."

"Just a minute," he panted as he flopped her over and began to unravel the Gordian knot at her wrists. He needed light for the work. She was a lot of woman. It hadn't been as easy to pick her up as he expected. He pushed the bra and the sleeves of the shirt up her arms and attacked the tie. "Hold still."

She managed to hit him in the eye with both hands. "Don't," she said through clenched jaws. "Leave that alone."

"I might as well. It's ruined."

"I suppose your wife gave it to you."

"She did as a matter of fact. It's the only thing she ever gave me that I liked."

"Isn't *that* a turn-on. Hurry up and get it off and get the hell out of here," she said in her courtroom voice.

The knot had been pulled tight and the bra straps kept slipping down her arms entangling his efforts to find the right loop to tug. Finally he reached in his pocket and pulled out a knife. As the blade clicked open she froze. She stared at him wide-eyed, her naked body rigid in the harsh light, her wrists tied in front of her like a victim's. Owen cut the tie with one quick stroke. The knife was very sharp. He snapped it shut, dropped it in his pocket and flipped off the overhead lights. He sat on the bed beside her and touched her arm. It was cold and trembled slightly. He gently slipped the two pieces of necktie, her rumpled blouse and the little brassiere off her wrists and tossed them on the floor. Then he rubbed her hands and arms. "That was a dumb idea," he said. "Do you want me to turn off the bedside lamp?" Since she didn't answer he didn't.

During the night Owen woke to hear the plows go by again. That meant it was a heavy snow, perhaps the heaviest of the winter so far. Her warm length was stuck to his as tightly as if their skin had been grafted. Her breathing was slow and deep. He loved the way she slept. His own slumber was shallow, sound or movement always brought him to the surface. Lately, for the first time in his life, he found it difficult to go back under. He spent hours some nights moving his mind's eye over the terrain of his life, observing it from far above. When he awoke in the morning he could not remember at what lonely canyon, what mesa, what bend in the road he had returned to sleep again. It didn't seem to make a difference. Each morning was fresh to him. He was not tired at the beginning of a new day. He put his arm over Demi's soft shoulder and cradled her head against his neck. Her breath was so warm it seared his throat. Her hair no longer smelled like Poison, it smelled like love. Suddenly he could not wait until morning to wake her. His arm tightened and she looked up at him.

Chapter 27

The day after the latest and least fulfilling meeting of the Strategy Committee, DePalma and Gland sought Miss Ontos in her office behind the front stairs. Through the partially open door they heard the disconnected rhythms of the Iguana and its impact printer, composition clicking away at the keyboard, a John Cage concerto pounding from the daisy wheel. "What an unearthly racket," said Gland to no one in particular as they entered the cozy little room. Then, "I donated all this equipment to the Club, you know," to DePalma, who knew all he wanted to know on the subject and more.

Miss Ontos lifted her little pink fingers from the keys in surprise. She was in the midst of compiling the events calendar for the month of March, 1988 while the printer produced the members' accounts for the month of February, her entry chore of the previous day. She rarely received visitors in her office except for the strained conferences with DePalma over the wine order once a month. Her heart rather sank at the unannounced entry of two of her least favorite members. It had been, until now, a productive, hence joyful, morning. The skeins of the Charles Club slipped from her hands and she smiled brightly, but did not immediately speak.

After a pause DePalma said, "Good morning, Ontos."

Gland grunted a greeting.

"Good day to you, Mr. DePalma, Mr. Gland." She reached over, shut off the printer, and the echoes subsided. Like some Escher construction the room was nestled in stairs beneath the front steps of the building and at the foot of another stairway that began from a door behind the lobby bar and wound down under the main staircase. A single window looked out at grade level on the tiny yard, the iron fence, the sidewalk, the street, and Sarmiento's shoes. The flat silver light of February shone in upon a space filled with carefully chosen objects, as decorative as their owner and as useful: an American Heritage dictionary, Roget, Fowler, and Bartlett; a Hewlett-Packard calculator; a fat orange Rolodex; long silver shears; a rookery of pigeonholes on one wall; soft carpet in a shade of pale green. A rolltop desk, whose carapace had never descended since Miss Ontos discovered it in a jumble of unused furniture in the old coalbin, filled half the room. Unlike such desks in other hands its multifarious contents were thoughtfully arranged. A bud vase with three forced jonquils sat next to the Iguana. Unfolding her white-stockinged legs, she detached herself from a semi-kneeling position in the computer bench and perched on its edge like a sparrow on the windowsill. "How may I help you?"

"At the Strategy meeting last night it was decided to invite the important Boston clubs . . . "

"Single-sex clubs," Gland interjected.

" . . . to a dinner at which we might share our views on the current crisis and our plans about how to deal with it."

"The crisis being the membership question?" Miss Ontos asked, crossing her short but shapely legs under their attentive gaze. She did not invite them to sit since there was but a single chair by the desk in addition to her bench.

"Of course, what other crisis is there?"

"Well, the rat crisis comes to mind. If it weren't for Kitty who spends the day in here," she smiled down at whiskers and eyes behind her wastepaper basket, "I should be quite at their mercy."

"Yes," said Gland. "The House Committee has promised a report on that at the next General Meeting. Have they talked to you about it?"

"Not as yet. The elevator crisis also suggests itself. We have had three incidents since Christmas. Our insurance company is decidedly unhappy."

"The House Committee plans to address that as well."

Miss Ontos began to describe her misgivings about the size of the oil bill, which did not quite qualify as a crisis, but she did not often get such an opportunity.

"In any case," cut in Gland impatiently, "we are planning a dinner about three weeks from today, early in March, a Wednesday or a Thursday evening I should think, but not on the ninth or the tenth when I will be in New York on . . . "

"Let me look at the calendar." She swung around, pressed several keys, and in a moment the screen of the Iguana displayed a crosshatch of thirty-one boxes. "The second and third are open. The seventeenth is St. Patrick's Day, recorded, but as you know, not celebrated in Boston on a Wednesday."

"When will it be celebrated?"

"From about the sixteenth through the twenty-third I should imagine."

"You keep the calendar on the computer?"

"Of course.

"Damndest thing I ever heard of," said DePalma.

"Let's shoot for Thursday evening the third," said Gland, "but we'll have to get the invitations out quickly." Both men looked down at Miss Ontos' curly black head. She nodded, quite familiar with their euphemistic use of the plural pronoun.

"And how many are we planning on?"

"Fifty or so."

"Twenty or thirty."

"Somewhere in there."

"May I have a list of the clubs you want to invite?" She was already plotting how to manage this latest effort to cripple a carefully planned schedule. She would call her counterparts at the several clubs, alert them to the date and the occasion, get an estimate of how many would likely attend, then send out the invitations with the knowledge that the event would be stored on the other club computers.

"I'll give you a list this afternoon. No, I can do it off the top of my head," said Gland. "The Tavern, the Somerset, the St. Botolph, and the Pilgrim, of course, representing the distaff side. What does that mean, by the by?" he asked, turning to DePalma.

"I haven't the slightest."

"A distaff is the stick which holds the unspun flax on a spinning wheel," said Miss Ontos as she enlarged the box for March third to full screen size and with a drumroll of the keys entered the information about the dinner party. "Black tie," she said firmly. "Cocktails at six-thirty and go in at seven-thirty. We'll need an extra waitress. I'll ask Old Jane for one. Over the years the distaff has come to symbolize women or women's concerns." She struck several more keys and after a gabble of code a menu appeared on the screen. "Here's the *carte* for the Founder's Day dinner two years ago. It was acclaimed as one of Anton's . . . one of Chef's greatest achievements. If you have no objection I'll suggest it to him." She looked up at them and smiled sweetly. "As opposed to the spear side, of course."

"The spear side?"

"Yes, symbolizing the male or male concerns."

"Oh, yes. Of course. The spear side. That's very good! But absolutely. The spear side." Gland pushed DePalma out of the office and Miss Ontos could hear Seymour's giggles as they mounted the stairs. She sighed and picked up the telephone; another burden for the broad muscular back of the lonely man in the kitchen.

"I've had the most remarkable telephone call."

The two men stood side by side in the Men's Lavatory of the Charles.

Silence greeted Walter Junior's pronouncement.

"It was from a man named, if I heard it correctly, Henry Handle. He was calling from a livery service in Somerville."

"A livery service?" asked Dormant. They surreptitiously waggled, rearranged, zipped themselves, moved to the mirror, inspected the ravages of the years, laved their fingers.

"Yes. Ultra Elegance, Inc., I think it is called. They provide limousines for all occasions."

"Did he tell you this?"

"Actually not. He put a musical recording on the telephone because he had to speak to someone else. I learned the details from the recording. I've never heard a recording such as that on the telephone before. It was set to the tune of 'Some Enchanted Evening.' "

"Why was he calling? Does he want you to rent one of his cars?"

"No, not at all. He wants to attend the dinner we are giving on the third." Walter Junior collided gently with his friend in the doorway of the Men's Lavatory.

"Mr. Handle, the liveryman, wants to come to dinner?" said Roger, immobile with surprise.

"Yes, and bring several of his friends. He is, uh, president, I suppose it is called, of the Benevolent and Paternal Order of Elks in Somerville."

"Walter, let us sit down over here. I'm not sure I'm following all this."

"Well, you see, it's quite straightforward. The Elks, uh, Lodge in Somerville is facing the same problem as we. They have been ordered by the Licensing Board to admit women as full-time, regular members, or lose their license to serve alcoholic beverages by the end of March. Or is it the first week in April?"

"How did they find out about the dinner?"

"Mr. Handle told me that one of the uh, brethren, is related to our Food Service Coordinator."

"Our what?"

"I believe he is referring to Old Jane. In any case, it seemed a good opportunity to see the question from yet another point of view. So I invited them to come."

"You invited them?"

"Yes. Do you feel it was a mistake?"

"Quite the contrary! I think it is a splendid idea. Just what the members need. Another point of view. Some new faces around here. Should make for an interesting evening. Are all the Elks Lodges under the gun?"

"No, apparently not. This is a prominent one and the Board is making it the test case."

"Test case, indeed. Let me buy you a preprandial something or other. Walter, you have not lost the capacity to surprise, to amaze, in fact. What will you have?"

"The usual."

"You're supposed to pick it up!" The angry cry echoed through the night from an upper floor of a building on the corner of Exeter and Commonwealth. Tasha had pulled to a favorite spot under the street lamp right at the edge of the curb. Her white hide gleamed in the light as she bent to her task, an air of ineffable dignity cloaking her face. Owen made no answer. He was seething with anger, as angry as he had ever been in his life, at least since that final fight with Abbie. The problem, he realized, was that he had nothing specific to be angry at. That was the ultimately maddening circumstance. There was no fight, no event, nothing Demi said. In fact that was the problem. She said nothing. He couldn't talk to her. She didn't return his calls. After a great evening, a great night, a strange night perhaps, but a great morning together, then: nothing. I'm not going to keep calling, he had told himself, then called again. She had changed the recording on her machine. Now there was no name, no preamble, no amenities. Just the admonition to leave a message. After the tone. Beep had changed to tone. "Fuck the tone," said Owen.

Tasha looked up at him inquiringly, then finished and moved on. "You're supposed to pick it up!" Again came the cry in the night. Generations of New England respect for the rule of law and the perfectability of the race resonated in the unseen woman's voice. It cast a challenge to the forces of evil, the enemies of society, the despoilers of civilization. It was shouted bravely into the darkness, like Farragut at Mobile or Jones to the *Serapis*.

Seymour and I are not so far apart, thought Owen, as the dog led him down the barren tract between tall tree shadows. It is easy to criticize him, to suspect him, but I'm not exactly on the side of the angels myself. He tried to remember if he had ever discussed this particular social issue with his friend. He thought not. I wonder what he would call me? Scoffshit, he decided. Somehow it made him feel better as the dog took him home, but the anger would not go away.

Chapter 28

Walter St. Henry Thomas Junior entered the library bearing his accustomed afternoon Amontillado, paused and looked helplessly about as if seeking some word of counsel from those assembled. "Roger, move over so Walter can sit down," said the Distinguished Poet a little testily. Dormant, his criminal status temporarily suspended, looked up from his first martini. "You're in Senior's chair. Move over one."

"Oh, sorry, Walter. Here, sit right down." He hoisted himself and moved, martini balanced with care, from one black leather chair with wooden legs to an identical one next to it. His departure revealed a brass plate affixed to the front of the seat he vacated:

PRESENTED TO
WALTER ST. HENRY THOMAS
ON THE COMPLETION OF
SIX TERMS
AS PRESIDENT OF
THE CHARLES CLUB
1936-1960

Walter Junior sank with a sigh into the chair now reserved by custom as his own. Large of ear and nose, his noble but somewhat sharply pointed head balanced on well tailored shoulders, its visage displaying an emotional gamut which ranged from pensive to melancholic. His father, universally remembered as Walter Senior, had during his lifetime been for many the embodiment of the Charles Club, his twenty-four years as Club president surpassing any before or since. During his tenure members of the Nominating Committee agreed that Walter Junior might some day succeed his father as president and, indeed, Junior was physically and emotionally prepared to both carry on the tradition of Thomas leadership and to inject the young blood many members felt was needed. Club tradition, however, allowed a president to continue in office as long as health and enthusiasm permitted. Senior's blood proved more durable than expected.

He was fifty years old and his son twenty-one when, in 1936, Walter Senior assumed the helm of the Charles. The great structural reforms of 1925 had been accomplished but the mortgage that made them possible proved an onerous burden after 1929. What shallow resources the Club treasury possessed were drained in the maintenance of the improvements, many of which—like the steam heating system and alternating current—were unfortunately invisible. Senior gained much credit for steering the Club through a trying period. Several special assessments upon the membership failed to tarnish his popularity. During the shortages and alarms of the Second World War fewer members used the Club, but Walter Senior, too old to fight but too energetic to stand still for long, stayed on the bridge. His son departed to the Navy and returned, a stoop-shouldered, tired, thirty-one-year-old Lieutenant Commander, to find his father in robust health and still the admiral of the Charles. When, in 1960, the expiration of Senior's sixth term neared, the Nominating Committee (now composed of sons and nephews of the president's contemporaries) felt that some action must be taken. Senior, a disciple of Bernar McFadden, whose regimen he followed faithfully every day, ran to the Club each morning in an era when urban runners were assumed to be escaping the consequences of illegal action. At seventy-four he could still out-distance most dogs and other pursuers. A five-course dinner, three wines, a decent port, and some of the Club's best Napoleon were required to soften Senior to the suasion of the Nominating Committee. Only the offer of the title President Emeritus allowed a compromise to be struck. Senior stepped down, his blood turbid as ever. Junior, however, could not step up since it was felt that two Walter St. Henry Thomases, one President and one President Emeritus, would not suit.

In 1974, at the age of eighty-eight, Senior graciously relinquished the Emeritus title after holding it less than fourteen years. Junior, now fifty-nine, wearing the bifocal eyeglasses disdained by his father, became president. Six years later Senior was cut down by a Cambridge taxi as he was bicycling on Beacon Street at the rush hour. No one occupied his chair in the Library until—after a decent interval—Junior assumed it, as all agreed, by right.

The President of the Charles Club, once seated, sighed and stuck his long nose in his sherry.

"My sentiments exactly," said the Distinguished Poet. "How much longer do we have?"

"A week past the next meeting of the Licensing Board, which is scheduled for the fifteenth of March," said Gland, standing back to the group, staring out the window like a martial cherub at parade rest.

Dormant finished his martini. "I believe the time has come to call a special meeting of the members and change the bylaws," he said, reaching over to press the bell button.

"Oh is that what you believe?" snapped the Distinguished Poet. "Well, pray believe as well that the Charles Club will become a local—no, a national—laughingstock. That expression derives, as I am sure you know, from the stock in which fools were restrained in the center of town and held to ridicule, which certainly will be the fate we deserve if we capitulate to that Greek fury . . . "

"What do you propose we do, then?" asked Owen.

"I propose we close the Club while we continue to fight in the courts. Or . . . or, keep the Club open for lunches and dinners. But without the alcohol."

"Balls."

"It wouldn't be the end of the world," asked the Distinguished Poet querulously, "would it?"

"It would be the end of the Club," said Walter Junior. "No one would come. They'd dine at home. Or at another club."

"Then we have no alternative," said Dormant matter-of-factly.

"As I am sure you recall it is the constitution of the Club that defines the requirements of membership, not the bylaws. It requires a two-thirds vote of the membership to change the constitution. I am almost certain such a measure would not carry."

"The alternative is, in fact, to close the doors."

"Sell the clubhouse, I suppose."

"Condominiums," murmured someone.

"How they'll all laugh," said the Distinguished Poet. "It will have been such an easy victory for her."

Gland continued his intent perusal of Commonwealth Avenue. "Hum," he said.

"Are you sure the members couldn't be persuaded?" asked Owen, leaning forward to address Walter Junior. "Are principles, outdated ones at that, worth the destruction of a great old institution?" He immediately wished he had not spoken.

"Hummm," said Gland, not unmusically.

"I think many of us feel principles represent the only value we are discussing," said Walter Junior gently. "An outdated principle is a principle nonetheless. The Charles was founded more than a century ago with certain ideas in the minds of its founders, as a gathering place for gentlemen of like tastes and background. What value has the Club itself if we abrogate the reasons for its creation?" Gland began to dance lightly on his rather small feet, his bulk rippling gracefully with each hop. "Are you well, Seymour?"

Gland turned to face them, his scarlet face radiant. "Beautiful," he said.

"Easy, Seymour," said Owen.

Gland's feet flew in a flamenco of unguessable emotion. His fat fists flailing, he strove for communication. "Listen to me!" he cried. "Beautiful!"

His audience sat expectant. Abel, a tray of drinks in his hand, paused in the doorway. The dark old room was silent except for Gland's insufflation.

"What do you think is so beautiful?" asked the Poet. "Sad is what I call it."

"God in *heaven* the answer has been right in front of us all the time."

"Seymour." Owen stood up and put his hand on Gland's shoulder. "Whoa, boy."

"THE PILGRIMS," he hurled the fateful words upon them. "The Pilgrim Club is the answer." He snatched a glass of scotch from Abel's tray and drained it. It seemed to unlock his larynx.

"What is the question?" asked Dormant.

"Give him a . . . " But Walter Junior's words were submerged.

154]

"The Pilgrim Club, why didn't we see it before? They have precisely the same problem we do, and that splendid investment portfolio, and no mortgage, no mortgage at all, on that big, beautiful, brownstone house on Clarendon Street. They will never change their membership; they see it as a matter of principle, just as we do. They are not as old as the Charles Club—we're some forty or fifty years older—but what matter? All we have to do is merge the two clubs, they keep their clubhouse, we keep ours, we'll all agree to abide by the rules, Ladies Entrance and what all, and we can have a party or two with them each year. Their chef is damn good, perhaps as good, but, no, I doubt that, still his way with veal is a wonder I'm told, and they have a place on a lake in Maine. We can try to negotiate the use of that on alternate months in the summer, and the Massachusetts cursed Licensing Board can go hang. But we've got to move fast, we've got to get to them before the . . . " He could not find the breath to get the S word out.

"Before the Somerset," breathed Walter St. Henry Thomas Junior. "Before the Somerset, I'll be bound, or salvation slips from our grasp."

Chapter 29

As it turned out, the table was laid for twenty-eight. Organized in a squarish U, it filled the Dining Room. After some shifting of chairs and tables, a fire in the occasionally-used fireplace was ruled out since the chairs along one leg of the U backed up to the hearth too closely for the comfort of guests or servants. While Abel and Old Jane conferred on the arrangement of the room and the younger women set out the best silver service, Gland and Walter Junior, surveyed the acceptances and plotted seating. Normally somnolent in the morning, the Club bustled.

The Pilgrim, which responded promptly to the mailed invitation, sent along six names, including the heads of the two committees in which true power resided, Garden and Activities, the president, and three senior staff officers. The Tavern promised three, identified as the full complement of their Standing Committee. Adam Winchester would represent the Somerset. Since he selected the Somerset's wine in consultation with no one except God, Seymour and Walter Junior were well pleased to have landed him. The St. Botolph offered two members of their Nominating Committee. The Charles would field all twelve of the Strategists. No word had arrived from the Somerville Elks, which assuaged Seymour somewhat, but Walter Junior insisted on reserving four places as a safeguard. "Shall we seat people in blocks?"

"Well, boy, girl, boy, girl is out of the question."

Walter Junior glanced up nearsightedly from the diagram he was carefully drafting on a sheet of Charles Club stationery. He had taken over the task after Seymour threw the sixth wadded sheet in the direction of an empty Chinese umbrella stand, a longish toss across the Library from the table at which they sat, a pot of coffee between them. Poor aim bothered the president of the Club less than the fact that the letterhead ordered from Shreve's was in perennially short supply. "I thought they might wish to confer as the evening's discussion progresses." He drew a careful line along the edge of a magazine to complete the diagram of the table.

"Confer? If I know this crowd they'll be conferring with the wine wherever you put them."

Walter Junior sighed. "This is an important, a critical gathering of those most affected. As far as I know there has never been a meeting of the Boston clubs."

"Not the single-sex clubs."

"I anticipate a brisk, uh, discussion of the issues. We should try to lead it to perhaps achieve some consensus before the end of the evening."

"I anticipate brisk swilling and gobbling. And if I know our membership we *will* lead it."

"In any case perhaps it is better to mix the guests in more traditional fashion. They can as well, uh, confer after the meeting."

"Where are you putting me?"

"Next to Charlotte Coupon."

"Coupon's wife?"

"Yes. She's a new member of the Pilgrim and they seem to have put her right to work. Interestingly enough, she never uses the Charles."

"Who is on my other side?"

"Well, I had not made it completely around the table as yet but whom do you . . . ?"

"Put Owen there." Gland helped himself to a fresh cup. Walter Junior, who had planned to tether an Elk there, followed suit.

Five Elks presented themselves, resplendent in the sort of clothing often rented from Mr. Tux for a daughter's wedding. A white Lincoln Town Car with six doors, a television antenna and black windowglass settled down to wait for them in front. Their arrival in the midst of the cocktail hour in the lobby was acknowledged by a burst of silence, followed by cheerful conversation all around. Abel helped them to drinks. Walter Junior came forward. "Greetings. So glad you could come. I am Walter St. Henry Thomas Junior."

The lead Elk, looking past his host for the others named, grasped the proffered hand.

"Henry. Henry, too. Henry Handle, that is. Nice to be here. Nice. Oh, thanks. Meet my fellow members. I'm the well, just say I'm the head guy in our chapter. Hell of a situation. We wanted to find out what you all're going to do. Nice of you to have us. Great place you've got here." For the moment they huddled together for protection and warmth, noses to the danger, tails to the cold wind which blew under the foyer door.

Adam Winchester stood stolidly at the other side of the room, his square figure encased in a black dinner suit of a cut not often seen since Coolidge's death. Abel extended a tray for his empty glass as the great man was approached by a Pilgrim from one side and a Taverner from the other. "Adam," they said in unison.

He stared at them impassively. "Peg," he said finally. "Dog-poop."

"Adam, isn't this a lovely idea? I haven't seen you since the Monet opening. Whose idea was this? You know, I haven't been here in twenty years."

"Nor have I. I'm George St. George," said the Taverner to the Pilgrim.

"Dogpoop," repeated Winchester. He seemed to be studying something about eighteen inches from the end of his nose which was the shape and color of a lightly boiled new potato. As Abel's tray floated by, however, hand unerringly sought glass.

[157

"Peg Cartright. I'm president of the Pilgrim Club. You're Walter Junior's cousin are you not?"

"Yes. One of the delegation from the Tavern. This is quite a summit meeting."

"Dogpoop."

"Thank you, Adam. He is reminding us all of my undergraduate nickname. I believe until a few minutes ago he and I were the only ones in the room who shared that important piece of information."

"What do you think of all this, Adam? The club business I mean. Are we going to have to elect men to the Pilgrim? Who would want to join? I mean we spend a lot of time on subjects like grafting fruit trees and genealogy and bridge."

"Sounds quite fascinating. I may be your first applicant."

"How many clubs do you belong to?"

"I have no clear memory. Perhaps a dozen. Some are no longer in existence. The India Wharf Rats, the old T&R." He sighed and swigged. "I am fascinated by genealogy. Dogpoop is actually Walter Junior's second cousin. The St. Henrys and the St. Georges are connected by marriage. Made in heaven one presumes."

"Can I refresh your drink, Peg?" asked Cousin Dogpoop, but Abel was ringing the chime and they began drifting through the sliding doors to find their places.

Abel had chosen three wines and a Champagne. A little recognized but well received California Chardonnay poured with the Petrale sole, which itself had been flown in from San Francisco the night before, vindication for Lapstrake if the members had known, provoked the first toast. Walter St. Henry Thomas Junior, in his role as host President, rose glass in hand. The room was resplendent with silver and red roses, ringed with flushed, masticating faces upon which the candle flames danced. He studied them as they fell silent rather as a headmaster might view his alumni grown older if not necessarily wiser. His voice, pitched low, barely carried above the restless cutlery. The Eldest Member cupped his ear ostentatiously. "We are here tonight to celebrate an experience, a, uh, pleasure, which is not unique to Boston, but is perhaps more precious here than in some other locales. The pleasure of which I speak is that of adult companionship and conversation with the friends of our choosing." Old Jane popped through the swinging door and headed for the nearest fish plates, but Abel caught her apron strings. "Boston has many clubs. Perhaps it is because we somehow need a special place to allow us to exercise those rituals of warmth and friendship which visitors often feel we lack." He stared at his glass, the Chardonnay golden green in the candlelight. "Something more than celebration brings us together this evening, however. There is a threat which hangs over this otherwise delightful dinner party. That threat could alter forever the nature of our club traditions. Certain, uh, forces threaten these traditions, certain forces such as politics and," he almost swallowed his words as his audience strained to hear him, "social change." With an effort, he drew himself up and ventured a smile which briefly lit the steep Yankee planes of his face. "Shall I make a confession? Politics alarms me. Social change is, of course, a fact of history, but one which at my time of life I do not often welcome." A long pause ensued. Owen found himself counting, he was not sure what, his heartbeats perhaps? Walter Junior swallowed and continued. "Howsomever," and he smiled again, bifocals twinkling in the candlelight, the unfamiliar exercise straining his jaw and neck muscles, "I welcome you all to the Charles and offer you the hospitality of this club." Abel released Old Jane as murmurs of appreciation rippled round the table.

Roger Dormant, registering this as the longest utterance of their acquaintance, applauded his friend then turned to Peg Cartright. "Hullo, Peggy. Nice to see you again. When was it last, the Monet opening?"

"It was Symphony two years ago. Leinsdorf was back. How is Celia?"

"I'm not sure. I think we may be separated. I haven't seen her in a month or so."

"Oh, Roger, how awful."

"She may be in California with Ann. But anyway I meant it when I said it was nice to see you. What's wrong, by the way, with meeting a woman friend at your club?"

"Nothing. I do it all the time."

The Bordeaux, an ambitious second growth which had reached adulthood in the Charles' cellar, was efficiently dispensed as lamb with mushrooms and truffles arrived. Seymour Gland seized the moment and his glass. "Single-sex clubpeople!" He did not have to wait for silence as the table gazed at his unsteady figure with fascination, "I give you the sturdy New England values which have always stood tall, and must continue in this grave era," he was shouting now, "to sturd against the resurgent dark fundamentalism of the hoathsome lordes," he sensed something awry but could not quite put his finger on it, "wholesome hordes." He looked around for Owen but could not find him. "The lonesome wards of the ancient world. In closing," he felt a hand at his coattails which pulled him inexorably down until he met the seat of his chair with an audible impact, "I thank you." Miraculously he had not spilled a drop so he poured it into his face in triumph.

The Bull Elk raised himself to his considerable height, the blue tuxedo lending emphasis to massive shoulders and a formidable midsection. "I certainly agree with both of the previous speakers, and I can only add that if GM in Framingham stays shutdown, we can blame it on the Japs and all of those who don't buy American." He resumed his place with dignity.

Abel moved like an athlete stitching the table together with deft jabs of Pichon-Longueville-Baron. He had committed two cases of the 1966 to this meal and was determined to use them to the fullest. He danced behind Owen, who had switched his card to put himself between an Elk and a Pilgrim. Owen turned to the former. "Are there any women Elks?"

"No, that's the whole point. Say, this is some kinda wine."

"What will you do if they make you add women to the, uh, herd?"

"I dunno. It's a tough one. Prolly go to the VFW. I don't think they can touch that. It's a real problem. We got such a great setup. Good bar. Big screen with the dish. Gets everything including Australia fergodsake. It's just the best place for an evening away from the wife and kids. Not that I don't love my family, don't get me wrong, but you need a place to get away. Am I right?" He leaned forward and addressed the Pilgrim, who had been following intently, perhaps in part because Seymour on her left was wrapping up Iran and Libya. "Am I right?"

"Yes, I think actually you are. Everyone needs a haven. I rather depend on mine. I don't use it too often, but when I need to get away for awhile, it's there."

"Exactly. Exactly my point."

"But look at us this evening." Owen gestured around the table whose acoustic power had risen dramatically in the past few minutes. "This is a great evening . . . Yes thank you just half a glass. Whoa! No harm done . . . Now what's wrong with a club that includes men and women?"

"Are you married? Where's your wife?" asked the Pilgrim.

"I'm divorced."

"Well easy for *you* to say," said the Elk. "No problem *there.* I'll tell you where my wife is. She's home and she's steamed."

"Does she want to be an Elk?"

"Hell no. She wanted to come here, but she wouldn't set foot in *our* clubhouse except it was the Christmas party or like that."

"My husband is not steamed, he's in London, as a matter of fact, and he may be boiled but that's another matter. He's never set foot in the Pilgrim Club and never will. The problem, young man, Owen is it, is that if you have men and women in the same club, do you have husbands or in your case," she nodded to Owen and the Elk, "wives as members, too?"

"No way."

"Then you have other women as members but *not* wives?"

"I'd be killed in my bed."

"Is that the way you feel?" Owen asked her.

"Not that I fear for my life, but he's right. It raises an awkward problem. What's the point of a haven if it's not a haven?"

"Exactly my point."

Adam Winchester struggled to his feet, a newly refreshed glass of claret in hand. He stared out into the clamorous room, a riot of candles and flashing forks. The roast lamb had proved a signal success and hearts of palm had just appeared. He stood immobile bearing his evening clothes with all the authority of an umpire in mask and pads. "I rise in praise of Yvonne," he said in his raspy voice. The din subsided as most of the audience with the exception of the Elks realized Adam, a bachelor badboy of repute, was about to do something naughty. "As I am sure you all know Yvonne has graced the grillroom of a certain Boston restaurant, a room which— until a few years ago—was traditionally reserved for men. Now, for better or for worse, but apparently forever, that room serves all and sundry. Yvonne is still there in her glory. What the new guests think of her is a matter of conjecture." He smiled a badboy smile and began to recite:

> "Demure despite her nudity,
>   She gazes quite sans crudity
> Upon the skulls both thatched and bald
>   Of patrons who are often called
>   Great Gourmets.

"She's not the Lady of Shalott,
　　She's what a wife is often not,
She silent hangs with mellow eye
　　Watching the world come and go by
　　　　Without Emotion.

"She is the ideal of our dreams,
　　When brain with wine and food careens,
Yet always does she stay quite chaste
And never does she make least haste—
　　　　The Lady of Locke-Ober's!"

Adam sat down to much clinking of glasses and raucous applause.

Charlotte Coupon, who had addressed not a word either to Seymour on her right or to her husband across the table, both of whom were so busy talking themselves as to be oblivious of this deprivation, leapt to her feet. With no preamble she launched into a sweet but forceful soprano:

"They talk about a woman's sphere as though it had
　　a limit;
　　There's not a place on earth or heaven,
There's not a task to mankind given,
　　There's not a blessing or a woe,
There's not a whispered yes or no,
　　There's not a life or birth,
That has a feather's weight of worth—
　　Without a woman in it."

She sat down flushed and breathless as the applause exceeded even Adam's, the Elks feeling clearly she more than held her own. Seymour, noticing her as if for the first time asked, "How many children do you have?"

By the time the Sauterne and the Baked Alaska made their appearance the American Flag, the Charles Club, the Boston Council for the Arts, the Crimson, and the Celtics had been saluted. Abel, now somewhat concerned at the obvious success of his efforts, sent Old Jane and her squad scurrying for coffee. Seymour, however, was calling for port and cigars. No one, least of all the Pilgrims, suggested the women retire. Abel returned from a hasty trip to the bar with four bottles of Cockburn's and a handful of glasses. He knew it would not be enough.

"Do you mind if I take a cigar?" asked Roger Dormant.

"Not in the least."

"Would you . . . ?"

"Thank you, no. I did once and regretted it instantly."

"Oporto?" Seymour asked Henry Handle, who had ingested whatever had come his way with enthusiasm and no apparent ill effect—in fact no effect at all. Lacking another glass, the Bull Elk extended his empty water tumbler and Gland topped it up.

Owen joined a general movement around the table. Glasses at the ready, reluctant to break the spell, the guests strolled from one conversation to another through a jumble of chairs.

"Did you play hockey?"

"I was in the Beanpot in 'fifty-two."

"Last real sport left. The rest is ruint with money."

"Do you garden?"

"Vegetables. Tomatoes and cukes. Carrots, radishes, beans. Squash. No zucchini, though. It's a weed."

"I miss mine so. We're in town now. I miss my garden so. And then we're in Maine and I never get things in early enough."

"Nothing like a fresh radish with some black dirt sticking to it."

"I hate goddamn windowboxes."

"Followme." Seymour shouted. "Ifyoucarepor. Ifyoucareporfort. There's a bottle in the cellar. We can. There's a bottle in the cellar we can find. No one knows where it is. We can find it because I hid it. EIGHTEEN NINETY-NINE." At this, the Eldest Member, who was resting his eyes for a moment, snapped to attention. Seymour and the Bull Elk followed by Peg, Cousin Dogpoop, Dormant, Charlotte Coupon, and Owen departed through the kitchen door. Walter Junior smiled at their antics from his place at the head of the table. The Eldest Member decided to rest his eyes again for a moment.

Anton, lolling on his throne with Miss Ontos standing close holding the great man's hand, watched as they trooped by heading for the basement stairs. Guest after guest hurried past the overladen sink and the cooling ovens. The Boston Cat stared at them with disdain from atop a cupboard. Down the old stairway they rattled, howling with laughter, clutching the remnants of the port, the Sauterne, the Pichon-Longueville, the Chardonnay, the Champagne,

[163

whatever in fact they could find; past the empty coalbin filled with furniture broken at forgotten parties, past an impassive Nilson, long since beyond astonishment, who set his wooden tooltray on the bench and watched them disappear into the wine room. It took a long time to locate the bottle of 1899. Several others were opened for good luck. The rats stayed in their holes.

Chapter 30

It was a strange evening even for March. The temperature had risen twenty degrees in the past several hours and warm air pushing up from some foreign place brought with it rain which would become dangerous if the temperature dropped back to normal. "Oh please," panted Leslie, running down Newbury Street as best she could in a heavy black wool coat with her purse and a Lord and Taylor box under her arm. She felt the coat, new and more expensive than she had planned, soaking up the warm rain like a blotter. "Oh come *on*," as the shower intensified then suddenly sluiced down as a whole pailfull was dumped out of the black heavens. She held the box over her head, then remembering its contents tried to shield it again under her arm. No one on the street had an umbrella, umbrellas were a month away. The trees offered scant shelter, their branches bare except for little white light bulbs and junction boxes. Just as she neared the corner of Fairfield—planning to dash to Boylston and the cabstand in front of the Lenox Hotel where she just might find a taxi—she broke the heel of her right shoe on an upthrust tectonic plate. The heel skittered under a parked car where the torrent bore it away to the Atlantic Ocean.

"Oh SHIT," said Leslie. She refused to let herself cry although tears would have been invisible on her wet wreck of a face. Rather, she acknowledged defeat at the hands of the Boston weather and staggered like a flood victim up the stairs into a restaurant she had never entered before. She stood dripping unevenly on the marble floor of the entryway.

The maitre d' opened the inner door and smiled. "Come in and catch your breath." Huge, handsome in a hunky way, a nice smile.

"Will you tell me where the Ladies' Room is?"

"Just upstairs to the left. Want me to take care of that?"

Gratefully, she handed over the box and trudged up the stairs, miserable from top to toe. In fifteen minutes she returned, limping like Walter Houston coming down the mountain from his diggings, the sodden coat over her arm, some damage control achieved on hair and face. She entered the restaurant looking for her box but neither it nor the man at the door were in evidence. A girl with menus and long dry blonde hair approached. "Would you like dinner?"

"No. I'm just looking for, I'm just looking for the man who was here."

"Brent? He'll be right back. Would you like to sit at the bar? Can I hang that up for you?"

Leslie surrendered the coat and climbed wearily on a barstool, at last on an even keel. "Perrier and lime."

"We have Poland Spring if that's okay?"

"Anything." She sighed and glanced out the windows at Newbury Street in flood.

Brent reappeared. "Your box is around the corner by the register. Just let me know when you want it. Would you like to have dinner?"

"No thank you. I think I'll just wait for a few minutes until it lets up. If it does. What's the name of this place?"

As he picked up the ringing telephone at the desk by the door he held up the menu, which said Ciao Bella, and smiled at her again. She looked around the room. The music was not great—show tunes or something—but the rest was nice. Those strange little light fixtures, lots of marble, very modern, very Italian. She reminded herself that she had decided to avoid things Italian. The people were friendly though. It had the feeling of a comfortable neighborhood place but upscale, definitely upscale, thought Leslie. The door burst open and Lawrence Owen came in, or was it Owen Lawrence, hair streaming down his forehead. He muttered something and brushed the water out of his eyes. A clap of thunder shook the building. Well, well.

He peeled off his coat, shook it, and hung it on a brass stand, holding on to a dilapidated, overstuffed briefcase. His eye wandering around the room fell on Leslie, and she smiled at him. He was the divorced one Ann had mentioned, she was quite sure. He had nice shoulders although not to be compared with the maitre d' who must lift weights during the daylight hours. Owen blinked at her several times. Was he nearsighted or something? Then he walked over to the bar.

"We met at the Charles Club just before Thanksgiving. You're Roger Dormant's friend."

"Leslie Sample."

"I remember, both the name and the voice. Owen Lawrence."

"Yes, I remember, too."

"Isn't it incredible out? If it turns cold again, we'll have two feet of snow. I just ducked in because I was drowning. Actually, I've never been here before. May I join you?"

"Sure. I did the same thing. Isn't it harsh? I must look a mess. I lost my heel, too." She extended one of her best features from which dangled the ruined shoe looking like a tiny boat without a keel.

Owen ordered a drink. This was nice. Really very nice. He smiled at Leslie and raised his Jack Daniel's. "Cheers. This is really very nice." She looked younger than he remembered with her dark brown hair pulled severely back in a bun. Almost no make-up.

"I think so, too." I'll stay if he asks me to dinner, she thought as she drank her sour water.

Owen wondered how much cash he had with him. He knew his Visa card was over the top because it had bounced back when he was trying to charge groceries at DeLuca's the day before. If I wasn't sitting next to such a pretty girl I'd feel sorry for myself. "Were you serious about wanting to join the Charles Club?" he asked.

"Of course I was serious. I wouldn't have gone there, to that awful whatever it was, reception, if I wasn't serious." Her husky voice was even lower than he remembered.

"I saw your picture in the *Sphere*."

"Oh, God, did you? I've given up hoping someone will take a good picture of me sometime."

"I thought it was great."

"I got a lot of calls from that article. Even a call from a reporter in San Francisco. And I got one sale."

"Sale?"

"Yes. I'm in real estate. A broker. John Coster and Co.?"

"I didn't realize that. I'll bet you're good."

"I am good. The best. Well, except for my boss and one other guy in the office. And they keep all the big stuff to themselves. I'm mostly, almost entirely, in residential. But I work in the high end of the market. Nobody beats me there."

"What made you decide you wanted to join the Charles?"

"Well, it's really too complicated to explain. My friend Ann, Ann Dormant, said I should do it. I had been there for lunch and I liked it, and I had run into all sorts of people who were, like, connected with it in one way or another, so I just thought why not do it? When I get something into my head I usually just do it." She looked into Owen's eyes, which she rather liked. "To be honest, Ann conned me into it. I had no idea what was involved."

"Well you certainly caused a commotion."

"I suppose they all laughed at me."

"No. No one laughed." Almost no one, Owen thought to himself. "Would you like another drink?" He waved his finger over their glasses to the bartender and she set up two more.

"I hope everyone has forgotten about it."

"Well, there are at least two members who are trying to get you elected, but it will take a change in the constitution of the Club to do it and that's a big step."

"You're kidding! Who are the two?"

"One is Roger Dormant."

"Who is the other one?"

"Would you like to have dinner?"

"Only if we go Dutch."

Roger Dormant was lying on top of the quilt in his pyjamas and bathrobe nursing a highball and wishing he felt sleepy. The television set in the corner, a concession to Celia's insomnia, was dark. A bedside radio mumbled quietly. Roger almost never watched television unless there was a golf match on a Saturday or Sunday afternoon at a course that had some passing resemblance to those he had played in his youth. Since many of the tournaments seemed to emanate from Texas or California courses with palm trees or mountains or cacti, he rarely kept a set on at all. I wasn't a bad golfer, he thought. Far from scratch, perhaps a twelve handicap at my best, but that was twenty years ago. When he realized by counting on his fingers that it was thirty-five years ago, he dropped golf as a subject of contemplation. Before he found a new one the telephone beside the bed rang.

"Hullo?"

"I was wondering if I would find you there."

Thunder, unusual for March, rumbled in the distance. Roger heard rain and sleet whipping the storm windows. "Yes. Hullo, Celia. Where are you?"

"I'm in Palm Desert with Ann. We're staying with friends of the Cartrights. They have a beautiful house here."

"I saw Peg the other night. She didn't say anything about Palm Desert. Where is it, in Nevada or someplace? I've been rather worried."

"Peg doesn't know we're here. I ran into these people in the lobby of the Beverly Wilshire. We saw them when they were in Boston a year ago. They just invited us and we came."

"It's good to hear your voice."

"What about the Sample person?"

He set his drink carefully on the night table. "What about her?"

"Are you seeing her?"

"Of course I'm not seeing her. What a strange notion. I haven't seen her since the reception at the Club. That was months ago. Why do you ask?"

"Do you know how many people have called me about that little evening at the Club?"

"No. How many?"

"So, now you have decided to be the one to overturn tradition and champion women's rights at the Charles Club."

Roger sat up and straightened his pyjama bottoms. "Well, not exactly."

"What exactly then do you think you're doing?"

"As a matter of fact, I just got tired of all the ruckus at the Club. You'd think the Redcoats were coming again. I believe the whole issue is stupid and irrelevant. So I am sponsoring a woman for membership. I think it will be good for the Club as a matter of fact."

"Why that woman?"

"Why not? She's a friend of Ann's. And she's charming." He immediately wished to retract the last remark.

"She's not a *close* friend. They weren't at Smith together. In fact, I haven't been able to find out where this person went to college, if she did."

"Can't Ann tell you?"

"She probably could but she won't. I'm not particularly pleased with my family at the moment."

Roger felt an unaccustomed pang of gratitude toward his daughter. At least she wasn't trying to make things worse. Then again, she had precipitated the whole situation.

"Are you there?"

"Yes, I'm here," he said.

"If you want to do something silly you might at least do it with someone we know."

"Would that make it better?"

"No, as a matter of fact, it wouldn't. It's just *bizarre* to think of you doing something like this. And don't expect me to sit around in Dover fielding telephone calls about it from my erstwhile friends."

"Aren't you coming home?"

"I don't know."

"What are you and Ann doing?"

"When we do anything we shop."

Roger shuddered and pulled his pyjamas out of his crotch again. "What are you shopping for?"

"Ann is buying clothes and looking for a horse. I am looking at antiques."

"What kind of antiques can you find in Nevada?"

"That's not a bad question. Perhaps we'll fly to Reno or Las Vegas and do some research."

Roger could not think what to say.

"I hear she is very attractive, young."

He still had no answer.

"Are you going to persist? To make yourself a laughingstock?"

That helped him. "Yes," he said and heard her hang up.

Chapter 31

The Music Room of the Pilgrim Club, because of the sunlight, the handsome French furniture, and the peach silk draperies, was the tea location of choice. Large formal teas were held in the Guest Parlor. Intimate teas for which some desire or need for privacy existed were poured in the cheerful little Conservatory, except in the summertime when the glass walls and skylight heated the room above the comfort level. The Mansion, as the older members called their brownstone clubhouse, was larger by one story than the Charles Club. Its kitchen had been redesigned by a master chef in 1942 and was conceded to be one of the best equipped in Boston, the equal of some of the better hotels and restaurants. A ballroom occupied half the third floor. The ten guest apartments on the fifth were pretty and comfortable. The mortgage had been burned in 1950. Even the cellar was orderly. An efficient thermostat which compared the outside temperature with those of twelve interior zones kept the heating system both economical and comfortable. The Pilgrims, three hundred and eighty women who lived in and around Boston and twenty-six who dwelt in other cities and maintained non-resident memberships, took their comfort serenely for granted. Peg Cartright had decided this complacency needed to be challenged.

"The evening was quite beyond description," she said to the twelve women grouped around her in the sunniest corner of the Music Room. "I have not had so much to drink since my son's wedding, and that was twenty, no, twenty-two years ago. I had no idea how I was going to get home. It was two in the morning and we were sitting on empty wine crates in this indescribably filthy cellar, passing around a bottle of port all covered with cobwebs and dust, the bottle I mean, gulping it down, it *was* delicious, or so I thought at the time, out of every sort of glassware imaginable, when . . . "

"How did you?"

"How did I what?"

"Get home?"

"In a limousine. Delivered to my door, thank goodness."

"How foresighted. But aren't they awfully expensive?"

"Not this one. It was 'on the house,' as he put it. I was the guest of the owner."

"The owner of the limousine?"

"The owner of the limousine company. He gave me his card. Told me to call them anytime. I must say, he was terribly ingratiating."

"What was he like?"

"Was he younger?"

"Was he a member of the Charles?"

"He was an Elk, and I found him charming, and that's all I'm going to say about *him*." Peg extended her cup for some hot water and tried to get back on track. She felt like Paul Revere but no one was looking out the window. "The point I'm trying to make, not very successfully, is that the entire evening at the Charles Club reminded me of nothing so much as a fraternity party out of control."

"Isn't that a redundancy?"

"In my memory it is."

"What do you mean, 'an Elk'?"

"It sounds like fun."

"It sounds like the old Tennis & Racquet Club."

"Now, *exactly*. I can remember my father talking about the goings on at the T&R," said Peg, struggling to advance the discourse.

"If you try hard, you can probably remember some yourself," said the tall woman sitting behind the coffee urn.

"Well, as a matter of fact, I can. Do you know they kept a suitcase in the cloakroom for couples who wanted to check into the Copley, or wherever, for the night? Adam Winchester was in the process of doing just that when the bellboy picked it up and the clasp let go and a dozen empty Champagne bottles went all over the lobby floor. His date, needless to say, fled."

"Who was she?"

"That's not important."

"Then why are you blushing?"

"Don't be ridiculous. I'm just not getting the message across, am I?"

"You are to me."

"What message?"

"Well," Peg picked up the cudgels again, "the Charles Club are a bunch of little *boys* whose clubhouse is in simply appalling condition. They may have the second best chef in Boston, and a huge stock of wine, which apparently barely suffices, but the place is falling down around their ears, and they have an *immense* mortgage.'' She paused and looked around the circle.

''Is that the message?''

''And they want to merge,'' said Peg.

''Merge? In what sense?''

''In every sense of the word if the behavior at the party was any indication,'' said Charlotte Coupon crisply.

''What did you think of it? Them?''

''Some of them were rather abominable. The rest were actually quite nice.''

''Which? That is, which were which?''

''Never mind that. This is an issue we *must* discuss. They have not put it forward in any formal way.'' Peg's handsome square jaw and lofty forehead framed in slabs of carefully arranged white hair gave her a resemblance not so much to Paul Revere as to Alexander Hamilton, who stood on his pediment outside the window. ''We can expect their proposal any day now.''

''Pro*pos*al? I mean, really.''

''It might be worth considering, a proposal, I mean,'' said Charlotte, to Peg's intense annoyance. The other women looked at her with varying degrees of surprise. She had only been a member for a few months and she rarely spoke unless spoken to. She was younger and not from Boston. Nevertheless, she gathered her courage and pressed on. ''You know why they want to do it. Seymour Gland was the one who explained it all to me. It's a question of survival.''

''Whose survival?''

''Certainly theirs,'' said Peg Cartright. ''They are one of the prime targets of that woman on the Licensing Board. They have less than a month to do something, or . . . ''

''Or run dry. A lot of good that wine cellar will do them then.''

''But this is our problem as well,'' said Charlotte. ''We haven't had all the publicity, those pieces in the *Sphere*, the jokes on the radio talk shows, but we will have to comply at some point or we'll lose our license, too.''

''Well, that would hardly be the catastrophe for us that it will be for the Charles.''

There was a murmur. ''I'm not so sure,'' said the tall woman behind the urn. ''It would certainly put a damper on things. How could we have a proper party? Remember the Garden Committee Dinner last fall?'' They all remembered the Garden Committee Dinner for a moment with the exception of Charlotte, who had not been a member then.

"My husband," she said, "who is a member of the Charles Club, still thinks there is some legal thing they can do. There's a case pending in the Supreme Court. About the New York Athletic Club. But Mr. Gland doesn't think there is any escape."

"None at all?"

"Except by merging the clubs."

"Well, he was hinting at that to me, too," said Peg, "at least insofar as he was able to communicate that night. Why do they not just come right out and ask?"

"I think they're feeling us, well, I think they're trying to discover what we think about it before they do."

Peg set her cup down firmly. "Well, I, for one, am against it. At best, it would be a marriage of convenience, mostly their convenience, and I'm not at all certain they're the best catch in town."

"What about the Somerset?"

"What, indeed."

"Why are we discussing this at all?" asked the woman behind the urn, who was on the Garden Committee but had not attended the fateful event down the street. "Why can't we just go on the way we have done?"

"Because we just can't," said Peg. "I know that much. But beyond that I'm not sure I know anything at all."

Henry Handle sat, hands wrapped around a draft beer, staring at the large screen. Skaters in black and red darted across it in haphazard patterns. Until a few minutes ago he had been following the game. The moment his attention lapsed the logic dissolved and Bruins and Canadiens moved in random choreography. The noise level in the Tap Room was high, usual for a Monday night, one of the busiest of the week, when many members sought recovery from the weekend and more than a few looked for reinforcement for the week to come. Henry's lack of concentration was interrupted by his son, who pulled up a captain's chair and sat down beside him at the scarred wooden table. Although thirty pounds lighter, Henry Jr. was six feet four, which put him two inches above his father.

Hockey was not the son's sport. Almost single-handed he had taken the Medford High School football team into the final playoff game against Archbishop Williams in 1979. Although they lost by three points, one brilliant run by Hankie, as he was called, generated an aura which still clung. Heroics on the playing field had a long shelf life in Medford. "What'sa matter, Dad? What'sa score?"

"I don't know," replied Henry. "I'm beginning to think I really don't know."

"No, I mean the score of the game? The Broons?"

"I don't know that, either. I lost track. Do you know, Hankie, that this lodge could be ruint, destroyed, messed up so bad we could lose half our membership?"

"Yeah? What'sa matter? Someone got AIDS?"

"You know, that's not funny? I'm serious. This is a serious matter. I don't think I know how to handle it."

"This is about the club thing, right? You went to that big dinner in Boston with all the rich guys?" A shout was cut off like a thrown switch as Cam Neely hit the post of the Canadiens' goal with a pointblank backhander.

"Yeah, the club thing. We're in it, you know. Can you imagine this place without a drop? I think we got to elect a few wives as members and then tell them to stay away."

"*Dad*, you know that's not going to work. You try that and your ass is grass."

"You watch your mouth. But you're right. Even as I say it, I know."

"First of all, you elect somebody's wife, all the others want to join, too. How'dya choose? What'dya say to all the others?"

"Right."

"Then you tell them to stay away? For*get* it. All that's gonna do, make em wanna come in, see what's going on."

"Right."

"Better think of something else."

"You better think of something else. I'm too old and tired to deal with this. It's a lose-lose if I ever saw one. I got a business to run. That's enough grief. You just drive a machine."

"Dad, you're the *guy* here. They're depending on you. You can't duck this." Another shout, followed by a collective groan, greeted a save by Moog, who couldn't smother the rebound, which was promptly stuffed back in the net by one of the Montreal forwards camping in the crease. The Forum went crazy. "Where's the HITTING?'' Hankie Handle asked God, the Bruins, the room at large, his father.

"You don't know who to hit when they change the rules on you," answered the latter.

Gland was talking on the telephone in the little cabinet off the lobby. It was stuffy in the booth, but he kept the door resolutely shut. Perspiration stood like drops of rain on the alabaster forehead, unmarred by line or wrinkle. His voice, however, was anything but smooth. A furious whisper, it contained as much emotion as could be expressed without being audible outside the door. "Lester," he hissed, "you gave me your word. You told me you could fix it. I have been working like a dog on my end. I *will* be able to get the license transferred. No, I haven't got anything in writing, but I can do it. Trust me in this. But I have to ask you, what good will it all do if they won't accept our price? You told me . . . "
Gland glared into the wall-mounted bakelite mouthpiece of the old instrument as he listened to the words pouring out of the receiver pressed like a black cucumber to his ear. A member peered in the window of the booth and was waved peremptorily away.

"Lester, I shouldn't have to tell you again that this is the deal of a lifetime. In six months Boston is going to wake up to the fact that some of the best located land in the city is underneath those sex shops and porno bookstores. For years everyone has thought of it as a ghetto, yes, that's it, a sex ghetto, right in the center of downtown Boston, and now the VCR has put them out of business. It is technology, you see, the march of technology which inexorably causes . . . " His eyeballs bulged as he stared into the telephone.

"How can you say that? How can you sit there in your Mercedes and tell me that we do not have a deal? I need this deal, Lester, I am counting on this deal, and I am going to have this deal, or you are going to be making your calls from some drugstore phone booth in the future . . . " He glanced around in apparent surprise, "No, I'm at my club. You can't meet me here. I'll be at my office in an hour. No, you better not meet me there either. Call me there and I'll tell you where to pick me up. We can meet in your car. We are going to *do* this deal, Lester, don't think for a minute that anything . . . " Gland pulled the receiver from his damp ear and glared at it. Then he slammed it down on its hook. He straightened his necktie which was slightly askew, examined his reflection in the window and stepped out into the cool tranquility of the Charles Club lobby. He ordered a drink and headed for the usual group gathered in the Library.

"What did you think of the party last evening, Seymour?" asked the Poet as Gland entered the room.

"One of the best dinners we've had in years," said Gland.

"It was useless," said DePalma, "a waste of time and good wine."

"Not much got settled," said Owen.

"At least a little spice got added to the pot," said Dormant.

"The Pilgrims weren't very spicy, except for Charlotte Coupon. Hidden depths there," Gland smiled enigmatically. "And, as a matter of fact, it *wasn't* a waste of time. A few seeds were judiciously planted."

"Whatever do you mean?"

"We'll wait and see, won't we?"

"We don't have much time, do we?" responded Roger. "I thought, if you care to know, that you rather made an ass of yourself in the course of the evening."

"Thank you for your comments."

"You were shitfaced, to be explicit."

"And thank you for all the constructive work you have put into solving this problem. I'm surprised you didn't try to smuggle that baggage into the party."

"Smuggle?"

"Smuggle."

"Baggage?"

"Baggage."

"I hope, Gland, that you are not referring to Miss Sample." Roger, badly hung over, felt his cheeks redden with anger.

"Who else would I have reference to? Are you trying to smuggle in other baggages as well?"

"I am not trying to smuggle in anyone. There is no question of smuggling. I have proposed Miss Sample for membership. Everyone votes on new members."

"They certainly do."

"And if the seeds you are planting are as productive as the ones you have flung about in the past, we can expect another crisis."

"You can't make an omelet without breaking . . . "

Owen stood up in the midst of the flying metaphors. "I'm going in. Does anyone want to join me?" He walked out of the room without waiting for a response. A sandwich with his dog seemed an attractive alternative.

Chapter 32

The first problem occurred on the street corner. Walter Junior and DePalma turned up Berkeley Street. Gland continued down Commonwealth a few paces, then stopped. "Hold on. Where are you going?"

"The entrance is over there."

"The entrance is right up here."

"Seymour, that is the main entrance. The Men's Entrance is over there." Walter Junior indicated a small door on the Berkeley Street side near the alley.

"We are going to use the main entrance. I am not going to sneak in the back way."

"Well, of course, the Pilgrim Club has their own traditions. We may not be off on the best foot if we ignore them," said DePalma in what he assumed was his reasonable manner.

"I am entering by the front." Seymour marched up the front steps and rang the bell. The other two watched him for a moment then retraced their steps up Berkeley. As they approached the unprepossessing doorway DePalma asked, "Have you been here before?"

"Several years ago. I attended a bridge lecture. Harriet thought we should get interested in bridge. Sheinwold was there. I didn't understand a word."

"Do you play?"

"My wife does. Not I." They paused then entered a foyer which opened into a small sitting room. "Isn't that a Marin?"

"I have no idea. What is a Marin?"

Walter Junior nodded at a small splash of color above the ornamental stone fireplace. "One of his Maine scenes. I've always enjoyed them."

DePalma was annoyed. "You know, you must recognize the importance of this meeting. I believe Seymour has hit upon a viable solution here. And it has unarguable advantages for the Pilgrim Club as well, of course. But I think we have to press for a timely resolution. A quick closing so to speak. I am prepared to address all the salient . . . "

"I wonder where Seymour is. I don't think we should go in without him."

The door banged and the missing member stamped in. "Do you know I was denied entrance?" He stripped off his dark blue cashmere coat and flung it on the sofa. "Some old harridan barred my way. Wouldn't even open the door. Just shouted at me through the glass. I've never had such an experience."

"I wonder which way we go," said DePalma. With some hesitation they started down a hallway, up a short flight of steps, then emerged into the imposingly columned central room of the Pilgrim Club. A dignified man in a white coat approached them. He said nothing but raised his gray eyebrows in question.

"Peg Cartright," said the President of the Charles Club firmly.

"Missus Cartright is busy at the moment, but she axed me to show you into the Guest Parlor. She will be with you shortly." He ushered them into a spacious sitting room with a view of the Mall. "You will be having tea with the president. May I bring you anything in the meantime?"

"I'd like a . . . "

"Nothing, thank you," said Walter Junior

"Madam President will join you in a moment." He nodded at a door off the main room. A brass plate beneath the richly engraved Victorian glass proclaimed it the President's Office.

"What a good idea," murmured Walter Junior.

Twenty minutes later, they were shown into the Conservatory. Peg Cartright was seated at a sumptuous tea table. After greetings they took the three chairs opposite her. "Tea, gentlemen?"

Seymour stifled his desire for something more substantial. Cups were filled and the requisite flavorings and dilutions added. A plate of tiny sandwiches was offered and refused. Another plate laden

with a variety of cookies was accepted by Gland and circulated no
further.

"I understand you met Miss Dana," said Peg to Seymour.

Gland took a hasty swig of tea to wash down a ladyfinger and
choked momentarily as it scalded his tongue. "Woo?" he asked.

"Katherine Dana. She said you were a little confused, seemed
to be lost. She lives here, you know, one of our senior members."

"Yes, I encountered her," said Seymour, swallowing busily.
"Lovely lady."

"We've come, Peg, to present an idea," began Walter Junior.

"An idea which will solve the problem which is confronting the
Pilgrim Club," added DePalma. "We've given a great deal of
thought to your situation, as a matter of fact."

"How kind of you."

"The solution," interjected Seymour, his voice pitched for the
boardroom, "is, of course, quite simple." A look on Walter Junior's face, however, interrupted his flow.

"Is something wrong?" asked Peg, noticing his expression,
which suggested a large species of dog asking to be let outside.

"Please excuse me for a moment." Walter Junior unfolded himself and bolted, ducking under the overhanging branch of a rubber
tree. The other guests sipped nervously as Peg made conversation.

"Is there a Men's Room?" he asked the majordomo.

"Downstairs, next to the storage closet. Right through that
door."

The President of the Charles Club ventured down a dark flight
and found an unmarked door. The Victorian elegance of the Pilgrim
Mansion was greatly diminished in the lower regions; the hall was
lit by a single bare bulb protruding from a converted gas fixture
on the wall. He opened the door to utter darkness. Locating a
switch, he revealed floor-to-ceiling shelves of linens, rolls of toilet
paper, unopened boxes marked Drano and BonAmi. He switched
off, ducked around the corner and tried a second, identical door.
This time, he found what he was looking for. "Hello, Adam."

Adam Winchester dried his hands on a little towel whose corner
was threaded on an angle of brass rod which directed it into a
wicker container when he let it go. "Walter Junior, as I live and
breathe. What are you doing skulking about in the bowels of the
Pilgrim Club?"

"The same thing as you, I'll wager."

"I was peeing, in point of fact. They fill you with tea here."

"Yes, I know. But that's not all you were doing."

"Is it any of your business what I do, or where I pee?"

"I saw you upstairs. I imagine you are here to suggest something to the Pilgrims."

"Perhaps I am. And perhaps you are as well. Great minds with but a single, et cetera."

"This was Seymour Gland's idea."

"Then I retract the observation."

"I'm sure you know the Pilgrims cannot join forces with more than one club."

"Of course not."

"I believe we made the first approach."

"You have already suggested such a proposal then?"

"Well, no. But Seymour has alluded to it."

"Is that so? Yes, I believe I heard him blabbing about something of the sort at that charming dinner party you gave the other night. What an original notion, to entertain the ladies in the wine cellar. The Pichon-Longueville-Baron was commendable, although as a rule I prefer the Pichon-Longueville, Comtesse de Lalande. Usually a very consistent performer. Alluding is one thing. Proposing is quite something else."

"And you have proposed?"

"Why, my good friend, surely that is a matter between the lady and myself? Or, at least between the Pilgrim and the Somerset?" He chuckled as Walter Junior clattered up the stairs.

When he rejoined the group in the Conservatory Seymour, impatient of delay and facing a conference with his private banker across town in an hour, had launched his pitch. It was whizzing at the batter who, when she understood what he was saying, hit it high and deep to left field. "I am afraid it is out of the question," she said as Walter Junior settled into his little gilt chair again.

"What, if you will forgive me, is out of the question?"

"Are you all right?" asked Peg solicitously. She had known him since dancing school. "You look a little flushed."

"I am all right, but Peg, please don't make a hasty judgment in this matter." Gland and DePalma, a little put out because they had not been able to give voice to the forceful arguments they had rehearsed at lunch, looked at each other.

"Hasty judgment?" said DePalma.

"Yes," said Walter Junior. "The Somerset has been here."

"Margaret. May I call you Margaret?" asked Seymour to their hostess, who detested the name. "Surely you recall we asked you first?"

"Yes, the night of the dinner party," urged DePalma.

"As a matter of fact I remember very little of that evening except singing some vile song when we were sitting around on boxes in the cellar, and being taken home by the nice man from Somerville."

"It *was* a lovely party," agreed Gland. "Reminded me of the dinners we used to have at the Fox Club when I was an undergraduate."

"Yes. That's what it reminded me of also. I haven't had such a headache in years. Really, Walter, it is out of the question. Please carry that message back." She patted his hand. "You are bad but lovable boys, some of you, but it was not to be." She rose.

Mouths slightly agape, they followed her into the grand hall. She shook hands with Gland and DePalma and gave Walter Junior a peck on the cheek such as Hamilton might have bestowed on Lafayette. "Please use the Men's Entrance when you leave. Sometimes you can pick up a cab there if you need one."

Peg and Katherine Dana sat together on a Louis XIV sofa in the Music Room. Two sherries were extended to them on a silver tray. "Thank you, Matthew. Well, Peg, you've had quite a day."

Peg smiled and knocked hers back then nodded in a meaningful way at Matthew.

"Two proposals within an hour of each other. Many girls never receive one."

"Katherine, I know you received a splendid one, which you have always treasured."

"Yes, I did. It was that boy, Walter Junior's uncle, his father's brother. He died of the influenza at camp during the World War. Never went to France, never fired a shot in anger, but he was a great hero to me, nevertheless." Her voice was little more than a whisper. "We lost so many of our set that year, and the next." She brightened a little and lifted her glass with trembling fingers. "But why are we being so blue? I thought you did a masterful job."

"Thank you," said Peg. "It's really quite comic when you stand back and look at it all."

"You're wondering if we should accept either offer. Perhaps we'll hear from the Tavern or the St. Botolph, as well."

"Perhaps we will. I think we should consider the Somerset proposal, discuss it with the members. Certainly not the Charles Club. That wouldn't do at all."

"Who was the fat one who tried to push himself in the front door?"

"Seymour Gland."

"Oh, yes, from Pride's Crossing? I don't really know that family. And the other one you said is a lawyer? You're right, it would be laughable if it weren't rather sad. It's the end of an era, you know."

"I suppose you're right."

"Not your era, Peg, mine. I'm afraid you are condemned to experience quite a bit of the new era. I, fortunately, am not."

"Oh, Katherine."

"Don't oh Katherine me. I've had the best of it. I don't want the rest of it, as they say."

"What do you think the Club should do?"

"Well, a merger with the Somerset would be a convenient fiction. It might serve for a while, but in the long run I don't think it would satisfy those who want to see these old relics dismantled. As an old relic myself, I know that compromise is not my fate. I'll have another, as well, Matthew. I know I shouldn't but I'm not in the mood to be good this afternoon." She smiled at the younger woman in the waning afternoon light, the structure of her face breath-catchingly beautiful beneath the old skin.

"Then what *should* we do?"

"Give up. Accept your fate, which is to be mixed and mingled. That is what society—I don't mean Society, of course, that's dead and buried—wants. Pick some one or two or a dozen men who are not uncongenial and invite them to join. You saw some candidates today. Adam is a charmer. Walter Junior is pleasant, if a bit of a stick. Roger Dormant has a streak of romanticism which makes him rather intriguing."

"Katherine, I didn't know you were so, well, perceptive about men."

"Oh, tush. I've known them all since they were children. That's really the problem. We're such a small group. The rest of the world wants in, you know."

"Not the men. Not really."

"Of course not. But the women. They're tired of looking at the outside of this old place."

182]

Chapter 33

Evening light lingered. The faintest intimation of spring hung in the air. Tasha could detect it not so much in the monoxide of the street, but from the old ground itself, which she read with insistent, repetitive sniffs. This meticulous study made for slow progress on the walk towards Hamilton, but Owen's mood was in tune with their halting progress. The high point of his day had been an unexpected encounter with Leslie Sample on the sidewalk outside the Vendome. She was emerging from the John Coster Co. office on the lower floor. He was walking home to the badger hole, thinking about a can of Progresso beef and barley soup preceded by six ounces of bourbon followed by homework as long as he could stay awake. Leslie read him like a listing: "Lighten up, for godsake." The sound of her voice, soft, rich, unexpected, almost accomplished her demand but she had to rush off to meet a client and he continued, preoccupied as before.

March was going out like a lamb, but the softening weather, the itchiness of tree twigs, the odd pioneer crocus hiding from the wind seemed to weigh on Owen's spirits. It's called depression, he told himself, it can be treated. But he recognized it as the sum of the parts of his life, which seemed not only untreatable, but unacceptable. His father had somehow accepted the unacceptable. He smiled sometimes in Owen's memory but the smile was more rueful than joyous. Isn't that the way, the smile seemed to say. I guess this is the way, Owen thought. I always seem to return to it. The hell with the way, he said to himself.

They rounded Hamilton slowly, Tasha inhaling the essence of each branch of the crippled yews huddled around the base, awaiting the next attack. Lights glowed from the grand *palazzo* across the street. The Boston Center for Adult Education was in full cry. Music from the miniature ballroom flooded the avenue. Demi came out.

For a moment Owen wanted to duck. No place to hide for a man with a white dog. She saw him and danced across the street. Faded jeans and a dashing leather bomber jacket. Blue sneaks, not the house brand, but perfect on her. She carried a Reebok bag and looked to him as if she had just stepped out of the shower. "Hello, Owen. I thought that was you." Tasha waved her plume.

"It is me. You look wonderful."

"Just finished my class. It's such a tough workout. But it feels so good when it's over. I just got out of the shower." She pushed the dog's nose away from her as Tasha took inventory.

"Where are you headed?" he asked. Why don't you return my calls, he wanted to say. What is the matter with me? Why isn't it us, instead of you slash me.

"I'm going to Copley Square to catch the T home. Will you walk with me?" The evening seemed suddenly softer, more insistent. She skipped and danced and bounced as if she still heard the aerobic music. She chattered like a girl about clothes and her diet.

As they walked up Dartmouth Street past the spot where he had bumped into Leslie a few hours before Owen saw a policeman's horse. The tall bay hunter was tied with a hackamore to the iron fence of a parking lot. The blue saddle blanket said BPD. "Handsome," said Owen.

Demi looked at him and smiled then noticed the horse. Her pace slowed.

Owen dropped the leash. "Stay," he said and walked over to the bay. "No, I meant the dog. Come here."

"I don't want to."

"Come over here. He won't mind. He's good with people, I promise you."

"No, Owen, I'm terrified of horses."

"Well, it's time to be unterrified. Come here." Reluctantly Demi moved toward them. "Give me your hand."

"Please, no."

"Just give me your hand." He took it and placed it flat against the red shoulder. The taut warm hide flexed and quivered as her anxiety entered the animal, was registered, then dismissed like a fly bite. Owen held her wrist and moved her hand slowly over the concavity of the horse's neck. The great head swung around and velvet nostrils took in her scent: soap and fear and Poison.

"Oh, God."

"He's a good boy. A lot of these animals are donated by private owners. Boston police are better mounted than most of my friends back home."

"Can we . . . ?"

"Come." Tasha trotted over and the horse leaned down to sniff the dog. Black nose met red nose. "Isn't he handsome?"

"He, is it a he?"

"A gelding."

"You mean?"

"Yes, but definitely categorized as a he horse. They can't use stallions on the streets for crowd control, traffic, things like that."

"Why not?" She had moved a few paces away from the horse but she could smell it now very clearly: ammonia and leather and iron.

"A stallion would just not be dependable. They have ideas of their own sometimes."

"Doesn't he have ideas of his own?"

"Not stallion ideas. Not many ideas at all, as a matter of fact. His brain is not very large."

"The rest of him certainly is."

"Yes, that's what is so wonderful about a horse. He belongs to us. Humans, I mean. He's here to serve us."

"Oh, really? And that dog?"

"She's much smarter. Learns faster. Remembers. Figures things out. A higher order."

"But still here to serve us?"

"I think so, although I seem to spend a lot of time serving her. If I had a sled or a travois, though, she'd be glad to pull it. She's bred to pull."

"What's a travois?"

"Two long sticks that carry a bundle or a child. Trail on the ground. Like a cart without wheels."

"And that one?"

"He's bred to carry, and to pull."

"Let's go. Let's get out of here. I have to get home." She hurried across Newbury toward the square swinging her little satchel.

"What's the matter?"

"I hate a world where living things are bred to pull, and carry, and scrub, and cook. What were you bred for?"

"I wonder about that. I haven't found out yet. What were you bred for?"

"I was bred to be a boy. When that went wrong, I was bred to breed. Goodnight, Owen." She vanished into the subway entrance.

"Lighten up," he wanted to call after her, but he didn't.

Chapter 34

"All right, creatures of the night, we're on the air, and all is fair, from Boston, the Attitude Capital of the World. Tonight we're going to talk live and lively with the latest of our state officials to appear in court, the Chairman of the Department of Motor Vehicles. He is, can you believe what I am saying, charged with *drunk driving*. Yes. You heard me correctly, the ever-popular DWI. The arresting officers said he smelled like Lynchburg, Tennessee, and he fell off every line in the street, including the sewer line. But he wants to tell you his side of the story. Don't laugh. There are always two sides to the story, as Ted Bundy said. I know that at least half of you have blown into the old balloon yourselves, and the other half just haven't been nailed yet. So, let's hear what he has to say for himself and we can take bets on whether or not it even comes to trial.

"Also tonight, we have with us the author of *Nuclear Spring*, a new book on arms control or something. No, I don't mean those AK-47s the kids play with in Roxbury and Dorchester. I mean the Russians, you know, NATO, all that stuff. Here's your chance to contradict a real expert, a Harvard professor, no less. What can he tell you about world affairs that you haven't already heard from your mother-in-law? But he's here in the studio with us tonight, and he's prepared to try to say something intelligent to this audience. Don't worry, I'll give you plenty of advance warning so you can hit the john or the refrigerator if you don't feel up to it.

"Tonight's first subject was suggested by Jane in Allston: Do you think men's clubs in Boston should be forced to admit women members? That's it. That's our lead-off topic. Let's kick it around. What do you-u-u-u think? Hello. Karen in Newton . . . Nope, sorry, you're going to have to hold your opinions of the Department of Motor Vehicles until later in the show . . . That's right. Sit on it. Hello? Sandy in Southie. All right, you're on the air."

"Hello, Dan? This is Sandy. Yes. I love your show. We all listen to you at work. We're on the second shift at Art's Hearts." It sounded like Ot's Hots.

"We pack candy for like Valentine's and Mother's Day and Christmas? Specialty things. And I know what you're going to ask.

Yes, we can eat as much as we want, but frankly we don't really eat all that much. When you handle it for eight hours a day, see it fall on the floor, you know what I mean?''

"Do you want to talk about our topic of the evening? Or your gut?''

"What was it again?''

"Men's clubs. Should they be forced to add women members. Say, are all you girls sitting around packing candy and listening to the show?''

"Sure are. Listen to this.''

Sounds of yelling and whistling were heard in the background also, "Turn him off,'' and "Get some music, for godsake.''

"Here, give me the phone, yes I want to talk about men's clubs. I think they should admit women, is this a free country or what? This is like a Constitutional thing. Women have rights, right?''

"Yes, but does it say in the Constitution you have the right to force yourself into an exclusive men's club?''

"Damn straight it does. What's their address?''

"Have you been nibbling on those brandy centers? You better wait and talk to our government official coming up next, who is out on personal recognizance. Next caller, please. Hello, Doris in Quincy.''

"I think this is the silliest thing. People are starving in Africa and we're worried about a couple of social clubs in Boston? Why don't you just leave them alone?''

"So it doesn't bother you that you can't go into their elite clubs?''

"No. And neither can you, by the way. They'd never let a slime like you in the door, let alone become a member.''

"All *right*. We seem to have a substance abuse problem out there tonight. Here's Jane in Allston. You're the one who suggested this topic in the first place, which is proving to be no worldbeater, by the way. What do you have to say about it?''

"Hello, Danny. Yes, well, they better let the women in. They're going down the tubes if they don't.''

"What do you mean?''

"Well, they don't have that many new members and except for the booze and the food, they don't get much income. It's just a bunch of old guys who sit around all day and night and argue and soak it up like sponges.''

"And how do you know so much about what they do, by the way?''

"I work at one."

"Oh, you work at a Boston men's club. Which one? The Somerset? The St. Botolph Club?"

"Never mind. They're not a bad bunch, but you wouldn't believe some of the things that go on sometimes. They let women in, might settle things down a little."

"What do you do at this club?"

"Food Service Coordinator."

"Does that mean like planning meals and so forth?"

"More on the delivery side."

"Wonderful. Well, Jane, please stand by. Since you have inside knowledge of the, I think it is fair to call it, outrageous things that go on in a Boston 'gentlemen's club,' maybe our listeners would like to ask you some questions. Hello, Henry in Somerville, you're on."

"You're making this sound dumb. It's an important thing. Clubs are important. You might not want to go to one yourself, but lots of guys do. So take this a little more serious. If the clubs get shut down as far as serving booze, then forget it. They're history. And then what happens? You're going to see a big increase in, whataya callem, Domestic Disturbance. Nine one one is gonna ring off the wall."

"Well, Henry, what is your solution? You want the Licensing Board to back off on this issue?"

"There's no way. It's not what I want, you know. It's politics. No chance they'll let go of it now."

"Then what's going to happen?"

"Maybe Jane is right. If we had a few women who didn't come too often . . . "

"Thanks, Henry. I've got Roger in Dover on line three. Dover? What made you call in, Roger?"

"I couldn't get to sleep."

"All right, I can accept that. What do you want to say?"

"I agree with the last lady. I think it's time to make a change. High time. Women will be good for the clubs. But, I'm afraid it isn't going to cut down on domestic disturbances."

"Why do you say that?"

"Just a little survey I took."

"Now, Roger, where do you get your information about this question? Are you by any chance a member of an exclusive Boston men's club?"

"Yes, I am, as a matter of fact."

"Well, you sound like you might be. Which one?"

"The, uh, Tavern Club."

"Oh, the *Tavern* Club. Is that the one . . . ?"

"Yes. We have a tradition of staging a theatrical production each year. The members take all the parts, including the females."

"You mean . . . ?"

"Yes. We dress up in women's costumes. Some of the members think having women in will spoil that, but I contend they can play the male parts."

"*Whoah*. What have we got here? Jane, what about this? Is this the sort of thing you see in your club, transvestite gamboling?"

"That's nothing. You should have seen what happened in the elevator a couple months ago."

"Well, Roger, let me ask you something else. Roger. Roger? I guess we lost him. O-*kay*, before we take a commercial break, let me summarize. We seem to have uncovered a rather steamy situation here. This raises the question, if women are ever admitted to these clubs will they want to join? To be forced to dress up in men's clothes? To be caught in elevators and subjected to who knows what indignities? Perhaps these hotbeds of what might be called post-Victorian prurience should be left to fester undisturbed. What do you think? Call in and register your vote before the show is over. Our lines are open and operators are standing by. And now this."

He flipped switches, turned wearily in his swivel chair, pulled the headset mike down around his sweaty neck. "Give me some fresh. This tastes like Tidee Bowl. Where's the goombah? Bring him in and we'll nail him to the cross." As his assistant started for the studio door he said, "That was better than I thought. What about all those old bankers and lawyers prancing around in pantyhose?"

"Kinda kinky," she said, "but kinda cute."

Chapter 35

The Special Meeting was well attended but unexpectedly devoid of passion. From the moment Walter Junior called the room to order at eight o'clock it was apparent most of the members' emotion had long been dispersed. They sat in folding metal chairs: gray of lock and bald of pate, well padded and cadaverous, clad in expensive suits and wingtips, clutching each his drink but strangely quiet. The President explained in his sonorous, patient voice the issues known to all in the main—if not in complete detail. Questions of nomination and admission were addressed by the Charles Club constitution. A change to the constitution required a two-thirds majority vote of the entire membership of the club. He had received proxies from thirty-seven members who for a variety of reasons were unable or unwilling to come to the Special Meeting. He would entertain any motions members cared to place before the house. A long mutterous pause ensued.

As the President surveyed the group like a collie eyeing his flock, waiting for one to break from the huddled mass, Abel leaned over and handed Owen a note. Owen balanced his half-empty glass precariously on his knee then, on second thought, drained it and handed it to Abel, nodding affirmatively. Two nearby members followed his lead and Abel departed telling himself for the hundredth time it was foolish to come near anyone in this club without a tray in hand. The note was from Gland, who Owen saw, to his surprise as he craned his neck to survey the crowded Dining Room whose tables had been shoved aside, was not present: "Please bring walking stick in hall stand to Ritz lobby at 8:30. Urgent. Seymour."

"If there is no motion forthcoming from the floor, I am authorized to present one from an absent member, who has submitted his proxy." Walter Junior unfolded a sheet of club foolscap and read, " 'I move that Article Four, Clause Twelve of the Constitution of the Charles Club of Boston in the Commonwealth of Massachusetts be amended to read "gentlemen and females," rather than "gentlemen".' Do I hear a second?"

The flock stirred. The Distinguished Poet stood up. "May I ask who offered this motion?"

He was followed by Roger Dormant. "Surely it should say 'ladies' rather than 'females'?"

And Owen. "Second it."

Walter Junior, unfazed by this burst of rhetoric, replied to the Poet, "Seymour Gland has presented the motion." And to Dormant, "I will entertain a motion to amend the wording of the prior motion."

"So moved."

"Seconded."

And to Owen, "We will withhold action on the first motion until we have voted on that which is before the house. Is there any discussion?"

"What difference does it make?" said a voice in the rear.

"If we're going to do it, we may as well be gracious about it," said Roger.

Appleyard stood up. "I move the question."

"Second."

"Gentlemen, we now have three motions pending. I assume you have moved the question of the amendment." Appleyard nodded. "The question takes precedence. All in favor of the question, please signify by saying aye."

"Aye."

"Opposed?"

"Well, what difference . . . "

"The ayes have it. We will now vote on the motion to change the language of the original motion from 'females' to 'ladies.' All in favor?"

"I think 'women' would be more appropriate," said DePalma.

The Distinguished Poet was on his feet. "This is another one of those wretched semantic diddles which have become so popular of late. Are we supposed to call persons of color blacks, or Negroes, or African-Americans? It seems to depend on which liberal Eastern op-ed page you read."

"The *Sphere* says . . . "

"I wouldn't wrap corn cobs in the *Sphere*."

"What are you, Owen, New Mexican-American?"

Walter Junior, his flock now streaming over the hill, barked sharply. "All in *favor*?"

"Aye."

"What are we voting for?"

"What difference does it make? It's all the same question."

"Now, gentlemen, or perhaps I should address you simply as members, it may not be too early to begin to change some of our old habits, I will call for a vote on the original motion, now amended to read," he hiked his glasses up his long nose and read, " 'It has been moved and seconded that Article Four, Clause Twelve of the Constitution of the Charles Club be amended to read "gentlemen and ladies," rather than "gentlemen".' Is there any discussion?" A silence without mutters followed these words. Then Roger Dormant stood. "I recognize Mr. Dormant."

"Well, uh, I have been on both sides of this question. I'm not sure that what we're considering is right for us, but I believe it is right for those members who will follow us. I have not much enjoyed the past six months. The old Club has not been the same. I hope it will return to some semblance of normalcy after tonight. But I fear, well, never mind what I fear, in any case, I think we should do in good spirit what we are being forced to do anyway. So I, uh, support the motion."

"Why did Gland present this motion?"

"Let's vote and be done with it."

"Is there any more discussion?" A pause, and Walter Junior, inheritor and conscientious guardian of fifty years of Charles Club tradition, uttered the fateful words: "All in favor."

"Aye."

"Opposed."

A scattering of nays rattled around the room. So, said the President to himself and to the shade of Senior looking over his shoulder, it is done. "The motion is carried." He adjourned the meeting to the backs of the members as they hurried in the direction of the bar, now secure for the foreseeable future.

"Where is Seymour?" asked Roger.

"Apparently at the Ritz. He wants me to bring him his walking stick."

"Imagine him sponsoring the motion! I mean, I *can't* imagine it. I'm still not sure we've done the right thing, and I had persuaded myself weeks ago this was the only answer."

"Shall we try to get Leslie Sample elected?"

"I think so. What do you think?"

"I think Jack Daniel's on the rocks, pardner."

A walking stick, especially one with an ebony shaft, a silver handle wrought to resemble a deer antler, and an amber ferrule which tapped smartly on the sidewalk made a pleasant walking companion. Not as comfortable as a Samoyed perhaps but not as demanding either. Seymour's affectation of a cane was usually an indication of an acute ego-seizure. Once he had taken one to the wedding of an old girlfriend and wound up breaking it over the back of the best man during the reception in the garden. He carried a stick, perhaps this one, to the ill-fated Monet opening at the Museum of Fine Arts. Owen had not attended himself, but the account of Seymour's depredations on the Champagne and the subsequent encounter with first Celia Dormant and later the museum security people had been often repeated at the Charles. It was pleasant to speculate on what might have set Seymour off this evening as Owen tapped along to the Ritz.

He was in considerably better spirits. The depression which had nagged at him in recent weeks was lifting. Tonight's meeting had surprised him. What had been deemed unthinkable not long ago had happened in a few moments. The club would change a little, perhaps, but the atmosphere of stress and acrimony would evaporate. The food would retain its high standard as long as Anton was there. Owen's favorite chair beside The Window would be as welcoming as ever. Even venture analysis might prove to be less onerous. He was wearing a new suit, his first extravagance in months not considering his club bill. It was a lightweight brown wool that fit him comfortably and would do well throughout the spring, which was definitely just around the corner. As he turned the corner he saw a line of limousines at the hotel entrance disgorging passengers in evening clothes. ULTRA EL-4 said the nearest license plate. Owen looked in but did not recognize the driver.

Inside the brass revolving doors he scanned the lobby, a heaving sea of furs, jewels and white shirt fronts. Gland stood in the center, arms clasped behind and beneath the tails of his coat, a rotund rock around which swirled *tout* Boston. Owen loped up the steps to his friend. "Seymour, how elegant. A tailcoat? Are you announcing your engagement?"

"Not yet. Not yet. Where did you get that strange suit, just a little party for the Governor and a few hundred of his closest friends, ah, you have it, feeling a touch of the old injury to my leg, many thanks, that will see me through the evening. Where is she, we should be going up." He extracted a gold hunter from his waistcoat pocket, flicked open the case, glanced unseeing at the time, snapped it shut and reinserted it in a series of gestures reminiscent of Bette Davis lighting a cigarette in her prime.

"Is that the injury you got when you fell off the dumpster behind the Wellesley dormitory?"

"No. It was an athletic injury. Ah, here she is. I believe you two know each other?"

Demi was spectacular in a black dress which partially covered her breasts but allowed the greatest exposure to almost everything else. Either she was wearing a collar of rhinestones around her neck or she would have to be driven home in a Brink's truck. The stones were so bright Owen blinked. "Hello there," he managed.

"Hello, Owen. Isn't this a crush? Seymour, I think we should go on up. Thank you for waiting. There was a dreadful line."

Gland now seemed in no hurry. "How did the meeting come out?"

"Well, Seymour, the Charles is no longer a single-sex club."

"Quite what I expected. As I was telling Demetria, I took a little straw vote a week ago and read the handwriting on the wall."

"There was a certain amount of surprise that it was your motion."

"Someone had to assume the leadership. It always seems to devolve on those who are most burdened. Well perhaps we should."

"What sport was it, Seymour?"

"I'm sorry?"

"What sport did you play? That caused the injury to your leg? It escapes my memory."

"Oh, that. It was nothing."

"You said it was urgent. That I should bring the walking stick to you. Here at the Ritz."

"Well of course it wasn't *urgent*. Just a figure of speech. Many thanks, by the way."

"If you don't actually need it, I think I'll use it myself this evening. You won't mind if I borrow it. Nice to see you, Demi. We must get in touch again."

"Yes, call me. Let's go up."

"No, I mean in touch. I'm sure you know what I mean."

"Seymour, please."

"Give me my walking stick."

"Good night."

"No you don't. HAND IT OVER."

Owen began to limp painfully towards the Newbury Street exit leaning heavily on the stick. Seymour looked at him in outraged astonishment, then followed. "GIVE it to me." He lunged at the ebony shaft and Owen staggered against the wall clutching the handle in apparent desperation. As Gland pulled Owen began to sag against the wall, his right leg extended grotesquely. "GIVE it."

The doorman hurried in from the street. "What is the problem?"

"It's MINE!" Gland wrenched at the stick and Owen groaned sagging closer to the floor.

"Here. Stop that. Can I help you, sir?"

"Please," said Owen, "I don't want a scene. Just get him away from me so I can get home. I'm afraid the stitches have pulled." As he dragged his leg through the door Owen glanced back to see Seymour in the arms of authority. A man in a three-piece hotel security suit had taken charge. Gland's patent leather pumps danced three inches above the floor. Demi was nowhere to be seen.

Chapter 36

"Do you do apartments?"

Leslie started then swung around from the screen of her PC. "Owen," she said with glee. "No, of course I don't *do* apartments. I *sell* stuff. Big, expensive stuff."

"Then I better leave." He made as if to rise from the plastic chair beside her desk. "I've come to the wrong place."

"No you haven't. We can take care of all your needs here." She grinned wickedly at him, swung back to the keyboard, jabbed it thrice and the screen went dark. "Now, just what *are* your needs?"

"Is this your office?" He glanced around John Coster and Co. in the big basement room filled with desks and filing cabinets and a copy machine holding down industrial gray carpet.

"Yes, don't you love it? All of this from here to here is mine."

"I thought you were a big shot in this office."

"I am. The biggest, except for, well, just say next to the biggest. We don't spend much on the furnishings. We'd rather see it in bonuses. And besides this pit just makes the properties look that much better to the customers. Why do you want to rent an apartment, are you moving?"

"I don't and I am."

"Then what do you want?"

"That's a different question. I'd have to try to answer that one over a drink."

"You're on."

"In an hour? Say six-thirty at Ciao Bella? Or at the Club?"

"I'd rather at Ciao Bella. I don't feel all that comfortable at the Club."

"Does that mean you don't want to join?" She ducked her head and Owen studied the white scalp where her dark hair was parted.

"Yeah, probably it does. Mean I don't want to join, I mean. But since my chances of being asked by the old farts are somewhere south of non-existent, it doesn't make a lot of difference what I want."

"That's very disappointing, because, by the power vested in me, I have the pleasure of inviting you to become a member of the Charles Club."

She stared at him, her red lips in a perfect O.

"Yes. It's true."

"Me? In the Charles Club?"

"Yes. Exactly."

"Owen! You did this. You and Mr. Dormant."

"Yes. But the rest of the Club voted you in."

"I can't believe it. Oh, now I'm sorry I said that a moment ago."

"Perfectly accurate. Nice old farts in the main."

"But I'd be afraid to. Am I the only one? Woman, I mean?"

"No. A woman named Peg Cartright who's old enough to be your mother. A few others."

"How did it all happen?"

"Have you ever seen the ice go out in a lake? One minute it's strong enough to hold you, or at least it looks like it. Then you notice a crack or two, and suddenly what was solid is a mass of little chips. As if winter were over in thirty seconds."

"Wait a minute. Sara, will you take my calls? I have to leave. Thanks, sweetie. Come on, Owen, we need to talk about this."

"Where?"

"Still Ciao Bella. I'm not psyched to handle the Charles Club yet."

"Now, tell me the part about the ice breaking up again?" They sat at a little table in the window. DeLuca's designer oranges were displayed for the early evening shoppers across the street.

"Well, one thing about ice going out is that you never know just when it's going to happen."

"But you know it will happen."

"Yes. And it did, about a week ago."

"But why me? You know and I know I don't really fit in there."

"Neither do I."

"Oh, come on, Owen, you love it."

"That's right, I do. The Club sort of saved things for me. It was my bastion against the world. I think, as a matter of fact, the Club I imagined was the Club I enjoyed most. I seem to have a very strong imagination."

"Where is the lake?"

"What lake?"

"Where you saw the ice go out. Or did you just imagine that too?"

"No. That's a little lake in the mountains above Taos. Eagle Nest Lake. We used to rent a cabin up there when I was a kid."

She studied him intently. "Tell me about it."

"My mother and father and I were up there early in the spring one year. We had trouble driving in, we didn't have a four-wheel, just an old Chevy pickup, because the road was soft, the frost just coming out of the ground, not wet enough for mud yet, but the earth can be soft as bread dough so you have to drive carefully. My dad kept to the crown, out of the ruts and away from the little ditches that already had some water in them." He stopped.

"What about the ice?"

"We stood out on the end of the dock and watched it. There was just a little breeze. You could smell the spring coming. It was a perfect day. The pines were razor sharp against the sky. Just a little breeze. We knew something was going to happen, but we didn't know what it was. Then we heard a sound like a great chandelier trembling."

"Go on."

Owen took a drink and cleared his throat. "The sound of a crystal chandelier. Tiny noises all around us, all over the lake, clear to the other shore. And what had been a sheet of ice was suddenly a ripple of little pieces of crystal. I couldn't believe it. Even my dad had never seen it before. He let me take a rowboat with one oar out into it and my dog and I paddled around the end of the dock in the ice chips. I wish I could tell you how it smelled."

"Tell me."

"It smelled old. Like something opened up to the air. Like a garden when you spade it for the first time in the year."

She felt a knot in her stomach. "You're going back, aren't you?"

"Well, yes, I think I am."

"You want me to help you get rid of your apartment."

"I know it's too small to bother with, but I don't know what to do about the lease."

"What about your job?"

"It never was much of a job. For a grown man, I mean."

"And what are you going to do back there? In Arizona, or wherever it is?"

"I don't know. Carry and pull, I guess. Take my dog off the leash. Do you ever take a vacation?"

"Sure, I take a vacation. That and clothes are my only extravagances. And my BMW."

"And now the Charles Club. It can be expensive."

"Oh, I can charge that to John Coster and Co."

"What a good idea."

"If I do it."

"Please do it. Roger and I worked hard for you. You're what the Club needs. Someone different. A breath of fresh air, as Roger says."

"You said there would be other women."

"Yes, but the members will pick women who are just like themselves. From the same, well, the same group."

"You mean class."

"Well, yes, class."

"I'm not from their class."

"Neither am I, but I found some good friends there. I spent some good times there." Owen thought of the chair beside The Window, tulip magnolias nodding outside on Commonwealth Avenue. "Anyway, class is what you are, not where you are from."

"Will you go over there with me the first time?"

"You've been there before."

"Yes, but I mean the first time as a, oh God I don't really believe this, member?"

"Yes, if you'll think about taking a vacation in New Mexico."

"Let's have dinner."

"Only if you pay. I'm unemployed." Brent, walking by, dropped two menus on their table.

Chapter 37

Abel sat over his second cup of coffee in the deserted Dining Room. Sun streamed in the windows. A smell of baking sweetened the air. The kitchen rattled and rumbled behind him, the sounds of luncheon and dinner preparation not only more audible to his ears than to others, but more descriptive. He fancied he heard veal being pounded, vegetables chopped. This moment was the pivot of his day. He had ten minutes before he began his rounds, before the telephone began to ring, before the first members arrived for the first drink of the day, before the luncheon service, before the inevitable and increasing activity of the afternoon and evening. His day sometimes ended well past midnight. They don't pay me enough to do this job, he told himself, but he knew he did not work at the Charles Club for pay. Most of his salary flew south to Portland Province on the eastern end of the island of Jamaica. It supported his elderly mother, his sister and her two young children, and perhaps one or two people he knew nothing about. If Abel had little to spend on himself his needs were commensurately few. He had a comfortable room next to Nilson with a big Air Jamaica poster and three watercolor paintings by his uncle on the walls. He ate well, better in fact than anyone else at the Club since Pesht only sampled and Nilson subsisted mostly on fish, preferably herring. Miss Ontos took only lunch unless she worked late and had a snack before going home. Old Jane, her wait staff, and the other kitchen help fared well but they had neither Abel's appetite nor his discrimination. Only the succession of long active days kept him from matching girth with some of the members.

Already he was pondering the choice between Cape scallops, the tender little ones which were becoming so hard to find, broiled under a flame with Anton's delicious garlic bread crumbs and butter on top, or perhaps a mixed grill—another Pesht specialty done in the English fashion. Because he scanned the luncheon menu in advance Abel had resisted the temptation to have the little dollar pancakes with Vermont maple syrup for breakfast that morning. Dinner would present another difficult choice between beef Wellington planned for a seating of twenty in the Large Reception upstairs or the choice item on the evening menu, sweetbreads *financière*. Abel sighed and finished his coffee. It was black and delicious and came from the Blue Mountain in Jamaica. If he closed his eyes he could see the Rio Grande at night winding down from the mountain to the sea under a full Jamaican moon. As a boy he had worked on the slender bamboo rafts lighted with luminarias and propelled by bargemen who were themselves powered by rum punch. Errol Flynn, he had been told as a child, originated the idea of rafting down the river and it had become a durable tourist industry. In those days Abel's shoulders were broad and his waist narrow, a Jamaican gondolier. As he stood up to take his cup and saucer to the kitchen he glanced at his reflection in the tall mirror at the end of the room. 'Tother way round now, my mon, he said to himself.

Roger Dormant sat alone, as well, in the Library. He looked up with a grimace as Abel entered to set out fresh ashtrays and match boxes and to straighten the periodicals on the reading table. "Ah, Mr. Dormant, I didn't see you arrive. How are you this day?"

"Passable, thank you for asking. In point of fact, I have a criminal headache this morning. What should I take for it?"

"Is it a headache related to the weather, caused by germs or bugs, or perhaps more of an alcoholic nature?"

"The latter I fancy."

"Is Mrs. Dormant still travelling, if I may enquire?"

"You may and she is."

"Then I suggest a sturdy base of vodka with V-8 Juice, Tabasco, Worcestershire Sauce, ground pepper, a squeeze of lime, and a raw oyster added. This is a mixture suitable to brighten your outlook before lunch."

"It sounds a little frightening."

"Strong measures may be required."

"You're probably right. Please have a second one underway before too long."

"The Cape scallops look excellent today."

"I don't think this is a scallops kind of day. It seems more like a corned beef hash kind of day to me."

Abel nodded gravely, finished his labors and vanished. Roger pondered the choices which lay ahead of him. For the first time he was not entirely certain of his welcome at the Club. He had stayed away for three weeks since he and Owen had forced the issue of Leslie Sample with the Nominating Committee. Now, he had heard, the floodgates were open. No less than five women had been nominated, whisked through the approval process, and invited as members. He wondered what effect this—there was no other way to describe it—tidal wave of females would have on the old place. Roger had expected a more gradual transition. It had taken a significant hangover to bring him back to the Club. So far all had seemed as it should be although it was only just past eleven o'clock. He felt no desire to open the *Sphere* or any of the other papers. To everyone's relief the Charles Club was out of the local news now, replaced in part by the Department of Motor Vehicles head who had been arrested again for driving with a suspended license. The Library was quiet, the light filtered by curtains thoughtfully drawn by Abel. The promise of the soon to be delivered medication had begun to alleviate the uproar in his head. He hoped this fragile equilibrium would survive the morning. He heard a step behind his chair and turned to take his medicine.

"Good morning. Do you allow women to come in here?"

"Why, yes. That is, I suppose so."

"Don't you know? Aren't you a member? You look like what I imagine members of this club to look like."

"Thank you. Yes, I am a member. Won't you sit down?"

Margo planted her expensively exercised haunches in Walter Senior's memorial and draped her Bill Blass coat over the back. "I'm grateful. It hasn't been one of my best days so far."

"Would you like a drink?" He rang for Abel. "I'm sorry to be a little vague about the rules of the club. I have been a member for, well, for a long time, but things have changed around here of late."

"Oh, really?" said Margo with evident lack of interest. "At least no one accosted me at the front door."

"Yes, we have women members now. And they use the front door."

"*Do* you? *Do* they? How advanced. Yes, I think I heard something to that effect."

"You don't sound very impressed."

"This *is* the next to last decade of the twentieth century, is it not?"

Roger picked up a copy of the *Wall Street Journal* from the table and glanced at the masthead. "Why, so it is."

Margo laughed, ordered a kir from Abel, and looked at her companion with a little more interest. "I am Margo Hunsikker. What is that extraordinary concoction?"

"Very pleased to meet you. I am Roger Dormant."

Abel said, "Called the Hair of the Jamaican Dog."

Roger took a gulp. "This is for a little headache. It has a raw oyster in it."

"My God. We never made them that way in Chicago. Have we met before? Your face looks familiar."

"People often say that to me. The other day I paid a visit to my lawyer and a young woman in the elevator asked me if I was somebody."

"What did you tell her?"

"Well, of course, I told her I was not, but she didn't believe me. She, well, she asked me for my autograph."

"How flattering. Did you give it to her?"

"I signed Adam Winchester, which seemed to satisfy her."

"Who is he?"

"Just an old friend. Not somebody."

Margo sipped her aperitif and looked about her. "What a lovely Sargent. This is a very pleasant room. I don't think an old friend is not somebody, myself."

"I didn't mean it that way. He looks a little like Margaret Thatcher, as a matter of fact."

Margo laughed again. "Do you know, the last time I was in your club an officious little man tried to throw me out? I swore I'd never set foot here again."

"Yes, I think I heard something to that effect. What made you change your mind?"

"I was invited to lunch today by a friend of mine, one of your new members. She persuaded me to come back and take one more look."

"With a view to becoming a member yourself?"

"Oh, no chance of that. But I said I would come. Out of curiosity, I suppose."

"I'm glad you did."

"So am I. I'm enjoying it more than I expected. Have you ever worn a moustache?" Abel returned and handed her a slip of paper.

"No. When is she meeting you?"

"As it turns out, she's not. She just called to say she had to go to the hospital. The baby is arriving a little early."

"She's having a baby?"

"Delivering. She's an obstetrician."

"In that case, would you care to have lunch with me? Afterwards, I can show you around a bit if you like. Although most of the members don't think so, the Sargent upstairs is even better than this one."

"How nice. I'd be delighted." Roger handed her a menu and they began to discuss the Cape scallop situation. The Hair of the Jamaican Dog had worked wonders.

Old Jane showed Margo and Roger to the Long Table, which was lively as usual with the unusual addition of three women engaged in spirited conversation with six men and each other. "Did you say you were from Chicago?" Roger asked as they sat down.

"Yes, I've been in Boston less than a year. I joined a bank here, the Old Currency, as a loan officer."

"Oh, do you know Avery Coupon?"

"He works for me."

"Well, if you enjoy Sargent, you have come to the right city. There are some wonderful canvasses at the Gardner, and at the Museum of Fine Arts, of course." He was about to describe the murals at the Boston Public Library when the member at his right introduced herself.

"Claudia Gammage. You must be Roger Dormant."

"Yes, indeed, a pleasure."

"I'm Peg Cartright's niece. She told me I'd meet you. You look just like her description. Are you sure we haven't met before? I see you're having hash with poached eggs."

"Yes."

"What is your cholesterol count? I'm working so hard on mine."

"I'm sure I don't know."

"I've come down from 249 to 221, but I'm determined to get under 200."

"Good for you."

"But now I've been hearing that the real villain is triglycerides, the neutral fats? I'm above 150 there, and that seems definitely excessive, don't you think?"

Roger put down his fork and waved at Abel, who magically produced another tall red glass. Dormant drank half and closed his eyes for a moment.

"Do your children like you?" he heard someone down the table ask.

"Well, the answer is yes and no. They're both at home again. It makes for *such* a trying situation. Our son has dyslexia and he's dropped out of Bates again. He's very, very resentful. I'm at my wit's end."

"Have you had him tutored?"

"Yes, we sent him to a special needs summer camp in Colorado a year ago, but he dropped out of that, too."

Roger turned to Margo, who was polishing off the last of the scallops and breadcrumbs. "Delicious," she pronounced, and smiled at him. "You haven't touched your hash. Has the Club changed much since, since you entered the twentieth century?"

"In little ways," said Roger. "Let's take our coffee with us. I want to look at my favorite painting."

"CIGAR?" The Eldest Member pushed the humidor to Walter Junior as he sat down in the appropriate chair. It was late in the day and they had the Library to themselves. A cocktail party was in progress in the lobby, the sound of laughter mixed with eager disclosures about winter vacations just completed.

"Thank you." Walter Junior picked up the nipper and nipped. He mouthed the end then clamped it between his long teeth. He opened a Charles Club match box, extracted a wooden match, struck. Fire applied, he drew it through the barrel of the last of the Havanas. It had stored well. Walter Junior sighed and settled back. The Library, already dim, slowly filled with blue smoke.

"Cayman Islands," shouted someone in the next room.

"Vail," came the sturdy reply.

"Do you feel the Club has changed much?" asked Walter Junior.

"IN LITTLE WAYS," said the Eldest Member.

"Some of the new members have asked that we not smoke in the Dining Room. Not the end of the world, I suppose. We can always come in here. Yes, I agree. Little ways. Nothing to be concerned about." He smiled at the older man but discovered he was resting his eyes. Walter Junior reached over and touched his hand. A pulse, all is well. He tried to extract the smoldering cigar from his fingers gently at first then with increasing force. Amazing how he doesn't want to let go of it, thought Walter Junior. Just like Papa.

Chapter 38

Spring, which had been fickle to Boston, spread her arms. From his taxi Leonard Lapstrake marvelled at the lushness, the greenness, the warmness. Spring was the coldest season of the year in San Francisco and in a microclimate dominated by clammy Pacific fog he had packed a protective wardrobe. Damn, he thought as he wound the window down to admit zephyrs flavored by cherry blossoms, dogwood and a myriad of tulips, I never seem to get it right here. Sitting comfortably sideways in the cab, his feet on the seat, his arms braced fore and aft to accommodate the tactical maneuvers of the swarthy lascar, can it be the same driver he wondered, he admired Boston for the first time. It's really lovely. Could I have missed something?

The flight had been wretched. He had been forced to book the redeye, which meant a late departure and an early arrival in Boston with whatever sleep possible en route interrupted in Dallas. The takeoff from SFO was delayed by "equipment" which entailed a sprint along the crowded venue of DFW to make the connection by a whisker. His stewardess friend had not been forthcoming with little gold stickers, so he had flown in the back of the airplane on both legs of the trip, crying babies and large men who wore their hats throughout the flight surrounding him. To lessen his discomfort he had ordered two martinis. Two on each flight, he recalled without remorse. At Logan next morning he floated down the jetway still airborne, into a cab with Iranian markings, a two-suiter—perhaps his own—firmly in his grasp. On this day late in April he saw a different Boston as they rocketed down Commonwealth, shaving the lights on yellow, sometimes on the cusp of red.

Fifteen more syndication customers under his belt, he now firmly controlled his destiny. Only the Great Caen, also known as Genghis to some of his peers, commanded more readers in San Francisco columndom than Leonard Lapstrake. Much as he loved the smorgasbord served to him daily by the City by the Bay, however, he wanted to vary his fare occasionally. Why not see other cities, write about other people? When he signed with his twenty-fifth paper—most of them west of the Rockies, he drew up a list of the cities he wanted to do: Paris, London, Moscow, Rome. Santa Fe, Jerusalem, Oslo, Venice. Inexplicably, Boston rose to the top of the list. The Hub had left a sort of gunpowder taste in his mouth. Something told Lapstrake he had only part of the story. In an attempt to recreate his first visit he had called the Charles Club and, speaking to Miss Ontos, arranged for a room within walking distance of a bath. The Iguana remembered him and she said they would be only too pleased to have him back. When the cab pulled up at the corner of Hereford he recognized the soberly graceful Georgian front. He gave the driver a twenty, got two dollars back and called it quits. The cab bounced away, the driver smiling, the passenger once again marveling at an airport only fifteen minutes from downtown. As if we built a flight deck on Alcatraz, he thought, liked it and decided to use it. The sun was up above the skyline, its rays diffused by the half-furled leaves of Commonwealth's linear wood. As he mounted the steps and reached for the doorknob he was almost knocked back to the curbstone by a bustling figure. "Sorry," Lapstrake gasped, although clearly not in the wrong.

"Quite all right. My fault, I'm sure. I was just leaving. But you can see that, can't you? Club's as empty as an old shoe. An empty shoe, that is," he added lamely. "By the way, aren't you . . . ?"

"Leonard Lapstrake."

"*Yes*. I knew it. We met the last time you were here from . . . "

"San Francisco."

"Quite right! But, here, I'm keeping you on the doormat holding your bag. Come in. Come in. Let me buy you a drink. I had about given up. No one to talk to. No one at all. Allow me." The Architectural Critic held the door and the traveller entered and looked about. Abel's impassive face greeted him from across the registration desk. The little brass lamp was lit, no animal of any description to be seen. Lapstrake rested his luggage and signed the book. Over the line marked "Sponsoring Member" he thoughtfully wrote "Seymour Gland."

The elevator was working. Lapstrake floated up to his room, washed, changed his shirt. In spite of only a few hours dozing fitfully in the shade of a Stetson he felt surprisingly good. He skipped down the well-remembered stairs and met his host at the foot ordering the first drink of his day from Abel. Nothing loath, Lapstrake asked for a vodka and orange juice and they strolled into the Parlor, which was sunny.

"I'm pleased to see you again. Are you here on another assignment?"

"Yes, my own this time. I'm going to visit two cities each year and write about them for the *Clarion*. That's the hometown sheet. And some other papers, as well."

"So you've come back to Boston. I thought you did us."

"So did I. Now, I'm not sure."

"Do you think you missed something?"

"Perhaps. And saw some things that may not have been there."

"All else aside, dear chap, I feel you were quite mistaken about the seafood. Have you tried the bluefish, by the way?"

"No."

"The halibut, the haddock, the flounder?"

"I had lobster."

"There, you see. Tourists eat lobster. Natives eat bluefish or scrod."

"What is scrod?"

"Well might you ask."

"Well, I am asking. I don't think we have that in San Francisco."

"Of course you don't. Scrod is one of the mysteries of Boston."
Lapstrake looked at him, pencil mentally poised. "There is no
species of fish called scrod."

"I don't get it."

"Yet you will find it on all the better menus. As I say, we locals
prefer it to the more exotic dishes. In fact, scrod is a market name.
It refers to any small, white fish of the cod family which comes
from northern Atlantic waters. If you will take lunch with me, we
will have it broiled with lemon and butter."

"All right, I will. There seem to be a number of Boston mysteries. The way people drive here, for instance."

"Do you find that mysterious? So do I. When I first went to
Paris, I was fortunate enough to meet a young Frenchman whose
English was better than my French. We had like tastes and I had
a little money. Bertrand undertook to show me what he called
'les mysteries de Paris.' Boston has its own secrets. Visitors don't
discover them on the sightseeing buses or the Freedom Trail."

"Tell me another one."

"You are sitting in one right now."

"The Charles Club?"

"Yes. This is a vestige. Perhaps in its terminal phase." There
was a pause in which Lapstrake had a fleeting mental impression
of a great flywheel gathering speed. "Boston has had its clubs since
it was a colonial capital," the Architectural Critic continued. "The
Revolution came and went, as did westward expansion, the Industrial Revolution, the Civil War, Bubbles, Panics, world wars,
Roosevelt, the sexual revolution, feminism, all those great forces
and events of the past two hundred and fifty years. Still, in spite
of all, a few of the clubs survive."

"But in somewhat altered form, surely?" Lapstrake was making
surreptitious notes on his vestpocket pad: war, Roosevelt, sex, he
wrote.

"No. No significant evolution. The men's clubs have been like
some of the smaller creatures, the Common Loon, the armadillo,
survivors from a much earlier age. Essentially harmless. Usually
unregarded, left alone. Tyrannosaurus and sabretooth were too dangerous to escape their fate."

"Yes, I used that metaphor," said Lapstrake as the great wheel
sped ever faster.

"They, we, have done little harm to society in all this time, and
little good. That, in fact, has been both our strength and our weak-
ness. Now, I fear, we have entered an era, even in crusty old

Boston, in which good, or the appearance of good, is expected from all social institutions. That is why we will soon disappear.''

"Surely not.''

"Oh, yes, we are not organized to do good, in fact to do anything of consequence. You might as well ask a bocce game in the North End to raise money for AIDS education.''

"Well, shouldn't they?'' asked Lapstrake, mindful that AIDS was discussed on milk cartons and cereal boxes back home.

"Exactly, exactly. They probably should, but they can't and continue to be the bocce club the members were born into. We don't even play a game. We're not a golf club, or a tennis club, or a bridge club, or a curling club. Aside from the occasional game of billiards on that table on the third floor, which is sadly out of true I fear, the table that is, but the floor as well now that I think about it, we have no club games. We exist as a club only to eat, to drink, to talk, to smoke, to read, to ruminate, to go away, to come back . . . ''

Lapstrake began to feel a strong urge to go away. As the Architectural Critic rolled on, his audience slipped notepad and gold pencil unobtrusively into his pocket and finished his drink. The headache which he had come to associate with Boston began to reassert itself. From somewhere in the region of the back of his shirt collar it lanced upward into the soft fatty undertissue of his brain. Recognizing this as an exploratory probe Lapstrake attempted an interruption.

" . . . to enjoy a fellowship, a clubship call it, which is not demanding of anything but a consistent absence of demands . . . ''

"I think I'm going to excuse myself.''

"What about lunch? What about scrod?''

"Thank you. I'll pass on the scrod. I think I need a nap. I've been up all night on an airplane.''

"Perhaps another time. I'm here most mornings.''

"Perhaps. It's been very interesting.'' Lapstrake walked carefully to the bar, pondering *les mysteries de Boston*. "Could I have another one of these?'' While Abel poured the orange juice Lapstrake said, "I think he was telling me that something has happened to the Club.'' It came out as not quite a question.

"Well, we now have a few lovely ladies as members.''

"Really? And has that changed things much?''

"In little ways,'' said Abel.

"What does that mean?''

"Nothing of consequence. The elevator is now in a current state. We installed a new device to regulate the heating system. Small changes which should have been made before."

"What about the men?"

"The old crowd is still here. Most of them. Most times." Lapstrake took a thoughtful drink. It seemed to help. "Will you sojourn long with us?" asked Abel.

"Just until tonight. Then I'm moving to the Ritz."

Chapter 39

The sartorial lustre of his new brown suit was a little diminished in Owen's eyes, but he wore it for lack of a better alternative. Before he left he stopped at the door to survey the badger hole. A stack of empty wine and grocery boxes from the morning pile outside DeLuca's sat in the corner. Earlier that evening he had begun to pack books, a melancholy exercise which brought depression back with a rush. What's to keep me here, he asked himself. What are the alternatives? To return to Santa Fe had not been much of an alternative until now. That it suddenly seemed his only real choice surprised him. The books might fill about six of the cardboard Chardonnay cases. Why am I still hauling around old MIT engineering texts? He lifted a tome from the pile on the birchlog table, *Digital Computer and Control Engineering* by R.S. Ledley. Its burgundy binding, its unmarked pages, the price of eighteen dollars and fifty cents on the inside cover in pencil evoked not the slightest flicker of memory. Might be worth a few dollars if it's not completely out of date which I'm sure it was fifteen minutes after I graduated. He dropped the book back on the pile. Tasha opened one eye, regarded him with an evident lack of enthusiasm since she knew she was not invited, and resumed her meditations, muzzle on outstretched paws. Owen glanced at the kitchen clock, opened the door to a cool spring evening and bounded up the mossy stone steps.

Since he did not want to keep Leslie waiting, he propelled his lanky frame, now mysteriously devoid of winter fat, at a lope across eastbound Commonwealth, cars honking at him, under the dark trees, then across the westbound side. In spite of his cheerless mood he smiled. This was to be the long-contemplated first visit by the new member. After discussion they had agreed it should be in the evening, usually quieter in the Club than at the middle of the day. Dinner, said Leslie, if you will show me how to do it. Do what, he had asked. You know, she said, like order and pay and where we sit. All those things. My treat, she insisted. If I can buy drinks, he responded. I'm unemployed, but I'm not broke—which was not the literal truth after he had purchased the Amtrack ticket to Santa Fe. He ran up the Charles Club steps and swung open the big front door to discover Leslie standing in the vestibule staring in dismay at the closet chamber, its door indiscreetly ajar.

"Is that . . . ?" she said, peering in to decipher the legend on the little tent card.

"Hello. Yes."

"But it looks like marble."

"It is."

"Is it for . . . ?"

"Any and all members. Feel free . . . "

She gave a shudder and took his arm as they entered the lobby. "I just *know* this is not going to work."

"Why not? It worked for me. Good evening, Abel. The usual," said Owen in his best imitation of a Boston clubman's voice.

"Then why are you leaving? Are you still leaving? Perrier and lime, I mean Evian," she said to Abel.

"Good evening, Miss Sample, Mr. Lawrence. What a pleasure to see the two of you. We're quiet tonight." He handed them drinks.

"We're having dinner, Abel," said Owen, signing the slip which he knew despite Miss Ontos' best efforts would not be reflected in a bill for at least a month then mailed to New Mexico, perhaps to be paid when he found a job. He would miss the Club float. He would miss the Club. "Follow me," he said to Leslie, cheerfulness draining away. "Yes, I am going back," he told her as they headed for the Library. Maybe they'll take me back at the library, he thought with a flash of the stacks and the oaken bookcart with its squeaky casters. Leslie clutched his arm.

"Not in there," she whispered as she took in the regulars framed in the dark windows.

"Oh, yes. You can't hang back. You're a member now. You've met them all, anyway."

"No, I haven't. I'm sure I haven't. And there aren't any other women. I can't."

"Stop thinking of yourself as a woman. Think of yourself as a member."

She was going to say I can't again, but Owen pushed firmly in the small of her small back and her heels clicked on the wood floor. Conversation ceased as four heads swivelled to the doorway. After a pause several voices spoke at once but Gland's was quickest off the mark.

"Well, Owen, I thought you were leaving us." He seemed not to notice Leslie.

"Miss Sample, welcome," said Walter Junior.

"I must be off," said the Distinguished Poet.

"I HAVE ALWAYS THOUGHT SO," remarked the Eldest Member, whose voice as usual filled the room. Owen propelled Leslie into one of the leather and wood chairs at the end of the semicircle, took the one vacated by the departing Poet for himself. Leslie, who was wearing a navy silk dress, pearls, and navy hose, almost disappeared when she sat down. As much of her as could be seen was spectacularly female against the dark leather. The Eldest beamed at the Youngest. "Well, I never thought to see the likes of you sitting here," he said, contemplating her superb blue knees.

"Neither did I," she whispered from behind her glass of water.

"Rather lights up the room, don't you agree?" He addressed the group at large, all of whom were staring at Leslie.

"Could I have some more, uh, Evian?"

"Just ring that bell," said Owen, "and Abel will appear." She did and he did. After ordering, she turned again to Owen and whispered something. "You don't pay," he answered. "It's one of the nice things about a club." The others listened with interest. 'You just sign a slip." She whispered again. "There's no tipping. At Christmas we all give something to the Box." She looked a question at him.

"The Christmas Box," explained Walter Junior. "It is divided among the staff as a year-end expression of our, uh, gratitude for their service."

"If that's what you choose to call it," said Gland, gesturing with his empty glass. "I really think the time has come to say something to Abel, Old Jane, in fact the entire . . . ."

"I am," said Owen.

"Going to say something to the . . . ?"

"Leaving you."

"So I've been told. And when can we anticipate your departure?" The walking stick was nowhere in evidence.

"Not to be permanent, I trust," said Walter Junior.

"Sometime next week."

"And where are you going?"

"Back to New Mexico. To spend some time with my father. I don't know how long I'll be gone." He looked at Leslie.

"Perhaps he'll stay there," said Gland. "I believe it's called the Land of Enchantment."

"Let's go in to dinner," said Leslie with a bright smile. "If you'll excuse us, gentlemen." She gritted her little teeth at them in her best imitation of a Boston clubman's manner, took Owen's drink as well as her own and marched out of the Library, heels clicking on the parquet, Gland smirking in her wake.

They lingered over *coq au vin* until the Dining Room emptied. Then Owen took her hand and led her into the kitchen. Feeling proprietary, he presented her to Anton. He bowed over her hand and stopped just short of clicking his heels. The aftermath of dinner surrounded them, but his apron and white shirt were resplendent. "Charmed," he said, eyes snapping.

"So am *I*," she whispered to Owen as they returned to the Dining Room followed by a curious Boston Cat. Owen showed her the paintings, the silver mugs and trophies, the guest book whose entries went back a century. They went down to the basement and into the wine cellar. Owen described the finale of the Single-sex Club Dinner as best he could reconstruct. it. They emerged laughing and climbed the main stairs to explore the upper floors. Leslie revisited the Small Reception Room and stared at the lesser Sargent as if searching for the face of a friend. She ran her fingers over the green felt of the billiard table but declined a lesson. Owen summoned the birdcage, explained its idiosyncrasies and to Leslie's delight they descended in state through the brass tangle of leaves and vines. It was late and Abel had retired. Most of the lights were extinguished save the brass banker's lamp burning on the desk. From its pool of radiance the Boston Cat contemplated their approach with an arrogance which melted as Leslie touched his ruff. "What is this?"

"The register guests sign when they stay the night."

The Boston Cat rolled on the open pages, extending his legs in the air, exposing a fuselage distended by years of Anton's cuisine. Leslie dug her nails into this ripeness and was rewarded by a display of toes and claws. "Have you ever stayed over?"

"No. I live right across the street, remember?"

Silence, broken only by a harsh rasping from the cat's interior, reigned.

"There are some, uh, guest rooms on the top floor," he added. After a pause: "Would you like to see them? We've seen everything else."

"Let's walk up," she said. "The elevator is so slow."

Owen turned on the light by the stairway, glancing curiously at the buzzing switch. An electrical short, thought the engineer as he followed her, followed in turn by the Boston Cat. When the light went out their excited laughter echoed in the old house as they groped their way from floor to floor.

Gland collected his topcoat from the hallstand. He had dined hastily and too well alone in the corner of the Dining Room, glancing often at the couple by the fireplace who seemed to think they had the room to themselves. He is quite absurd in his Robert Hall suit, thought Gland. Who does he think he is bringing that, that . . . none of the words which popped into his mind seemed exactly to fit. Seymour remembered the renegade Dormant was the one who had actually brought her into the club. He dismissed the train of thought, pulled on his black gloves—incongruously perforated at the knuckles motor-racing style—and retrieved his stick from behind the coatrack where he had hidden it to forestall theft. He had become more cautious, more *street-wise*, a phrase he had lately added to his vocabulary, since the ugly incident at the Ritz. No one had spoken to him about that evening, but he was sure it was common gossip at the Club. Gossip, he knew, was the second most popular activity of the Charles Club. But he had hardened himself, having seen the lengths to which an erstwhile friend would go to cause pain and public humiliation. When would he learn the lesson? Seymour let himself out the door and, checking to be sure it was locked behind him, walked thoughtfully down the steps. When would he finally learn to be less open, less trusting, less vulnerable to the attacks of supposed friends and the ruthless schemes of business associates?

Seymour decided, since it was neither cold nor raining, to walk down the Mall and catch a cab in front of the Ritz. A few blocks would do him good although he was in excellent shape. He stepped out briskly, breathing in the night air, tripping along with a flourish of his stick. Demi had complimented him on his prowess on the dance floor. She had looked quite smashing at the party. He could still remember the expression on Owen's face when he saw her in the lobby. There were real possibilities there, not for something foolish like marriage; but the advantages which could accrue from a well-managed relationship might well help to solve the problems with which he was struggling. What matter if she were a little taller? Gland knew his own stature in the city. He no longer needed the lifts he wore in his shoes in college. A man's true height had to do with other things: money and power and women and clubs and cars and boats and houses and offices and favors owed and coerced from others. He knew what he could do to people. He was actually, now that he thought about it, as invulnerable as anyone in his acquaintance except, perhaps, the governor, who, it was rumored, might seek the presidential nomination. Gland had no need for public office. *Private* office was more to his liking. By the time he had walked from Sarmiento to Morison to Garrison his mood had lightened. His false friend was gone, exiled. Demi had promised to come to a reception at the Four Seasons next week where she and Gland would certainly be noticed. He had London to look forward to. Perhaps Demi would accompany him. He glanced at the lighted windows on either side, some bare student rooms, some elegantly decorated. His thoughts drifted to real estate, always a stimulating subject, and he smiled.

Chapter 40

Abbie looked terrific. He almost walked past her, not recognizing the short haircut, the unexpectedly stylish suit, the billowing raincoat. What the hell, Owen asked himself. It was as if she had disguised herself as a knockout. She was paying off a Weston taxicab on the corner of Newbury and Dartmouth attracting a certain amount of attention. Owen wondered why the sight made him angry. Then she caught his eye and frowned back at him. "What are you doing here?" she asked.

"I more or less live here." She stared at him, apparently expecting a fuller explanation, which he supplied in spite of himself. "Going to the liquor store, to the drug store, buy a copy of the *Sphere*, go home and walk my dog."

Abbie was peering into her leather bag fiercely rearranging its contents. "So, how is she?"

"Bored. Doesn't get enough exercise. She's at me all the time."

"I don't doubt it." Her purse closed like a trap. "Quite beautiful, I imagine."

"Yes, she always looks good. Her coat is amazing."

"I really don't want to talk about her, or her damn coat."

Owen looked at her, puzzled. "Nice to see you again, Abbie. You're looking great. I've got to be going."

"Yes, well, I'm meeting someone myself and I'm late. We're going to see something at the Colonial this evening, I can't remember what it's called, Penn and something, I think. It's so hard to get into the city. Thank God he's driving me home."

"Well, have a nice evening."

"Oh, it's no one you know. He doesn't get his name in the newspapers. Like the ones you date," she added.

"How do you know who I date?"

"You'd be surprised how much I know about you. Hear about you." They looked at each other for a moment. "Father asked about you." He was afraid she was going to cry.

"Give him my regards."

"Do it yourself." She started to walk away. To Owen's discomfort, she was walking in the direction he was going. He could turn and run or he could go on living his own life. Clenching his teeth, he walked beside her toward the liquor store, looking for an opportunity in the traffic to bolt across the street.

"Where are you heading?"

"I'm meeting him at the Copley Plaza. Is that far? I got out of the cab too soon."

"It's right over there. Why did you get out of the cab?"

"I thought I saw someone I knew. You should call him, you know." To his consternation Owen saw her eyes were brimming.

"Call who?"

"Daddy, you idiot."

"Good-bye, Abbie, you really look nice," he said as she ran unsteadily away from him on her high heels. She usually wears short heels in the city, he thought. Why should I call old man Sells?

By the time he had completed his errands, dumped his few purchases on the birchlog table and picked up Tasha's leash, the thought occurred to him: why should I not?

The next day Owen was to meet Roger Dormant at the club for lunch. Having no job to fill the morning and unable to confront the half-filled cartons any longer, he decided to cross the street a little early. Before he left the apartment, however, he picked up the phone and punched the number of Portman and Sells into the keypad. Staring at the clock over the kitchen sink, he suddenly found himself connected to John Sells. The gruff voice was so familiar it took him a moment to bridge the chasm. Sells was talking to him in a worried tone, as always, chopping his words like carrots into a stew.

Owen remembered how he had met him almost fifteen years ago, two months before Owen was to receive his degree. He had been summoned to the office of Doc Martin, Chairman of the Electrical Engineering Department. Owen had been surprised by the invitation and unsure of the reason. He knew he was not in trouble. On the contrary, he was fairly certain he was doing well. How well he hadn't guessed until Doc introduced him to Sells, who was sitting in the shabby window seat drinking tea. Sells, although not as tall as Owen, looked bigger than he was. His large head seemed shaped by a rough file. Wisps of red hair were pasted to his pate. Owen was the young man, said Martin, he had been telling him about. John Sells had asked to meet some of the more interesting of the new crop. The two of them should get acquainted. Martin had a lab seminar down the street. Stay in the office as long as you like, Doc said, and ambled out the door. Before Owen realized he was being interviewed he had been offered a job. Small wonder, he thought, staring at the hands of the kitchen clock, the big hand at nine and the little hand at twelve, that he was no good at job hunting. He had never tried it. "Sorry, what did you say?"

"Concerned. Didn't have a chance to talk. Wondered what you were doing. How it was going." A pause. "Hello?"

"Yes, John. Well, I've been doing some business analysis lately."

"What's that?"

"Ah, business analysis, looking at investment opportunities in second and third stage companies, some startups."

"Why?"

"Why what?"

"Why are you doing that?"

"I'm not anymore. I decided it wasn't for me."

"What's for you?"

"I'm in the process of deciding that."

"How long does it take you? Hello? Want to do engineering?"

"Yes."

"Come in and see me."

"Well, I'd be happy to talk to you if . . ."

"When?"

"I'll give you a call next week, John."

"Good. Don't worry about the, about the other thing. Between you and her. Hello?"

"I'll call you, John. And thanks." As he walked over to the club, Owen thought it might be extremely pleasant to get his hands on a set of engineering drawings again.

He found Roger and Walter Junior leaning over the library table. The president of the Charles Club seemed unusually burdened. He acknowledged Owen's greeting, and the two turned again to some sheets covering the periodicals on the table. "What, for instance, is that?" asked Roger pointing.

"I really don't know. I think it is the bar."

"Well, it seems to be marked 'cellar egress.' "

"Then, obviously it is the basement stairway," said Walter Junior, with unaccustomed asperity. "I am quite at sea with all this.

Owen, please take a look." Owen leaned in. "Are you mechanical, structural, or civil?"

"I'm electrical."

"Pretty much all the same thing, I'm sure."

"No, actually worlds apart," said Owen studying the ancient set of blueprints. "This is the Club," he said after a moment. The sheets were limp and mildewed.

"Yes, Miss Ontos found these in the back of the storage closet off the Billiard Room." Walter Junior cleared the extensive passages of his throat. "I believe, Owen, you are the only person with engineering training of any sort among our entire membership."

"They're beautifully drawn." Owen leaned closer to trace the faded outlines with his fingers, trying to read the identifications and specifications.

"Walter is appointing some new committees," said Roger.

"One is an Architectural Committee."

"Perhaps Owen would consider . . ."

"I'd be happy to be on it," said Owen, admiring a rendering of the portico in the corner of the topmost print.

The two older men looked at each other. "We need a chairman, as well," said Walter Junior, "but we are also forming a Long-Range Planning Committee. Perhaps that would be more to your liking?"

"I'll take the Architectural. And I'll be the chairman, if you like." Santa Fe popped into his mind. "Perhaps on a temporary basis. I'm not sure about my own long-range plans at the moment."

"Most of our appointments are on a temporary basis," said the president.

"What's the purpose of all this?" asked Owen, as he floated one sheet in the air and deftly extracted the print beneath it.

"The Long-Range Planning is to examine the future, uh, evolution of the Club now that we have, taken the, uh, step."

"Now that the women are in," said Roger. "Someone's already proposed that we stop smoking in the Large Dining Room. I mean, we have to go slowly here."

Owen smiled at his friend. "Roger, you've been one of the firebrands."

"That's a little strong. I have been, still am, in favor of change. But it has to be gradual. We need to look carefully at things, discuss them."

"Sounds like Roger should be head of Long-Range Planning."

"He has declined, I'm afraid."

"What do you want the Architectural to look at?" asked Owen. The minute the words were out of his mouth he knew the answer.

"Bathrooms," replied Walter Junior, gloomily. "One Ladies' Room won't suffice now. Perhaps we should combine the two committees. Would you take them both?"

"Good idea," said Roger. "Call it Bathroom Planning."

Owen and Roger sought a private corner, avoiding the Long Table which was half full. Women were present. Both men could not refrain from counting them. "Six," said Roger in a low voice. Conversation in the room was subdued, reflecting the weather which was cold, and damp, and dark. Spring was on hold. As they set their drinks down and seated themselves, however, Owen felt his spirits lift. He looked across the threadbare but brightly starched cloth at Roger. "Good to see you, pardner. You look a little down."

"It's good to see you, Owen. Cheers."

"How's your family?"

"Ann is still in California or Nevada or someplace. Celia is back in Dover."

"That's nice."

"Actually not. Things are rather strained. I didn't realize the club business would cause such an uproar."

"Why is she upset? I'd think most women would see it as, well, as a victory of sorts."

Old Jane hovered over them. They looked hastily at menus, elegant as always in Miss Ontos' crisp typography. Roger wrote out their order slip and handed it to Old Jane. "Celia often sees things in a different light. She is, as my daughter would say, pissed."

"About what?"

"My leadership role, as she puts it. By that she means Leslie Sample. By the way, I haven't seen her at the Club since you brought her by the other evening."

"She's a little shy. She's coming to New Members' Night, though."

"So is Margo Hunsikker." Roger brightened a little. "She just joined, you know. I'll be blamed for that as well, no doubt. But at least we're finding some interesting people. You and I, Owen, we've changed this old place." They started on the fish chowder. "What did you mean about your own plans a few minutes ago in the Library?"

"I'm thinking of going home to Santa Fe. To look around. I'm not working for Seymour anymore."

"So I heard."

"There seems to be a lot going on in Boston, but I think maybe I need a change of scene."

Old Jane, looking out of sorts herself, set eggs benedict in front of Roger and sole in front of Owen. They glanced at her in surprise, at each other, then began eating. "What do you want to do, Owen?"

"Get back to engineering. That's what I'm good at. Good for. I want to get back in harness."

"Why don't you set up your own firm?"

Owen looked at him in surprise, a morsel of fish poised in mid-air. "I'd like to do that, but I haven't the resources."

"What resources are you lacking?"

"Financial resources."

"Could you make it work?"

"Oh, I see what you mean. Yes. Damn right. I have the energy and probably the brains. But not the rent money. It would take a while to get some clients, to get myself established."

"I might know some people who might invest in an engineering enterprise."

"Are you one of them?" asked Owen, a smile breaking across his face.

"Yes, and the rest are related to me in one way or another. I more or less manage a family investment trust."

"Roger, I don't know what to say."

"Give it some thought before you decide to go back out there, wherever it is."

"I certainly will. And thanks. No matter what happens, thanks."

"New Members' Night should be fun," Roger said finishing his drink. "Margo and Leslie and Peg Cartright and the Pilgrims and the brethren all mixed up together. I wish Celia could be there to see it, but she won't."

"Why not?"

"Because spouses are not invited," said Roger smiling.

Chapter 41

The Charles Club was incandescent, light spilling from every window. A passerby on a dog walk or returning late from work took refreshment from the beauty of the house illuminated. Through the lacquer portal, its great brass hand gleaming like a jewel as the door opened, passed a stream of black-clad men and dazzling women. Dazzling mostly by comparison, amended Owen, as he watched the scene from the sidewalk. A few indeed dazzled. Margo swept up the steps from her cab in a long red coat which caught every ray and every eye. Most of the women, however, wore what Talbot's told them to wear to a party. But they were brighter to Owen's eye, more animated than the men, who showed only a spark of white collar or a patent leather reflection to relieve the black. What was the symbolism of the doorknocker, Owen wondered not for the first time. He remembered his surprise when one of his schoolmates identified the weathervane above the library cupola at Holderness as the Holy Ghost. Owen had seen it as an iron feather. Did the finger of the doorknocker warn sinners of their ultimate destination? It seemed unlikely. Many passed through the front door of the Charles beyond doubt, but they were minor sinners in Owen's judgment. An exception or two certainly came to mind, but he thought them unlikely to be intimidated by a doorknocker. Perhaps it said something about New England housekeeping. Wipe your feet, Owen's mother had always called to him when the screen door banged. By then, of course, it was too late. It was a routinely affectionate greeting, mother to boy, who always glanced down at his dusty boots as he headed for the kitchen. He knew a little grit would pass unnoticed in the house beside the river. But now, reflexively, he rubbed his shoes on every doormat over which he passed. Blessed with a good mother, he reflected. A good father as well, I guess. Stand up straight, he always said. I think I'll call him, thought Owen. He thought of the boxes of books stacked in the apartment. Hell, I'm not going back. Why should I go back? Everything I want is here. But I should talk to him. Is he lonely? I should ask him to come to Boston. He always seemed so self-sufficient. So was I until recently, Owen thought. Leslie popped out of a taxi. There she is! ''You're dazzling,'' he said with a wide grin.

He took her elbow as they mounted the steps, but she shook it loose and threaded her hand through his arm. "That should be my line," she said, looking at his tux appreciatively. She was wearing an emerald dress under a stiff white evening coat. He had never seen her so spectacular. "You really are," he said close to her ear as they entered the confusion of the foyer.

"A little Fiandaca something," she said happily.

"What's a Fiandaca?" he asked.

She laughed, a good beginning for New Members' Night. "Owen, you *do* look wonderful. I've never seen you in anything but a brown suit or a gray suit."

"This is my black suit."

"You should wear it more often. Thanks for waiting for me," she whispered as he helped her out of her coat and struggled with the crowded coatrack. Making their way toward the bar, they found Margo with Roger Dormant. "Hello, Mr. Dormant," said Leslie laying her hand on the sleeve of his tuxedo.

Roger found himself unable to make introductions. He looked beseechingly at Owen. "Leslie Sample, Margo, is it Hunsikker?"

"Yes, with two k's. Nice to see you again, Owen. I'm delighted to meet you, Leslie. You don't look anything at all like a Charles Club member."

"Oh, thank you. Neither do you. I love your dress. These are my two sponsors. Aren't they gorgeous?" No one had ever called Roger gorgeous. He vibrated quietly. "They're the reason I'm here. I really never thought I'd become one. I'm still surprised. Aren't you?"

"Well, yes I am. I was recruited. Like an athlete. They didn't quite offer me a contract, but," she looked at Roger who seemed incapable of speech, "pressure was brought to bear." She took Roger's other arm. "He's one of my sponsors, too," she said as she led them through the press to the bar. "I don't usually respond to pressure, but this time I did."

Abel was dispensing Champagne with the assistance of one of the women from the Dining Room. "Good evening, Ms. Hunsikker, Miss Sample," he said, not missing a glass, "Mr. Dormant, Mr. Lawrence. I expect you ladies will have Champagne." He suited action to words, then grounded the wine bottle to quickly assemble Roger a dark scotch and Owen a similar bourbon.

They moved away from the bar and stood together, sipping. A dozen women and some forty or fifty men were doing the same. A knot of Pilgrims clustered in a corner. The noise level was moderate, even a little subdued.

"Cozumel," said a quiet voice behind Owen.

"Sun Valley," someone responded thoughtfully. No one disturbed the mushrooms wrapped in bacon cooling on the sideboard.

Margo's eye swept the room, then fastened on her companions as if unwilling to let them slip into the general lethargy. "Tonight feels like spring," said Margo. The little group looked at her in silence. "One of my favorite seasons," she added resolutely.

Roger managed to regain the power of speech. "Mine too."

"Then let's kick back," said Leslie.

Abel moved into the Dining Room to forestall placecard swapping. The tables were to be as eclectic as possible, and he was determined not to allow the groups which had already formed to continue through dinner. It did not look to him as though this party had happened as yet. He glanced at his remedy being uncorked at a serving table by one of the temporaries. Anticipating problems with the first New Members' Night of the New Era, Abel had spent the morning in the cellar. He had emerged with six cases which he knew to have been overlooked and undervalued. A ferocious Napa Cabernet Sauvignon had lain in the corner since its acquisition ten years earlier. Abel had been the only one to try a bottle. The first glass opened his eyes. The second closed them in gleeful appreciation. Titanic was the word which came to mind. As the diners straggled in, he was ready. He began filling glasses as soon as a table was seated. He knew that if conversation lagged people reached for whatever lay in front of them. Nothing happened for almost five minutes. Then the room began to buzz.

Margo found herself seated next to the Eldest Member. They ignored the mulligatawny set in front of them as they sized each other up. "WOULD YOU GET ON MY GOOD SIDE?" he asked.

"I'll do my best."

"NO, I MEAN MY GOOD EAR. THANK GOD I'VE GOT ONE LEFT." He rose, pulled her chair out with a courtly gesture and seated her as they traded places. "SO YOU'RE A MEMBER. IT'S AMAZING."

"What's amazing, if you don't mind telling me?"

"OF COURSE, I DON'T MIND. I'M DELIGHTED TO TELL YOU. YOU ARE AMAZING TO ME," he said, the rising noise of the room overriding whatever acuity might be left in his good ear. "THIS PLACE HASN'T CHANGED SINCE I WAS THROWN OUT OF HARVARD. NOW IT'S BEEN TURNED DOWNSIDE UP. OVERNIGHT."

"And you find that troubling?"

"NO. I'M DELIGHTED. DELIGHTED. TO BE SITTING HERE NEXT TO A BRIGHT, BEAUTIFUL, YOUNG," Margo glowed, "PERSON AFTER ALL THESE YEARS, ALL THESE SAME OLD BORING YEARS. IT'S WONDERFUL." They toasted each other and took a sip of wine which caused them to lift eyebrows and glance down at their glasses. "YOU CAN'T IMAGINE HOW BORING IT IS HERE SOME EVENINGS. WE'VE BEEN SAYING THE SAME THINGS TO EACH OTHER, TELLING THE SAME STORIES OVER AND OVER FOR YEARS. NOW IT'S ALL CHANGED."

"I'm sure your stories aren't boring. I'm looking forward to hearing them."

"NO. NO, I WANT TO HEAR YOUR STORIES. YOU'RE OUT IN THE WORLD. A WOMAN IN THE BUSINESS WORLD. WHAT IS IT?"

"Banking."

"YES. WELL I MUST DISCOVER WHICH BANK. MY BANKER IS OLDER THAN I AM, IF YOU CAN IMAGINE SUCH A THING. HE REMEMBERS MY MOTHER. I THINK THEY HAVE PREVENTED HIM FROM RETIRING JUST TO DEAL WITH ME."

"I'll give you my card later, but I don't want to tell business stories. Isn't there a rule about that at the club?"

"OF COURSE THERE IS. WE HAVE RULES FOR EVERY-THING. THAT'S ONE OF THE THINGS THAT MAKES IT BORING. I LOVE TO TALK ABOUT BUSINESS." He drained his glass, which was mysteriously refilled before it touched the table.

"Well, we will not talk about business at this party. We'll talk about you. Are you married? Do you have a family?"

"OF COURSE. OF COURSE I DO. DID. ONE SON LIVES IN SWITZERLAND, ONE IN JAPAN. HAVEN'T SEEN THEM FOR YEARS. MY WIFE DIED TWO YEARS AGO. SO I COME HERE FOR WHATEVER AMUSEMENT I CAN FIND. WHICH HAS BEEN PRETTY THIN UNTIL RECENTLY."

"I'm sorry to hear about your wife. How long were you married?"

"THIRTY-FIVE YEARS, ALTHOUGH IT SEEMED LONGER."

"Oh," said Margo, sipping her Cabernet. "Well since you've had so much experience at it, perhaps you should get married again." She smiled sweetly at him.

"NEVER GAVE IT A MOMENT'S THOUGHT." One of those vagrant hushes wafted across the room as almost everyone took breath or food at the same instant. "WILL YOU MARRY ME?"

"What an attractive proposal. I am immensely flattered." Margo's cheeks were as bright as the wine. "I'm afraid, however, I must decline your gallant offer." She leaned closer, as did every guest. "My heart, you see, belongs to another." A collective sigh was followed by conversations resumed. The Eldest Member grinned like a boy who has had his cake and tasted it too.

Leslie emerged from the bathroom on the second floor which, in the current concern over allocation of facilities, bore a card affixed to the door by an upholstery tack. The card said LADIE'S ONLY, the calligraphy and the punctuation Nilson's. As she pulled the beaded chain which extinguished the ceiling fixture, she caught sight of a figure framed in the light at the end of the hallway. She tasted the humiliation of the Candidates Reception in the back of her throat as she recognized Seymour Gland's silhouette. For a moment she thought of slipping back inside and locking the door but only for a moment. Squaring her almost bare shoulders and giving the green taffeta a hike at the bosom, she advanced.

Seymour did not move, his rotundity effectively blocking the passage. She could not see his eyes but she thought he was smiling. "Good evening, Mr. Seymour."

"Gland, Seymour Gland. Call me Seymour."

"I did." What a colossal turkey, she thought. So I got the name wrong.

"It is *such* a problem to learn all the members when one joins a club. Have you ever joined a club before?"

"Of course. Several," she said. "If you'll excuse me I think I should get back to my table."

Seymour did not move. "Really? How fascinating. I belong to a few myself. What clubs, if you don't mind my asking?" He extracted his watch by its chain, flipped, clicked, glanced, clicked, and tucked away. "It's early. We have plenty of time before the speeches begin."

Leslie took a deep breath and smiled sweetly. "CYO, Rainbow, Cheese of the Month, CDs Unlimited, the Woman's Industrial and Educational Union for the cooking class, and the BCAE for Great Buns." She studied him and them attempted to squeeze by. He stood, thumbs and forefingers in the pockets of his waistcoat, his elbows just at the level of her breasts. He did not move. "The Charles Club was someone else's idea," she added.

"Not a very good one, I'm afraid. I don't see it working out for you. Not unless you become a little better acquainted with some of the, well, more influential members." Seymour's face was as smooth and shiny as an apple. As was his custom, he had shaved that evening with meticulous care. Although not hirsute, he often shaved twice a day and always before a dinner or a party. It made him feel *ready* for a social occasion. Others were seldom as well prepared as he. Usually, he thought, quite unprepared.

"I am very well acquainted with several members."

"I suppose you are referring to Dormant and Lawrence. They are hardly the leadership of the Charles Club. Lawrence is dropping out, as a matter of fact."

"Well, I'm not." She stamped on his instep with a needle-like heel and gracefully eluded his spasm. Once on the stairway side of him she turned and looked at the fat figure, standing like a dancer one foot on point. "I won't mention this to Owen. He'd dim your lights."

"Owen is a coward. I've known him all my life. Owen just watches. He doesn't participate."

Leslie swept down the stairs, the odor of Gland's heavy cologne in her nostrils. A blast of sound greeted her from the Dining Room. Abel had indeed found the key. The evening was happening. Leslie paused for a moment to control the trembling in her clenched hands and to locate her table. Maybe I haven't known Owen long, she thought as she threaded her way to her chair next to Walter Junior, who was grinning at her like a horse with a digestive blockage, but I know he sure as hell can participate. Before she sat down she swept the crowded room with her glance. There he was. She felt a little twinge as Owen looked up and smiled. The knot in her chest dissolved as she smiled back. Later, she thought, I'm going to straighten *you* out. She sat down at her table and looked at the president of the Club, who simpered back at her. In the meantime what do I do with this one?

The speeches had been unremarkable, the effects of the Cabernet almost overriding Walter Junior's tentative welcome to new members and virtually trampling Paul Subito's lengthy response on behalf of the newcomers. The Eldest Member was resting his eyes at the close of these remarks, so Margo rose glass in hand to look for Roger. Leslie was about to leave her table when Owen dropped into the empty chair on her left. "Congratulations, kid."

"Yes indeed, from all of us," said Walter Junior. "By the way, Owen, Margo Hunsikker expressed a wish to join your Architectural and Long-Range Planning Committee. She seems to have some provocative ideas to contribute. She mentioned," he leaned forward frowning, "bidets."

"All of architecture is provocative," said a voice behind them.

"Would you consider joining us?" asked Owen.

"Delighted," cried the Architectural Critic as he grabbed another empty chair and refilled his glass, beaming at the fresh audience ranged in front of him. "Yes, architecture has throughout history provoked the very strongest emotions of any of the arts. Unlike painting, sculpture, music, poetry, the dance, it will not, cannot disappear upon command. Those who live with it are destined to live with it forever. Unless . . . "

Owen leaned forward and made a determined effort. "Actually, I was wondering if you would join this new committee. We're looking at the need for some structural changes in the clubhouse and some issues of . . . "

" . . . one happens to live in Boston. Then the terms are seemingly less onerous. One has but to wait the requisite four to six years before dynamite, the wrecker's orb, and inflated land values combine to remove the source of provocation, alas only to be replaced with something almost sure to be worse." He paused only to lubricate the machinery, then the great wheel rolled on.

Owen grabbed Leslie's hand and they bolted. Before they reached the lobby they bumped into Margo and Dormant. "Come on, we're leaving," said Owen.

"We are?" asked Margo and Leslie together.

"Yes. We're going out on Newbury Street to celebrate the end of winter."

"Well, I've hardly had a chance at the Charles Club yet," said Margo. "I want to sit in the Library and complain."

"Plenty of time for that," said Owen, searching for coats. "I'm staying," he added in Leslie's ear as he helped her into her white evening wrap.

"Excuse me? Well then, I'm staying too."

"I want to play billiards," said Margo plaintively, as Roger held her red coat.

"We're already beyond the vernal equinox, halfway to the summer solstice," said Roger with some urgency. "The sun has assumed a northerly motion. We haven't much time."

"Of course, *you*'re staying," said Owen, pushing Leslie out the door. "I'm not *going*. It hit me tonight when you got here."

She stopped in the front door, people crowding past. "*Owen*, what are you saying? Will you make *sense*? Stand up straight."

Instead he leaned over and kissed her, then pulled her down the steps, his raincoat flapping behind him, Seymour's walking stick magically in hand. Margo and Roger followed more sedately. "How do you know so much about spring?" she asked him.

"Inestimable advantages of an expensive education and late night radio."

Abel stood behind the bar and watched the last of his guests blow noisily out the door. It slammed for the hundredth time that night with a sharp metallic rap as the hand tapped its finger against the plate, the stroke echoing in the empty foyer. He switched off the lights and the almost-Bulfinch ceiling receded into darkness, relieved only by the yellow shade of the banker's lamp on the desk. Abel plucked an empty wine bottle from the sideboard and automatically wiped the mahogany with a napkin. He glanced at the label and filed it in the cellarbook of his memory. Titanic is the word, mon, but definitely a fast finisher. The dinner had ended more quickly than expected. His people had peaked, then departed in a rush. It was just past nine o'clock as he walked into the Dining Room, where most of the tables were cleared. He noticed the Eldest Member alone in the corner resting his eyes. One of the women came in from the kitchen with a tray to clear the last tables. An impulse prompted Abel to wave her out of the room.

He walked over to the figure slumped in a chair, studied him intently for a moment then sat down beside him. Abel reached for the half-smoked cigar between the blue veined fingers. "Against the rules now, you know," he said gently. There was no response. He carefully extracted it and set it on a plate of macaroons next to a half-empty pony of Cognac. The old man was quite still. Abel saw that he was not breathing. Abel glanced at cigar, glass, cookies, sighed, patted the hand, and rose to go to the kitchen for help.

[229